To.
Sharon,

A fellow writer,

John Talisker

aka: Doug Reid

GATC'HH'EN'S RITE

IF THERE IS NO MEANING, WE LIVE IN HELL

Gatc'hh'en, pronounced "Gat-chin", is not of this Earth. He is part machine, part living being. One thousand years ago, he began to learn the ways of humanity, and in 15th Century France, he fell in love with Catherine, who was later burned at the stake for witchcraft because of her association with him. He retreats to the outer reaches of the solar system to nurse his guilt. Six hundred years later he returns, now cynical and half mad. Determined, and to get Catherine back, he selects Emily, a woman who is near death, and genetically modifies her into the woman he remembers as Catherine. Emily loves her beautiful body, and her new lease on life, but as she and Gatc'hh'en soon discover, there is a steep and unexpected price to pay.

GATC'HH'EN'S RITE

JOHN TALISKER

Wolfe Island Press

Printed and Bound by Createspace, Charleston, SC, USA.
Book Layout © 2017 BookDesignTemplates.com
Cover design by Terry Belleville: terrybelleville.com

Gatc'hh'en's Rite/ Talisker, John. -- 1st ed.
ISBN: 978-1542593120

Margaret Joyce Beckett
and
Clarence John Reid

Gatc'hh'en: Pronounced: *Gat-chin:* <u>*kætʃ :lən*</u>

> *G – Guanine*
> *A – Adenine*
> *T – Thymine*
> *C - Cytosine*

CONTENTS

Beginning

In the beginning. What a notion. There is no beginning, no end. Time goes on, and on, into the past as well as the future. Truth: another concept with no meaning since there is no such thing as truth. There is only the physics of how things work, and how things work is arbitrary. If everything is arbitrary, there is no meaning. If there is no meaning, then there is no God, and we live in Hell.

A first conscious thought: He awoke sitting on a rock the size of a small moon looking out at hanging foliage and glooming trunks of trees narrowing upward into a scattered sky. The hollow hills stretched into the distance and beyond that the encompassing grey sea. He was not alone. He was surrounded by sound, and scent, sensation, color, light and dark. The cyclic sound of the sea against the shore: water washing over rock, rock chattering against rock. He searched for the pattern, found it, and then folded it within himself, an endless quilt of geometrical shapes. He could calculate it. He could lift it in his hands and turn it from side to side to study it. He could understand, actually know — completely know, deeply know — day and night, summer and winter, rain and cloudless skies, snow and sand, with all the endless paradigms colored, convoluted, by the stochastically predictable patterns.

In the beginning — that is before he met the people; before he knew the patterns of day and night; before he understood what the revolution of the planet about its sun meant to the people — he had flown over the face of Earth, skimming over blue oceans beneath the stars and a bone-white moon. Following shining rivers as they spilled down from high plateaus and meandered across plains to the sea. Soaring and then rising like Phoenix above dark, snow-capped mountains to greet the sun once again rising. But then turn around and repeat. Spring. Summer. Fall. Winter. Rain, Wind, Snow, Black Earth, Gray Sand. Hurricanes. Tornadoes. Tsunamis' wiping out entire coastlines. Volcanoes belching up the interior of the planet turning the sky dark, the day colder, the nights darker. Turn around and repeat. Tossed seas. Blue. Lonely ice-capped mountains. White.

The interesting thing, the only interesting thing to experience had been a self-sustaining carbon and water-based process enveloped within a myriad of physical forms that he knew was called Life. In the oceans, on the land, in the air, the highest peaks, the deepest crevices, it was everywhere and all built on the same pattern, the same twisted string that encoded not only the form but also the beginning and the end of the organism. He understood how the pattern came together: Simple nucleotides, only four of them, geometrically arranged in a double helix, each strand storing the same information while running counter to one another. The information replicated as the two strands separated and then rejoined, slight errors in the encoding ensuring evolution. Dynamically complex and amazing. Amazing because the process is fantastically improbable. Amazing because it led to countless forms most beautiful.

His people had once had been composed of a nearly identical organic structure, the original building blocks similarly sourced from vast dust clouds of ionized matter, heavy metals, and carbon-based molecules that would ultimately form new stars and new solar systems. The fundamental mechanisms were different, very different, but had the same function in that the resulting lifeforms could each metabolize, and replicate, and, most important, evolve.

He had thought long and hard about it and always came to the same conclusion: Existence is a miracle that suggests a purpose.

"But aren't you confusing miracle with merely being rare, or suggesting there might be purpose only because you cannot stand the notion of living without it?" he would ask, careful to be as precise and emotionless as possible.

He would reconsider his self-posed question and rephrase, sitting back, cynically and grimly smiling. "What's it all about if not a miracle?" with the corresponding answer: Everything. Nothing.

He knew how empty the stars were: stone cold most of them; not all, but most. How many planets were there with people on them? He did not know. Not many, he guessed. It was why he had been placed on Earth, he decided, but without knowing if it might be true, since no one had thought it necessary to explain what his Rite of Passage — if that was what it was instead of mere abandonment — was all about. He understood this much: *The Rite* was reserved only for a select few. Lucky him, then: *Lucky, lucky, lucky him.*

But what was it all about, though? As far as he knew, his Rite had but a singular purpose, and that was to learn and then presumably humble himself. "You may breathe the burning flames of a star, but in the end you are the same as this cold, liquid water, and carbon-based creation. You may slip through the starry mists like a wisp but, in the end, you are not all that different from the flame of life that is burning on this planet." The notion that that might be the purpose of his Rite led him to yet another potential answer to the question posed.

Yes, life is sacred; all life, no matter where found and how put together.

Was that it, then? Was that all he had to learn? He would have struck out for home at that point, stupidly and naively, with no way of finding his own way, and would have done so except for one thing: quite by accident he met his first person. What happens when two different beings meet, greet, confront, and collide? Is there a spark? No, there is no spark, how could there be? One is a blaze of light, energetic ions, and electrons that can spread itself out over half the solar system; the other a repeating pattern of carbon, hydrogen, and oxygen at a temperature and pressure in which water exists in liquid form. And yet there is commonality, not only in the desire to live, and not just to procreate as some might think. So, no, he soon understood that he was not going home, at least not anytime soon, not until he understood who the people were and what their fragile existence might mean. All this... this *Rite*, was, after all, only about him, was it not?

Of course, he had known about the people right from the start. They were everywhere. He, at first, had avoided them; they had seemed like an unnecessary complication in an environment already complicated enough. What did they have to offer him, after all? He could see they were social creatures. He could see they were intelligent. He could see they were excellent builders. And yet they were the product of the unique evolution of the right-handed double helix encoded life, and in that way, no more unique, or special, than any complex lifeforms that had evolved to find a niche in the planet's Eco-system. What had changed his mind was not the tools they built; it was not the combination of their art and their science, nor the fact they could look forward in time as well as back, learn from the past, and dream of the future. No, it was simply because he could talk with them.

The first person he met was a dead person. A woman. Naked. Her garments removed. Sexually violated. Her skull battered to fragments. He slipped down between the trees and hovered beside her and carefully examined her broken body. Recently dead. He slipped back and slowly rotated about the clearing, taking it all in, keeping her central to it. Others of her kind mingled nearby. The male of the species. It was clear they had brought her life to an end. They were in the process of doing the same to another using a similar technique. He observed them carefully. Sex and violence. They dragged another woman forward and another. It would take them a while to process them all: a day, perhaps. They took turns.

A pillar of black smoke had drawn him there; and where there's smoke, there's usually fire, and fire is always interesting. It represents change, disassociation, and rapid oxidation; it is an aberration in a world where order predominates, or a catalyst in a world where it does not. He had thought later, too, after reviewing how he had come to this understanding and recognizing the irony of it, that the killing of the women had not been unlike fire.

Of course, he knew all about the people's wars. He knew how brutal they could be, and almost always were. But it wasn't the rule, in that their wars did not dominate their culture. It was the balance between war and peace that dominated: good and evil, as he later learned to describe the fine balance that kept the people from destroying themselves. If that were not true, their society would be open-ended and there would be no villages or any people at all. No, they cooperated with one another far more than they fought. It was one of the reasons they were people, and not just another living creature, as remarkable as they, too, could be.

He had been so clever, so rational, and so eager to return home that he had not bothered to check up on the people before then. He thought the definition of life and the recognition that he and his people shared a common bond would be enough to end his isolation.

"Did I pass, did I? Good! Let's go! I want to go home!"

He had not understood the many opposing and seemingly random contradictions that often tore the people apart and separated him from them. The people on this planet they called Earth had not been designed. They were the product of random mutations filtered by evolution, an imperfect process.

He had watched until the men finished. They raped and murdered all the women. It took hours and not quite a day as he had predicted. They were quite exhausted by the end. They piled the bodies atop the body of the first. There was a rather large accumulation, both young and not so old. He was about ready to turn away when one of the women groaned – and that was the second person he had taken the trouble to reflect upon, also a woman. He slipped down beside her. The gray matter of her brain spilled out. They had killed them all by a single blow to the head with a metal weapon: copper and tin. She would not last long. She groaned again and struggled to extricate herself, and after having managed that, began to crawl toward the safety of the tree line. She could see it just ahead. She reached for it. It was amazing she could see at all.

He could not quite understand why she struggled. She would die no matter what she did. Her wounds were too great. He hovered close.

"Hello, hello... Let go, let go..."

He could see she understood. It was a complete surprise. He had not expected she would. He had only been echoing aloud his internalized thought and feeling, but when she acknowledged him — a nod, a grimace, and then the denial of her imminent death — he had been taken aback; and then, later, reflecting upon the moment, astonished.

Of course, he knew about pain — he was not always devoid of it himself — but he had never experienced it like she had been experiencing it at that moment. One cannot live pain-free — that is death — but the pain she had felt was uncommon, unnatural, and he would not have it. He picked her up and rose above the trees blazing as bright as the sun with her in his arms. She fainted. He rose higher, stopped her pain, and mended her wounds. He clothed her. He returned her to full life and health.

On seeing him ascend, the men jumped to their feet and grabbed their weapons, but on seeing him descend in shards of stabbing light with her in his arms they fell to their knees. He set her down before them and gave her the power to do what she would. She killed them all. They fell where they kneeled. She cut off their heads, turned them over, and gutted them.

No mystery there, he supposed. He had merely shifted the balance of power. He vowed then not to interfere again in matters of war, not because it was immoral, but because anything he might do would be just as pathetically arbitrary as what they could, and would, do to themselves. What would be the point?

Still, after that, he could not quite let go. He remained for a while and spoke to her, and she answered. After that nothing could ever be the same. She asked if he would burn the bodies of the men and spread their ashes over the hills as if they had never existed, and he did so. She asked if he would bury the women and children that the men had murdered, and he did that as well, finally placing an upright stone as tall as any man to mark the place. She thanked him and asked him to take her home, and he did that too. She asked his name, and he told her. Her name was Judith. She believed him to be an angel, she said, and called him Michael because she could not pronounce his name.

In retrospect, he wondered if he could have found his way home before then. Or, if he had, would he have been welcomed, given that he would not have reached the expected level of understanding demanded of him? He did not know. He would never know. The truth was, it took years to assimilate what had happened, and what it meant. Isn't that often true: the things we learn the best are often those things that we take the longest to comprehend? That's what Catherine would have said. He instead did something entirely unexpected, surprising himself in the process. It had been relatively easy. He took water and a handful of clay and transformed it. He utilized the patterns held within the double helix from the woman. He had needed it to heal her wound. He became her twin brother.

2

Catherine

Belief came each time he looked up into the night sky. Belief came when he recognized a sign, like a beacon in time, guiding him from one moment to the next. Belief headlined by a water color sunset resting over the green hills. Belief orchestrated by a golden sunrise lifting from the sea slowly washing away the hollow immortality of the stars. Belief amid laughter and joy. Belief in the blazing strength of the people; and, above all, a belief fueled by the incalculable beauty and wisdom of Catherine, her body and soul.

There was once a warm summer day, undulating grass beside a flashing river, not a cloud in the sky...

So, what was it about that day amidst the pantheon of days that define the great reach of the past that he should take such note?

That day changed everything, of course.

It was his fault, really — his delusion, to be exact — to think the grass — such a common plant — was something especially luxurious. Four billion summers so far, some warmer than others as Earth wobbles on its axis and the sun wanes and waxes, and the grass seventy-million years old at least. Even so, the exceptional grass — outstandingly fresh and photosynthetically green — that would be the chlorophyll — was interwoven with blood — red poppies that followed the breeze, and then, as the draft abated, straightened and danced in the sun as the running river flashed.

The river: a large natural stream of water flowing to the sea, a lake, or another such stream. Water: very ancient, water. It is the low energy state of bonded hydrogen and oxygen and originates from the earliest times. Like the grass, there is nothing particularly exceptional about water, except when it flows beneath a yellow sun hanging in a blue sky as seen through eyes that he now possessed.

The child wandered outside the comparative safety of the small group gathered by the cusp of the river. She meandered through the tall grass, up a steep hill, the river adjacent. She saw him, turned and ran. She ran out of her own will, out of pure delight. What did she see when she looked his way? Something bright, suspended in midair, following the bank as it meandered along. She should have been frightened, but she wasn't, only curious. He followed her, ducking beneath the bank of willow to skim the sparkling river, then up again to see if she noticed. She turned and waved and called out. He picked up the path she was on, keeping his distance. She immediately ran in the opposite direction, leaving the path, looking back occasionally to see if he was following. Not afraid, just curious; it was just a game. She tripped and fell. He scooped her up before she hit the ground spinning her through the air before setting her gently down. More of a puzzle: he had not anticipated he would be so affected. Those patterns within patterns again that mean so much but are difficult to fathom because they are more often tied to the heart than the mind.

He asked her name.

"Catherine," she said.

He echoed it, relishing the sound, dwelling on each syllable and the anticipated memories he knew her name would later invoke.

"Catherine…," he had said.

Perhaps he should have been more circumspect; if only he had known the future. But then that is never the case, is it?

And just as well, too, for all that.

Catherine loved to run through the tall grass amidst the summer poppies. It felt as if she was flying, she told him later. He had watched from the shade of the forest, hour after hour, marvel upon marvel as she and the other children chased, laughed, and tumbled. She had a brother. Daniel. Daniel later drowned in the river. Tragedy. He had been unable to prevent it, but he might have if only he had not wandered about, his mind adrift, wondering about this, wondering about that. Daniel's head went under. His lungs filled with water. He had felt the boy's panic. The dimming world collapsing to a point. Death came quickly after that. He had felt life going out of him.

He never told Catherine he could have returned her brother to her, although by the time she had turned her back on him that one and only time, she might have suspected. She accused him of negligence and much worse, and it was true, too. He should have plucked the drowned and very dead Daniel up and out of the river and set him on the bank, dripping wet but breathing. He still did not know why he had not. He loved Daniel. He did know his inaction had left the body of Daniel without life. He could, and should have breathed new life into that still form. How many times had he imagined doing just that? A thousand? Two thousand?

It was true that her brother's death was only one of the many regrets he carried. He had lived then as he lived now, in a life of guilt and remorse with no real attempt, just the odd gesture, the occasional feint now and then, toward redemption. He was learning to be human as he suffered.

But he knew sarcasm well enough. "Redeem thyself, my love; turn that water into wine," she had said to him bitterly a year later, and he had done so to spite her, because by then spite was not unknown to him. The worst of it was, he had been so wrapped up in it all by then that it was almost impossible to pull back and return to his previous self. He had become a slave to his new-found passions. It was his physical self that drove him; that damnable blood and tissue, and his human heart that betrayed him more and more.

"Your human heart does not betray you, my love; it provides you with meaning. It helps you understand," Catherine said later having completely forgiven him.

Catherine's heart had been so large and so encompassing that she could forgive him almost anything. Still, he had to think about it, and it wasn't until long after her death did he know it to be true.

But he should never have let Catherine die in the way she had. He often thought he should have killed them all for it. The priest for slapping her, the tribunal that tried her, those that tied her to the stake, those that lit the fire — perhaps the entire planet. And why not? They were all equally culpable. Did they not allow such travesty to exist? Was their sin not in the turning away from what they knew was right?

Is that not right, Catherine? Is it not always the turning away from what one knows is right that is our sin?

• •• ••• •••••

But it is not the big things that draw us into the past but the little things. He recalled a moment taken from near the end, before he stupidly let her go; the time just before L'Batard. The nearly invisible trail swept upward through the meadow and into the trees. He shifted his weight on the horse. Catherine was ahead, already halfway to the tree line. He called after her. She stopped, turning her mount about, and then with a sigh climbed down. She held onto the harness for fear of falling.

He called out to her, approaching, "I have had enough, Catherine; we rest here this evening."

She swayed on her feet. "I can go on," she muttered as she threw herself onto the ground.

He dropped the pack and threw himself down next to her, pretending equal fatigue. The vista before them was one of green field and the darker forest stretching along the length of the horizon. "Open your eyes, Catherine; drink in the world surrounding you." Thinking of nothing else to say — he had been devoid of mind and common sense in those days — he had echoed what she had said days earlier when her heart had been lighter and she had not been so burdened.

She opened her tired eyes and looked upon the valley. "My God," she breathed as she idly traced the silver thread of the river with her finger. "My beautiful Loire, so perfect." She immediately berated herself, hanging her head, her profound weariness making it difficult for her to concentrate. "I am sorry; only God is perfect, my love," she said dropping her head to her knees and leaning into him. "The rest of us... The world..." She did not finish, exhaustion carrying her voice down to a whisper and then extinguishing it.

She had suddenly straightened, turning to him, her eyes, half closed, mirroring her fatigue. "You, my love, have been marked by God, as I have," she said with rekindled energy. "And God knows I love you as much as I love Him!" The flame ebbed as quickly as it had been borne and she sighed and closed her eyes and fell again against him.

He did not have the heart to argue. She was far too exhausted. Not in her body — he could have mitigated that — but in her heart.

· ·· ··· ·····

But what is it to be alive? The ability to metabolize and temporarily thwart universal entropy? The ability to reproduce and adapt? Consciousness: "I am Gatc'hh'en therefore I am?" Catherine taught him how to see, hear, smell, taste, and touch; and, more important, how it felt to see, hear, smell, taste, and touch. Without her, he would have remained as hollow as he had once been. Perhaps the real reason he had been sent to live amongst the people was to learn just that: to comprehend the final truth of just how empty of any substance he was? He would not be surprised. But he shook his head. No, no, no, no, he was no less hollow, no less in existence, than any person, he concluded. Not that we are all that deeply here. Bodily, yes; the essence of us, no. It is funny how we pretend otherwise.

• •• ••• •••••

There wasn't much she could teach him about the sense of sight. He had far better acuity, sensitivity, and range than she. She described what she saw as composed of color, and shadow. The sun was gold, the ocean blue; the fields green, flowers yellow, and red.

She tested him. She held up a frog — she was only fourteen years old. "This frog is green with black spots, and slimy clear goo. What do you see?"

"I see a living object. It breathes; it has sight; if you are telling me it is green, then it is green — and the spots, if they are black then they are black."

"Do you mean you do not see the colors?"

"Of course I see them: The colors I see reflect the environment the frog lives within. It means the frog is adaptive its environment. The creatures who prey upon the frog cannot easily differentiate the frog from its environment — if that were not true there would be no frogs; they would all be eaten."

She had thought about that. "I suppose that's true." She lay it carefully back into the shallow water, and it swam off disappearing beneath a golden lily floating on the surface of the river stippled by the summer wind. The lily was one of hundreds, perhaps thousands that lay like a green and yellow mat upon the dark water, ringed by tall stands of reed with their soft tips of brown encompassing them.

They stood up to their knees, she closer to the bank while he was further out where the current ran. The water felt cooler than the air, but not uncomfortable. His feet sank into the mud, the soft mud oozing up through his toes. She pointed to where the river gently flowed past and around them. It was sparkling in the late afternoon sun. She had her dress hiked up so it wouldn't get wet.

"What color is the water?" she asked, looking up.

"It is clear. All light passes throughout without dispersion or absorption."

She scooped a handful and let the water trickle away through her fingers. She looked up again and queried, her eyebrows raised. "It is clear but also silver. Do you not see the dancing silver?" she said.

"It is not the color: it is sunlight refracting through, and reflecting off, its surface — it is not dancing."

"But it is still silver, bright silver," she had said. She had then thought. "Like glittering jewels?" she suggested, smiling, probing, her head canted to the side.

He could not imagine what she meant. He looked more closely, the sunlight glittering on the surface that lapped against the mud bank: tall reeds, spotless blue sky, with the sun over his shoulder.

"Yes, it is," he had said, not wanting to disappoint her but then suddenly seeing what she had meant and laughing with her, she catching the sudden shift of understanding in him.

"Told you!"

· ·· ··· ·····

After she had taught him how to see, she taught him how to listen. Unlike sight, his human hearing was almost a new sense. He had a much wider range but not nearly the sensitivity. He could detect the vibration of the roiling surface of the sun before it erupted upward; he could detect the faint whistling of the interstellar wind, and the sharp snap of the sun's magnetic field as it suddenly broke free and then violently reconnected. He detected vibration propagated through a medium, in his case most commonly magnetically trapped protons. What he had learned from Catherine was not the physics of sound, but the experience of it.

Late one night, summer, no moon, the stars piercing a black sky, she sneaked out of the house to visit him, a familiar enough ritual. She knew exactly where he would be. She ran right to him, having an explicit memory of every stick and rise and fall of the land about her home. An innate instinct made it possible for her to do so, he knew; not just memory. She could not see the ground but she could run over it without tripping, while he would have mapped out the terrain in precise detail, scanning ahead as he moved.

She had found him then pretending she hadn't, paused by an oak, hiding behind it. Her fingers kept to the rough bark as she circled, waiting for him to acknowledge his presence. She was nearly seventeen.

She finally called out whispering. "Mon Coquelicot? Mon cher Coquelicot?"

He stepped into the zodiacal light to stand close behind her.

"I know you're there!" she called out in a more normal voice, albeit with an edge to it.

"How do you know?" he asked softly, right behind her, so close the wisps of her hair tickled his face.

She whipped about. His human eyes could not see her smile, but he knew it was there by inference.

She laughed. "I can hear you, of course!"

"Hear me?"

"Your breathing!"

"Ah!"

He had not thought about that — but, of course, he was breathing. He had taken the form of a person. What else should he have expected?

Of course, she had known he was there for another, a more instinctive reason. She had found him because she had known he would be there. And she had known he was there, not because she had heard him breathe, but because she had felt his presence. But those series of lessons came later. The lesson of the day had nonetheless been given and learned.

• •• ••• •••••

The sense of smell was not entirely alien to him. He recognized it for what it was; that is to say, he understood the details. Many objects, in particular organic compounds, give off molecules of themselves; the density varies but is usually quite small: in the parts per million. What Catherine did not know was that in his natural form he had a primary sense similar to her sense of smell and taste combined, and just as difficult to explain. He could easily tell the difference between a pure plasma composed of pure hydrogen and helium, and a plasma mixed with heavy elements, or organic compounds. The more purified, the greater the delight. He had never tried to describe that to her. What would be the point?

She held up a flower. It was the color of gold and glowed like the sun. She had seemed surprised by his description.

Catherine had smelled like newly mown hay, he remembered. She was eighteen.

"What do you smell?" she had asked, carefully handing it to him, anticipating his reaction.

He had a human nose; the molecules released by the dandelion interacted with his olfactory senses, the molecules laying on the cilia connecting to the neurons in his nasal passages, creating an electrical signal that went to his human brain to be experienced.

"I don't know what that is," he admitted.

"Well, you know its color, you can feel its texture, you can taste it if you wish, and now you know what it smells like. It is a dandelion."

He tasted it, and then quickly spit it out. She laughed. "You are a great puzzle to me," she said still laughing. "You have seen and walked upon millions of dandelions — and yet you do not seem to know them at all!"

She had continued to laugh, teasing him, he knew, her eyes sparkling. Later, she included yellow buttercups, purple lilac, pink honeysuckle, blue iris, red roses. He learned quickly; he smelled them and had the sense not to taste them although each time she suggested he should, laughing.

• •• ••• ••••••

The first time he had kissed her was the first time he understood how much he had changed. How much more of a person he had become. Spring. It had been a cold winter, but it was over now. The sun peeked out through dark clouds, strands of blue sky — the size of man's shirt, she said, certain with those signs the weather would continue to improve. They were walking along a dirt lane, just drying from the rains. The road was lined with crocus and early daffodils not yet open. The day smelled of the newly opened Earth, verdant with a promise of spring. She kissed him in broad daylight quickly on his lips, just once, her hand remaining in his as she stepped back, her arm stretched between them. She was nineteen years old.

She was blushing, uncertain of herself. She brushed a strand of hair back off her face.

"Sometimes a woman must take the matter into her own hands," she said, smiling and blushing, and again brushing a lock of her blond hair off her face with her free hand.

"What does that mean?"

"It means I fear I might have grown into old age waiting for you to kiss me!"

They had kissed from then on; after that, neither of them could stop themselves. The kissing led to more intimate connections. He learned about the sense of touch then. Her soft neck, her breasts against his cheek, the texture and curve of her thigh beneath his hand. The sex. Her hips reaching up to him, her back arched. The kisses, the thousand kisses in accompaniment. And he, what was he? Nothing but protons and electrons held together by a magnetic field. And she, what was she? Nothing but flesh.

3

Re-entry

F ive hundred years later with Catherine long gone, dust to dust, her soul to nothing, he hit Earth's magnetic field aligning his own magnetic field at the last moment. He broke through the frontal bow shock and dropped along the magnetic lines toward the magnetic north pole, the surrounding radiation ionizing the upper atmosphere, the oxygen glowing green, the nitrogen blue. Brighter and hotter than the sun he impacted the atmosphere at twenty times the speed of sound. Not wishing to be seen, he dropped his altitude to only a few meters above the frozen ground, the resulting sonic boom lifting a rooster tail of melted ice that fell in a rain of frozen crystal behind him.

He plotted a great circle arc that stretched from the Arctic, skirted across the Greenland ice fields, then swept across the open North Atlantic. It entered the airspace of the United Kingdom above the Shetland Islands, and then continued onward traversing the entire length of Scotland, and then England, then across the channel and onward toward his destination, Paris.

He checked his position. He was two hundred thousand meters above Ellesmere in the Canadian Arctic. He increased his altitude, and the rugged mountains of Ellesmere resounded with the resulting sonic boom. He glanced behind: cascades of ice and snow shattered, lifted, and then released, tumbled from the frozen peaks into empty valleys of ice. He lifted higher and slowed. A moment of carelessness on his part could cause considerable damage to the surface and the life on it. He should be more careful.

He opened his wings to embrace all that stretched out below him, from Ellesmere to Iceland. It was cold, winter had settled, and yet he knew that everything below him breathed and lived. He had learned that from Catherine. When in his impatience, or outrage, he had felt like destroying whoever, or whatever, might cross his path, she had quietly asked, knowing very well the shape of his heart and the turn of his young mind, "Who are you to break apart what is clearly meant to be? We are nothing compared to all this." He had not known how to answer her at the time, confused as he had been about the responsibility of the power he held in his human hands, but knew her meaning well enough now. He was nothing in all this. Nothing.

He lifted higher yet and slowed further. He was already over the ice fields of Greenland. He dropped his speed and increased his altitude yet again. He could feel the long-range radars paint him. They would be scrambling their fighter aircraft to intercept him, he knew. It was the same as last time — well, almost the same; the modulation methods on the radar pulses were different; their reaction times faster. He smiled but without humor. There were so many destinations the people could choose: extinction being one, mere survival another, ascendancy out of ignorance yet another. He had listened to their endless talk: Talk, and talk, and talk, almost always about themselves, and their progress in science, health, and military might describing it as destiny, often evoking their God as if they and they alone had God's ear.

What did it mean?

Nothing, really.

There was that word again.

Nothing. Nothing. Nothing. Nothing. Nothing.

Well, at least he and they, fleeting alive as they are, and he, too, for that matter, had that in common: that and the flesh and blood he had wrapped about himself as if a pupa in a cocoon.

As always, whenever he thought of mankind and destiny, he thought of L'Batard. How L'Batard had ridden out into the open plains at a full gallop to save his brother, his escort following close behind, their banners flying against the golden fields stretched out before them. A beautiful place. The willow-lined Loire a ribbon of blue. L'Batard a great man. Sometimes the place and the times define a man and not the other way around, or so Catherine had once said, and which he now suspected to be true. But, then again, he only suspected; he didn't know really. He knew only what Catherine had told him, and L'Batard to a lesser extent.

He cleared the snowfields of Greenland and was now over the North Atlantic, Iceland to the South, the Shetlands only minutes away. He was once again making somewhat of a spectacle of himself but, then again, who cared, really? He had no one to answer to, no conscience to guide him. He had no blood running through veins.

Okay, maybe he should care a little… Just a little, perhaps. It was just that he had nearly come to an end, and no longer had the luxury of pretending to be anything other than who he was; that is, not made of flesh — and, despite Catherine's best efforts to suggest otherwise, a mind without a soul. She had been quite wrong about that. How could he have a soul? He was not a person. He wasn't even alive in the strictest sense. A fact he had not bothered to explain to either Catherine or L'Batard.

What would they have said if he had, he often wondered.

Four F-35 fighter jets intercepted him approximately one hundred kilometers north of the Faroes. They came from above and below. He dropped his speed below Mach 1 and they immediately shifted their vectors. He correspondingly picked up his speed to match theirs, nearly Mach 2, then dropped his altitude. They followed. They were addressing him on all frequencies, as they say, both narrow and broadband. He didn't bother to listen — he had a good sense of what they might be saying: something about whose airspace he had entered and please follow the escort.

He was fifty kilometers from Inverness. He dropped his speed to one hundred knots and lowered his altitude to fifty meters. Inverness jumped into view then in a flash was suddenly behind him. He dropped to five meters and entered the Loch, raising a rooster tail of the pure loch water behind him almost as high as the five new fighter jets that followed him in, the original interceptors having broken off. The new ones were a new design capable of both vertical and horizontal flight, but not as fast as the interceptors. He banked sharply right then followed the high terrain clearing *Ben Nevis* with only a meter to spare. They followed. The closest had his fire control radar locked. They wouldn't dare. He dropped down into the Loch again and cleared the end at *Fort Augustus* ten meters above the town just below the speed of sound. He then abruptly shifted his bearing and raised his altitude to one thousand meters, then continued back on course leaving his escort far behind.

He noticed for the first time how crowded the airspace was. There were at least a thousand aircraft at various altitudes and ascent-descent profiles within range of his senses. The density was an order of magnitude higher than the last time he had dropped in like this. Since they were most likely passenger aircraft, their presence inferred an extended period of peace, although you would not guess it from the way the interceptors had performed.

More fighter jets were waiting for him: entirely English this time. No Scots allowed. The dirty buggers.

Five seconds later, he entered their gantlet and this time they fired: Five air to air missiles traveling at Mach 3 set to detonate on impact.

He let them hit, all five.

He dropped his speed to no faster than the ground transportation vehicles he could see following the highway below him, and waited to see what they would do next. Six out of the seven flew past at Mach 2 but one dropped next to him, nose pitched up, flaps fully deployed, landing gear extended. The pilot stared. He would see only a ball of fire less than a meter across.

Dropping all pretense, he accelerated to twelve times the speed of sound, and less than a minute later was over the English Channel. Thirty seconds later he swept across into French airspace.

There is something soft and gentle about the French countryside, ancient too, he felt. It was like going home, green fields and hedgerows into the distance.

But how ridiculous he was, how sentimental: he had no home, not anymore.

But wasn't that what this was all about: no home, no love?

Yes, of course.

But, then again, what does one know about the inner workings of one's own mind, the twists and turns, or the hidden layers? Only slightly more than nothing, he suspected. We are a complete mystery even unto ourselves it often seems; not the mechanical parts — they can be understood well enough — but the underlying tricky interactions that are often more than the sum of the parts.

Funny how that is.

No, not funny but unfathomable.

He glanced about. He had been momentarily distracted. Thirty fighter aircraft — Mirage 2000 and French, obviously — waited for him as well as a cluster of ground missile batteries, their radars already locked on.

Enough was enough. He shifted his polarization and dematerialized, leaving a gaping hole where he had once been that almost immediately collapsed in a tremendous roar of inrushing air and rematerialized over Paris directly above the *Isle de la Cité* and *Cathédrale du Notre Dame de Paris*, oriented exactly to the left and right banks facing the heart of the city, the tourist crowd of early May looking up, startled by his sudden appearance. He was as bright as the sun: compact, and spherical. They would no doubt feel the heat. He ensured that was all he was radiating: just light and heat, the heat consistent with the early morning and slowly descended to the stone pavement just before the Cathedral, then coalesced back into the man Catherine had once known. He breathed deeply in, luxuriating in the sensation and looked about, feeling the pangs of history and the eyes of every citizen of Paris, both living and not, upon him. He breathed in deeply again and slowly exhaled. It was where they had burned her.

4

Remembering Jupiter

It is the emotional context of remembering, is it not, that imbues one's memory with relevance? The rest is merely detail. Functional. Like a machine's memory. There were many things he remembered in near perfect detail, such as the time he rode one of the greatest Coronal Mass Ejections he had ever experienced all the way out to Jupiter. He spent nearly a month riding the shock wave of energized particles that had originated from the thin surface-layer of the sun all the way out. He knew what was waiting for him, and had been looking forward to it. Jupiter's magnetic field rivals the sun's field; it is a maze of twisted currents and seas of radiation that Jupiter's Galilean moons sift through in their nearly perfect circular orbits about the giant.

It was then that he had stumbled upon the schools of single cell life deep beneath Europa's thick ice. A plume of water ice rising from Europa's surface, reaching almost as high as suborbital levels drew him to that brightly mottled world, frozen methane on the surface, ice beneath. He had assumed the plume had been caused by a meteor strike but, even so, it was most unexpected and breathtaking to observe. The polarized high energy protons captured by Jupiter's magnetic field drew the liquid water upward to form the frozen plume. It was an exquisite blue, and in the frozen wasteland of space about

Jupiter as crystalline as water can be when near absolute zero. When struck, it rang like a bell. He rang it twice, the first-time marveling at the pureness of the resulting note; the second-time marveling again as the second note beat with the first creating an enharmonic third — a beautiful sound, mid-C, taking days to fade. And, oh yes, it was horribly cold around Jupiter; while taking up energy from the magnetic field, he had to keep himself tightly bound to maintain his temperature.

It had been quite an adventure. Adventures like that make one glad to be alive — an uncommon sensibility after Catherine, he had often thought at the time. He returned many times after, down through the thick clouds of radiation, through the ice, just to gaze upward through the near darkness to see the swarms of silver drift by, the heat from the thermal vents warming the water as well as himself. It was a time of peace when he needed it. Catherine had been gone then a hundred years. The people amongst whom she had once lived, brave as they are, frustrating as they could be with their priests accompanying them, were in the process of exploring the vast continent of North America in their little wooden boats.

• •• ••• •••••

He remembered an infinite number of things — no, not infinite, for his mind was not unlike the human mind, at least in the way it could assimilate concepts and then make them real. A billion, billion neurons constitute the human brain, more than there are stars in the galaxy, but the engendered memories held within and between furnish no proof, have no substance; they are merely fleeting electrical impulses in a framework of temporary order. They fade with time and disappear entirely with death. When people die, they exist only in the memories of those that remain, and when they inevitably die too, all is lost. There is no such thing as the soul or life after death. Catherine's opinion notwithstanding.

His memory in the instance of what he was thinking, and feeling too, was precise. He could recreate it in detail, and would be able to do so until it all disappeared with his inevitable dissolution. It was the day Catherine's patients, her *Jacqueries*, the hot sun making anything seem justifiable, had crashed through the gate like animals kept too long from cool water. Inside, blinking in the darkness, realizing they were about to spoil the holy, they had then jumped, maddened, insane for her touch. It was a two-edged gift, her power to heal. Give, and the world takes. Give more, and it takes more. They clutched at her clothing, pulled open her coat, tore at her blouse, holding their hands to her body until there was not one square inch of her flesh she could claim as her own. Bruised, bleeding, there was nothing she could say that had any effect, had any meaning. They were deaf to her pleading and soon deaf to her screams.

They had loved her and nearly killed her with their love. She was lucky he had been drifting by. No, not lucky — he had been searching for her, wondering where she had gotten to. He knew the risks even if she didn't. No, that's not right, either. She, of course, realized the risks, but refused to let them rule her: Anything for others. She had been brave like that.

There was nothing he could have done but remove the building's roof and walls and then lift her free. He would have destroyed them all but as tired and hurt as Catherine had been, she would not allow him to do so. Indeed, she had been outraged that he had even suggested as much. He had instead ensured that each suffered at least as much as she had suffered — he well knew the pattern and depth of her bruising. She had stilled his hand when she heard them scream, angry with him, but too wounded in her heart as much as her body to complain with any force.

He often wished he had not given her the ability to heal but her desire to expunge the traitorous ruin of bodily sickness was so powerful, and seemed so right, at least to her, he had been unable to refuse. He should have instead swept her away and settled them both on an uninhabited island deep in the heart of the ocean on the far side of the world. He would have kept her just the way she was, forever young and beautiful. They would have had children together who would live forever.

Ah, but there is the rub, is it not? Everything dies, including himself, the highest mountains, and the widest seas. Noble, or ignoble, nothing lasts forever. It is not meant to.

· ·· ··· ·····

And yet, the medium through which time moves is called irony. A long time ago, even as he measured time, Catherine reached for his arm. Their eyes met. It had grabbed at his heart then, and even now too, belatedly perhaps.

"Tell me what you see, my love," she had pleaded, the night settling, the first stars appearing. "Do you see our deaths?"

He wondered why she insistently asked him about the future; he knew no more than she.

"I see only our long life together," he had answered, and had then pointed upward to divert her attention. "Look… Your lucky star."

She looked up and sighed. "Ah yes… What is its name again?" She turned again to him to await his answer.

"Deneb."

"It is in Cygnus."

"Yes, it is."

"Do you see the cross, my love? And the mist of light, a thousand candles held by angels that it overlays?"

"I do."

"It is surely God's mark upon creation," she said. "It is a reminder, possibly." She thought, her quiet smile nearly invisible in the growing darkness. "I tell you it is Heaven and you insist that each one has worlds of their own," she said, then turned to him and smiled. It was a game they played. "You expect me to believe that?" she added softly. "Look how tiny the stars are."

"They are far away."

"Where is Heaven then?"

"All around us, within us, here and now."

That is what she wanted to hear.

"And Hell?"

"It is the same: all around us, within us, here and now, like Heaven."

She nudged him to draw him back. "You also say Earth moves around the sun instead of what we all know to be true which is the sun, like the moon and the stars, moves above the solid Earth. You could burn for contradicting the word of God, my love."

"Would you light the fire that would burn me?" he had asked, turning to face her, not yet having heard of the practice.

She was bathed in gold from the fire. "No, not I; I love you. You are a mystery to me. But I know you say such things for a reason."

"You should always search for the truth in things."

"Do I not?"

He drew the blanket about them, holding one edge she the other, keeping the warmth of the fire in and the cool of the night at bay.

"I need to know something, my love," she asked after a moment.

He remembered poking the fire.

"I have known from the first moment I laid my eyes on you that you are not of this Earth," she had said.

"What would that make me then?"

"You are my Guardian Angel. I have said so many times. We are just talking of what we often talk of."

He brought her hand to his lips, kissed it. She smiled and kissed the palm of his hand in return.

"I ask again, who or what are you if not an angel?" she asked.

He looked away not wanting to answer but she would not let him escape.

"God sent you?" she asked. "You can heal with a mere touch. I have seen you do so."

"As can you."

"God gave me that, I know, but through you. And you can fly through the air as a bright light," she calmly added. "God gave you all that power. It is truly amazing."

He would not pretend nor deny.

"When we first met, years ago, in the fields with the poppy," she added to remind him.

He had again refused to comment.

"So?" she prompted, not allowing him to escape.

It is always better, is it not, to tell the truth? Does the truth not set us free?

"You should know that I planted a device within you," he said not caring if she understood or not. "More than one, in fact: an entire array, one for each cell — more than there are stars in heaven. The devices give you the power to heal, not I. They also ensure your health."

She smiled, accepting his confession with a slow nod. She then quietly offered a confession of her own.

"Sometimes — you know it is more than sometimes — I believe I am running less from those who would cause me bodily harm than from my God," she had said. "I thought my touch could heal like His — and as I know your touch can. I have sinned against God, my love. My pride..."

He had abruptly turned to her and stopped her with a finger to her lips.

"You know nothing of sin."

"Oh, but I do, I do."

5

Jacinth

Twenty-four generations of people had gone by and he found himself looking for echoes of Catherine's genome in the throngs of people that populated Paris. So far he had found little that resembled the resonance that would indicate the presence of even one living relative. It might mean her line had ended and if so it would mean failure. He would never be able to reclaim her. Then what would he do? Die, most likely. Fade away. He had come close to that fate already, and more than once. It was that *nothing* thing again.

He turned about to verify his surroundings. The crowd of tourists, almost three deep, stepped back. He bowed low then slowly straightened. The response prompted the rapid taking of photographs with their electronic devices. He bowed again and slowly straightened as he had before. No response. He would have to suffer them then.

He turned to the Cathedral — it had barely changed — but the *Ile de la Cite*, *Quai Saint Michael*, and the *Parvis-Notre Da*me had changed dramatically; only the stone and bronze of Charlemagne on his brave steed appeared to have remained unaffected by time. He slowly entered through the big doors into the darkness encapsulated by the ancient stone. It was cooler inside than out. No ghosts, only cold stone. He strolled through the central nave, the *La Rose Occidentale* behind him, the arcades and the high arc of the ceiling imitating heaven enclosing him. He paused to reflect upon it all. The skill and craftsmanship. The majesty. The quiet. Time resonating. He felt it all.

He glanced at the striking blue and red stained-glass Rose at the end of the South transept and nearly bowed to it, then proceeded onward toward the white marble Altar, all the while glowing as if illuminated by the sun. He stepped over the velvet rope barrier and climbed the few stairs. The sadness in the eyes of the bronze saints belied their holiness. Those whose only sin was to see the world differently had been burned alive only because of the same unwavering faith that, ironically, had inspired the construction of Cathedrals like *Notre Dame* throughout Europe. Perhaps that was the source of the sadness in their eyes.

He slowly turned about, absorbing the quiet, the hush in the stone including the whispers of the ancient dead high up amidst the arches. Catherine had once stood in this place; she had prayed beneath its dome believing in everything she had been told. If only the stones could talk; if only the stones could show him.

He turned away from the Altar, the sadness of time grabbing at him, and suddenly realized he was not alone. A murmur of a dozen languages pervaded the nave. The tourists from outside had followed him inside. Photography was prohibited, but they clicked away with their iPads and smartphones, all aimed at him.

"Puis-je vous aider Monsieur?

He turned to the source of the question: a young priest. He did not like priests. He was quite biased in that regard.

"You are not supposed to be here, Monsieur," the young priest explained. "There is a line there, a rope. You are not allowed to cross it."

He looked. It was true.

"My apologies."

The priest was shifting his weight from foot to foot; he was flushed red. They were a prissy lot.

"Is there something else wrong?"

"You have no clothes on, Monsieur — you are quite naked."

He looked down. He was as bare as those at birth. That explained, at least in part, the tourist's curiosity as well as the young priest's evident embarrassment.

"Forgive me, Father, for I have sinned," and clothed himself in the garments of the saints, the same who lay guard over the altar. Whoever said he didn't have a sense of humor?

The young priest jumped back and tripped over the rope barricade, landing hard on the cold marble tile, as he transitioned into his natural form: brilliant white, two suns bright, hovering about a meter above the tiled marble floor. The young priest scrambled for the protection of the darkened apse as the crowding tourists, their camera and cellphones momentarily forgotten, bolted for the exit in a mad clash of language dragging their children behind them. He flew out through the high doors and ascended only high enough to suspend himself above the ancient city, *Ile St Louis*, *La Seine* below him; *Musée du Louvre*, *Jardin des Tuileries*, and the *Arc de Triomphe* and the *Eiffel Tower* in the distance.

He scanned the city below looking for the tell-tale resonance that would indicate traces of Catherine, the city lights going out, traffic coming to a halt, the sound of sirens. There were some faint traces but not nearly enough. Disappointed, he ascended until he could see the curvature of the Earth, misty white against the brown and green of the faded horizon and scanned again this time in a much wider arc — still nothing.

He turned about and went dark. That is, he became invisible to whatever sensors the people might bring to bear. He flew toward the French City of Blois in the heart of the Loire Valley, dropping to a few hundred meters off the ground, keeping his speed low, remaining perfectly silent, invisible to radar, eyes, and ears. He had returned to Blois many times since Catherine's death looking for the echoes of both her and L'Batard, and so he knew about the Chateaux, reconstructed and now twice the size. He hovered over the old bridge with the *Loire* flowing beneath, but it was the same there as in Paris — nothing, only near silence and faceless people who resonated outside the pattern he was searching for.

He departed Blois, and disappointed, slipped off the old bridge, skimming over the surface of the fast running Loire, lower than the tree-tops, bright as the sun, the silver waters of the Loire flashing, and the limbs of the willows rising and falling as if waving goodbye as he passed. He gained altitude to clear the city of Orleans, then cut cross-country eastbound, maintaining a speed of three hundred kilometers per hour at an altitude of five hundred meters: high enough to ensure no damage from the collapsing column of air behind him but low enough to just clear the forest-clad crests of the rolling hills. He passed the ancient village of Troyes at one thousand meters, dropped again, and then followed the terrain, hugging it close, skimming the natural lakes, barely clearing the tree tops of the *Foret d'Orient*. And then rising again over rolling farmland and into Lorraine where he crossed the open farmland to the *Village du Domremey*.

The village remained as he remembered it: the same grassy turn of the La Meuse; the same tumbled fields, and the softly rising tree-clad hill beyond. It was the same but not the same; roads cobbled and filled with traffic now; wires leading to bright lights — forests cut but regrown; open fields with similar boundaries. And there, finally, he had better luck. A faint signal but it nonetheless resonated, turning his head as he slowly wandered about in a crowd of tourists. They were everywhere these tourists. Was there nowhere within France that remained sacred?

The source was a young girl walking hand in hand with her mother. It astounded him how much she physically resembled Catherine: blonde braids, summer dress, sandals that clicked on the cobblestones as she skipped along. That the smallest pattern within the far larger pattern of her DNA could bring out the physical appearance of Catherine so vividly was truly amazing. But, then again, perhaps the real resonance was within his own mind and expectations, the similarity perhaps not as pronounced as he imagined. Again, and again, we see patterns where there are none. He was no more immune to that affectation of the mind than the people, it often seemed.

He turned to follow the child and her mother. He felt like a predator. But should he not feel exactly that way? Was he anything else but? She should not fear him, though; she would be safe with him. He would never harm her. He would destroy himself first. Catherine would insist on it.

He dissolved his human form and followed at a distance, high up in the eaves of the old buildings, keeping himself invisible. Child and mother entered a schoolyard. Her mother was taking her to school. He looked about: a light mist hovered amongst the chestnuts and elm that lined the street leading to the lush grass of the open yard, dotted with swings and slides and climbing apparatus, and a modest building made of brick. A host of children, their mothers and fathers, clustered about exchanging parcels of lunch, the parents bending to kiss their children goodbye for the day, their cars parked, some double parked, along the street.

He broke the child's grasp of her mother's hand and swept her up, holding her above his head. He examined the details that defined the child, both the Catherine and the nearly overwhelming individual components of the little girl, half of which was her father, the other half her mother, the process of the mixing creating something entirely new, not just the average of the two. There would be no future without this newness, he knew, as he set her down, returning her to her sobbing mother who lay on the roughened school yard face down begging for her daughter's life. He saw immediately there were traces of Catherine in the mother as well but, as with her daughter, she, too, was quite impossible, for to change either of them would destroy them, not only their bodies, but who they were, and he could not, would not, do that. They were living people, each with a future, as short as it might be. Catherine, when reborn in the bodies of either of these people would accuse him of murder, and rightfully so.

He felt somewhat foolish. Caught out by his own stupidity. Why had he not thought of that? He had a conscience, it seemed: a facsimile of Catherine's conscience, perhaps, but a conscience nonetheless. He had quite forgotten. Good ideas, as good as they might first seem, are often incomplete, the unforeseen only seen when the reality of the idea begins to take form. Still, it's annoying that the unforeseen is often sourced from your own weakness. Annoying because there is no one to blame but yourself.

He turned about to take in the details of his surroundings and found himself surrounded by children, their parents, and the teachers. They huddled together, shoulder to shoulder, staring at him, open mouthed, on the tips of their toes, ready to bolt. He showed them the form Catherine knew, this time dressed as the children's fathers dressed: leather shoes, white socks, jeans, open neck shirt, leather jacket.

He bowed, looking up and smiling, his hands clasped behind his back, then slowly straightened continuing to smile. No one moved, shouted out, pointed, or otherwise spoke, but nor did they run.

Mother and child scrambled back, the mother defiantly wiping her tears away with the back of her hand boldly face him.

"Je suis appelle Gatc'hh'en — je suis Gatc'hh'en," he indicated, pointing to himself. He slowly approached, his hands raised. "Je m'appelle Gatc'hh'en," he said again, trying to sound reasonable, even friendly.

He dropped to his knees and drew the child to him with a gentle touch, extricating her from her mother's grasp.

"Quel est votre nome, mon cher?"

He could barely hear her response.

"Jacinth."

He gently and carefully removed her glasses and her hearing aids.

"Qu'est-ce que c'est?" he asked.

"Ils me aident a voir et entendre," she whispered back.

He put them aside, smiled up at the mother, nodded, then smiled again, and then pushed himself upright and backed slowly away. He waved then transformed again, returning to his natural form. He flooded the schoolyard with light and ascended straight up. At one-thousand meters he broached the speed of sound; at ten-thousand meters, he pitched over and increased his speed to seven point eight kilometers per second and entered low Earth orbit.

6

Low Earth Orbit

He placed himself in an elliptical orbit that under the influence of the Moon and the sun as well as the small imperfections of Earth's gravity, caused his orbit to precess so that the Earth slowly swung below him. Oceans, continents, mountains and plains, ice caps, and deserts. Beautiful blue, green, white, from the dark of night into the brilliance of the day in only moments. The cities of the people glittering in the night; the brilliance of the sun reflected from the oceans and ice.

He thought of the child and her mother. The child's impaired hearing, her reduced eyesight; the mother's love for her child. Was that not what makes the world go around? He had almost wept when he saw how much the mother loved her child. He was glad he hadn't taken them; it would have been a travesty of all Catherine had taught him. What had he been thinking? Best laid plans… Once again, we never know how we will react until the moment comes. The heart betrays us as much as it remains faithful, as Catherine liked to say.

He could feel the radar beams paint him. They would have no doubt tracked him all the way up from the heart of France into orbit. They were probably engrossed in a lot of pondering and theorizing and scratching of heads, and had probably linked his entry into the atmosphere only a few days earlier to his recent return to orbit. It would fit the same flight profile. They might even correlate the incidents at the cathedral and the school if they were paying attention at all, and he was certain they were. The people were not stupid. They would assume that any sequence of improbable events occurring over a short period are most likely related.

He closed his eyes and turned so that he faced the sun. He opened his wings and basked in the radiative energy, luxuriating in it. Let them correlate his coming and going; he was done with hiding. He was done with making a point — if ever there had been a point, and he was not sure there ever had been. He was just fumbling in the dark. First we have a plan and then we fumble about. Is that not the way it usually goes?

He sighed his frustration and looked down upon Earth: beautiful; achingly beautiful. He adjusted his attitude, feathering himself to the sun as he fell along the lines of his orbit, the blue and silver Earth slowly shifting below him. He felt for a moment as though he were an integral part of it, the motion, and the silence. He felt as if he could spread himself upon the ocean beneath him: the Galapagos beneath the broken cloud washed in the newly born light of dawn. He would open his wings and embrace the planet from golden horizon to the silver night, with the entire Pacific shining in sunlight below, thereby becoming part of the greater world, simultaneously intermeshing himself with the oceans and icecaps, the plains and mountains, rivers and deserts. His spirit swelled thinking of it. We are so lightly here, as the poet says.

He didn't believe in Catherine's heaven, or life after death. It was a ridiculous notion, and quite impossible, and he had often told her as much. But she had only corrected him, insistent that he understand canting to the side as she did so, her free hand brushing back a strand of her hair loose in the wind. He loved it when she did that: she was entirely unaware of the affectation. Of course, there was some irony in it, too, for did that not mean she was alive in some fashion. Still?

Despite her death? In his mind, at least, as much as in his heart? Was that not the fundamental reason for all of his... fumbling about?

He waited for the next dawn, and then bathed in sunlight and feeling once again hopeful, he recommenced his search using a precise frequency and a raster scan pattern covering a two-point-one degree swath of the habitable surface of Europe and then North America in one-point-two milliseconds. To suggest someone on the planet's surface might detect the bombardment might also be an understatement. The peak power output was nine-point-one gigawatts, and it was sourced from low earth orbit only a few hundred kilometers above Earth's surface. For a moment, there were some on the surface of Earth who imagined their sun had gone nova. He could not have cared less; let them guess; let them make their plans.

Emily

He found her on the third floor of the New York Presbyterian Hospital, West 168th Street, New York City. She lay in a private room waiting for death, the curtains drawn. Lymphoid blast cells had resulted in an overproduction of beta lymphocytes, which in turn inhibited the production of normal red and white platelets in her blood. Her disease was called *acute lymphoblastic leukemia,* and for her it was fatal. He could not help but notice how beautiful she would be in health: blond hair, blue eyes, full lips; not unlike Catherine. He had waited for her father to leave — he would only be gone for a moment; he had heard him promise her that — and then had entered the hospice room through the window, slipping between the tightly bound but geometrically arranged molecules of silicon dioxide that comprised the glass.

The hospital complex, as was much of the city, and indeed the entire Eastern Seaboard, was still reeling from a complete breakdown of the power grid, including computer networks. Lighting had been restored; computer systems were in the process of rebooting. It seemed his exploratory scan had had an effect after all. Concerned for a moment and checking, he noted it had no or little effect on aircraft, or on automobiles; the electronics within their more critical systems seemed to be more rugged than the statically based versions in the cities and for personal use. He didn't know why — cost-based engineering, he suspected. He did know he had applied a similar scan on the military aircraft he had first encountered over the green Downs of England, and it had had absolutely no effect — at least as far as he could tell. It certainly had not stopped them from firing their missiles. He had thought his deep scan would have been similarly safe over the cities. It was time, perhaps, to be a bit more discrete, and perhaps a bit more attentive. On the other hand, if that's all it took...

Once in the hospital room, he assumed the form Catherine would have known, dressed as Catherine would have last seen him in those last days, and bent and kissed her. It felt odd and indefinably wrong; the woman lying before him was, after all, not Catherine. Perhaps he felt that way because he had never kissed anyone other than Catherine. He kissed the unknown woman again, her forehead, cheeks, nose, her mouth. He was kissing the dead, or the nearly dead, he knew.

Her eyes flickered — his close presence was already helping. He placed his hand on her chest — it felt stranger still putting his hand where usually only lovers are invited — and made the necessary repairs to the broken strings of DNA that were the cause of her disease. As expected, her body heaved and jolted but then after a moment peacefully settled, breathing regularly. If she had been conscious, the pain would have driven her to madness. The repairs, such as they were, were not enough, though, he noted: Her body required energy, and quickly. Her cells were starving. He gave her what was necessary, stimulating what he knew to be her cellular ATP at the level of her mitochondrial DNA. Her body temperature increased accordingly and he stopped the infusion before it became dangerous. They could only handle so much these bodies; they were often delicate — but robust, too; surprisingly so sometimes.

He watched over her. Her breathing became regular; her heartbeat, too. He stepped to the end of the bed and checked the name on her chart: Emily Elizabeth Dupuis. A French name, and logically so. He returned to her side and peered down, and then not knowing why absently ran his finger along the curve of her cheek and then kissed her again. It still felt wrong; wrong but necessary, he thought, as he straightened, still looking down at her.

She stirred, opening her eyes and then closing them, unable to keep them open. She sighed quietly and then settled.

"There now... That is better, isn't it?"

He said no such thing but it was, after all, what Catherine would have said if their roles had been reversed.

He almost changed his mind. He should leave now. Let Emily puzzle over the return of her life and thank her god for it. She was a living, breathing person, and the plans he had for her were on the problematic side of Right. That and the fact today was not the same as yesterday; yesterday he had been in search of Catherine hoping to begin again. But today, or least some time during the time the sun had remained hidden on the far side of Earth, he had received a most unexpected message, coded only for him. It was a message from his brother. He had almost forgotten he had a brother: a mother, father, and now a brother too; who would have thought? He barely recalled him, but he knew he was older; older and presumably wiser.

The message had been simple and clear but also presumptuous in its simplicity. It was as if he had not been gone that long at all; as if his Rite of Passage amounted to a passing of little consequence or meaning. He had been placed with great ceremony, but his return was apparently nothing like that.

I hope you are well, Gatc'hh'en. I'm looking forward to seeing you again. It has been a while.

Soon,

Arra'll'en.

His brother's message engendered a tremendous sense of relief. He had not, after all, outlived them all in a relativistic time warp as he had once feared, and they had not forgotten him. And yet, it was such a simple message, almost half-hearted in the paucity of words employed to say hello after such a long shift of time, and from his brother at that, a brother he barely recalled. Did it mean he had passed his so-called Rite of Passage? Presumably so. Did it infer his time with the people was over? Presumably so. Did it mean he had a choice in all of this? Not really. And what of the things he should have done, and then all that he had done and perhaps should not have? There was no time for that. No time to correct his sins of the past. More important, what of Catherine?

.. ..

He held Emily's hand in his and kissed it, and addressed her as if she was already Catherine. "I see you within," he said and imagined her replying, "As I do you."

But, in truth, there was no reply; it was all in his mind. Emily lay peacefully, her breathing regular and sure. "I will help you emerge from this chrysalis of a woman; we will leave together," he said aloud, to the empty room and the words once said seemed right. What was Emily if not a chrysalis?

He straightened, backing away, releasing her hand. Should he go? Should he go?

Yes, he should.

Voices in the corridor: her father returning with an attending physician. There was some urgency in their purpose. He turned to the door and froze them in mid-stride as they entered, suspending all electrical impulses to their muscles. They didn't collapse; they remained standing, perfectly rigid. They could see him and think, but not speak. Their hearts were equally locked. In a moment if he did not release them, they would be dead.

He released their hearts and the muscles that controlled their breathing, and then leaned over and read the name-tag on the doctor's white garment: Dr. Robert Norris — Of English heritage, then. He leaned back and examined him more carefully: young, Caucasian, dark hair, dark eyes to match; his mitochondrial clock registered almost forty years, give or take a year or two.

He turned and studied the other, presumably the father — Yes, the father; his DNA proved his fatherhood. And he had a French heritage, as would be the case. He noted, too, his damaged heart; he had only weeks or a month or so before it seized. He corrected the corresponding damage and the old man staggered slightly. His arteries had been clogged; clearing them so abruptly must have felt odd, if not a little painful.

He allowed them both to track him. Their eyes blinked rapidly and swiveled in their orbits, revealing frustration and fear — mostly fear. He could kill them, again by stopping their breathing, or their hearts, or by any number of means. He could cause them to disappear entirely: dust in the ventilation system.

But, "*Shhh, Shhh,*" Catherine had once whispered, imploring, calming him, her hand on his arm. "Are these men somehow less than you?" she had asked him then as she would ask him now if she were present. He had been ready to strike at the priest and his aspirant for their arrogance and threatening postures, to say nothing of the fact the young priest had just slapped Catherine because of her so-called blasphemy

"I fear the kind of power you possess will ultimately corrupt you," Catherine had anxiously added but her voice still gentle, holding him back while the mark of the priest's hand blossomed on her face.

Of course, she had stayed his hand; she could stop his hand anytime she wished, for any reason whatsoever. But did not tell her then or even ever what he had done to the man's mind, saying nothing of it so that she would not gain the benefit of his hypocrisy and his own special brand of arrogance.

"If I were a person perhaps that would be true," he had replied moments later as the two of them watched the priest carried away in a fit of madness, a madness he had imposed upon him in revenge.

"What did you do?"

"Nothing."

He was not accustomed to lying but he did then. Catherine knew, of course; she knew everything about him.

He glanced at Emily; she was still asleep. He took her free hand in his, and holding both kissed each of them, each in turn. He then turned to address the good doctor.

"I am Gatc'hh'en," he quietly informed him, letting his name settle and gather, to be recalled later if need be. He didn't like doctors, especially. They could be as insufferable as priests. He added for Norris's benefit, letting the words tickle his mind. "First, do no harm? Is that not your credo as well?"

No response. The good doctor feared for his life. That was all he could think of.

He had only moments before the doctor and the father would remember in any detail what had happened. He could wipe their memories clear but then there would be residual effects harder to explain. He released them. They dropped to their knees with relief, the father immediately scrambling toward his daughter.

He carefully placed Emily's hands on her chest one over the other so her father could take them up. He watched him do so, and then hold them to him, kissing her open palms each in turn as he wept. The doctor had meanwhile rushed to the electronic device monitoring her condition. "No, no, you were wrong, Marcel! Your daughter is okay; she's good! There is nothing wrong with her!" Norris pointed to the device to prove it. "Look at the heart! It is strong and steady; her breathing too!"

"Thank God! I don't how I could have been wrong, but thank God, thank God!" her father cried in an American accent —he had imagined her father's accent would be French; there was a good probability it might have been. Her father kissed her hands again leaning over her, and openly wept. His heart would have given out at that point if he had not repaired it.

Enough was enough. He would let them figure out what had happened, if they could. Not caring what they might see, or what they might report back if they should be asked, he transformed back into his natural state and once again passed through the thick glass as if it did not exist.

8

Brother

It is frustrating sometimes, this tedious repetition of life and death, hope, and delusion. He felt sorry for the people but proud too. Is that what he would say to his brother when he asked what he had learned? Would he say that while their mortality defines them, they carry on as if they live forever? Would he say that they often sacrifice their lives for one another, but then in the very next breath murder their kind for paltry reasons? It would be easy to show what excellent builders they are, but just as easy to demonstrate how they inevitably tear it all down in a fit of self-destruction. It is odd. They tear it all down only to build it up again, over and over. It makes no sense: no sense at all.

He would have to tell his brother that he had learned nothing. He would have to say he understood almost nothing. He had only a myriad of observations to share, for in the end there is no rationale to explain what the people do, or how they feel, other than what their biology defines for them. Their lives are random, even meaningless. They fool themselves to think otherwise.

But was he and his brother any different? When it came right down to it? Truly?

• •• ••• ••••••

Bathed in Earthshine, the sun piercing the depthless black like a hole in space, the moon a ghost reminding him yet again of the lost past as much as the past that still lingered, he rotated slowly about to find his home. It was still there — not that he expected it to have moved. The star associated with his home planet had at first ballooned outward and then a hundred-thousand years later went nova. The explosion created a halo of hydrogen and helium and all the metals that had once comprised their star, leaving only a small white dwarf where their sun had once been.

He recalled a short ceremony preceding his departure that would begin his Rite. He remembered his mother's tears and his father looking down with pride, and then his brother suspended high up above gathering up his wings, keeping to himself; and, yes, he recalled his brother when he thought back — he had just returned from his Rite. It was a privilege to be chosen and very rare for brothers. But on reflection, that, too, seemed a revelation: his brother had gone through, and supposedly passed, his version of the Rite; it meant that his brother's message had been contrived; he would know what the Rite was about and what it was like. Why had he hovered off to the side otherwise?

He remembered everything, every detail, everything that passed through his eyes and ears on the way to his mind. It was a curse, really. He remembered his mother despondent and hesitant but determined to follow through. "This is necessary," she had told him when he had asked why he had to go through with it, taking him off to the side to say, "This is how we remember."

They approached a singularity — something so small, and so singular in shape and structure that the name although not mathematically correct becomes appropriate. Perfectly spherical. Time trapped within. Light unable to escape. He understood the mathematical details as well as the physics, so what he ultimately experienced was not much of a surprise, or necessarily unexpected; it was just that it was so much more powerful an experience than he had imagined it would be. The singularity — if one should call it that — was not just dark but perfectly black. It was spinning faster than he had been told and calculated. And nor could he see the nucleus in all its fullness. It had been only a black speck in the distance at first but he could feel the force of it, the relentless pull of gravity, the only one of the primary forces to escape its singular heart.

They had dropped over the edge of the vortex and were swept inward, picking up speed and massive bursts of energy. He had never felt such violence, such force until then, and not since, admittedly; it had felt as if he might be pulled apart. The power of the transit made them nothing. Nothing. There was a powerful jolt and when he had opened his eyes found himself alone, and in case there was any doubt about what he should focus on, found himself in orbit about Earth, the first time he had ever laid eyes on it. In his first few seconds of his Rite, he found himself weeping from the emotional trauma of the trip, and the wondrous beauty of the world floating before him.

· ·· ··· ·····

History is the lie we have all come to agree upon, and yet there are undeniable facts upon which it pivots. His people had first stood upright and looked up at the stars less than a million years before their sun would traitorously turn their home to cinder, and even though they had by then managed to relocate to the outer planets further out within their solar system, there was no air to breathe and nothing would grow on those worlds without a sun. They had looked around carefully and thoroughly for another home orbiting about another star like the one they had lost, but as luck would have it, there were no habitable planets within five hundred light-years. They could look but not touch, it had seemed, for the harsh truth was that before the development of the Tunnels they could not travel faster than the speed of light, or reach out further than light would take them in a lifetime.

They had built starships built upon a hybrid approach, accelerating the ships using a locally generated electromagnetic field powered by their star that stretched out as a spiral with a diameter equal to their solar system. Once in interstellar space, the ships employed ion-drive engines powered by matter- antimatter combined with solar-system wide ram-scoops to gather up local ions to supplement the onboard fuel. Twenty-six so-called generational ships — generational in the sense it took a generation to build each one of them — were launched toward five different destinations at intervals of one hundred years, each with better technology, and, presumably, a higher chance of success. None were ever heard from again. The ships had communication devices; the crew could have called, and of course they did, but as they accelerated outbound the calls became fewer and fewer. A thousand years went by, and the transmissions stopped. It was rumored there were some of the old people still out there somewhere wrapped up in their cocoon of metal with their artificial sun still shining. More likely, they died somewhere out there between the stars. If so, it was probably a very slow death for they would not have given up easily.

It was not lost on him, though, that that was exactly his own situation upon arrival at Earth. The people's solar system was not unlike an island to him. He could not navigate much beyond it, at least not very far beyond because of the same limitations that once nearly ended his people, namely the inability to travel faster than the speed of light. It was neither ironic and nor a coincidence that it should have been arranged to be like that. He was certain it was an intentional part of the fabric of his Rite.

In those early years, with his heart rent with loneliness, it had been tempting to disperse himself as the old often did. And, indeed, he might have attempted to do just that at least once, or twice. Time, it does everything to you; you can experience it directly but can understand it only theoretically. It adds up to this: no matter how perceptive one might be, or how profound the understanding of the world, if one cannot share one's life, then what is the point? If there is no one to love, no one to listen or listen to, then you are nothing; life becomes meaningless.

He eventually overcame his despondency and had come to reason, and correctly now, too, it seemed, that he never would have been sent on a one-way trip by those who loved him. It is ironic, though; he barely remembered his brother: what he was like, his sense of humor, his strength, and weaknesses; what he liked, and didn't. But it didn't matter. The mere receipt of his message confirmed more than the few words that comprised the content that his home and family remained intact and were waiting for him.

Of course — or not so 'of course' since in his profound ignorance he had no idea about what was what, just a jumbling together of what he did not understand — he had, before he had reached a true understanding of the laws that govern space and time as well as his heart, made a misguided attempt to return home using only his internal resources. The farther he drew away from the sun, the weaker he became and only managed to get as far as Saturn. Cold, lonely, his velocity dropping, and at the very end of his strength, he had followed Saturn's magnetic field and swung through the rings and clipped Titan before heading sunward again, the full truth of his isolation and the finality of his Rite finally understood.

It had been foolish of him to make that attempt, really, but he had done so in his early days long before Catherine and L'Batard, and long before his eyes had been opened to see the people for who and what they are. Namely, not so different from him in the fact they, too, are intelligent and mortal in the face of an entirely indifferent universe they both try to understand and live within, each with their fear and loneliness in hand.

• •• ••• ••••••

He lifted his human face to the night sky and one more time tried to imagine his brother's face. Would his features be like his own?

Would he possess wisdom, kindness, or both? He sighed not knowing whether to laugh or cry out his frustration. The existence of a society of people that can communicate to another a society on another star is rare both in the fabric of space but also in time, and with no imminent rescue in hand his forbears had been forced to come up with a new plan. They understood matter and how it was put together. They could manipulate it, change it, seamlessly exchange energy for mass, and vice-versa. It meant the ultimate solution, and the only real solution open to them was to change themselves. To redesign their bodies but not their minds in such a way as to allow them to survive in the tenuous remnants of their star, not just bodily but also in a way that enabled them to remain whole. That is, whole in both heart and mind.

Irony convoluted by irony: Would he not have to recreate himself as well? Is that not what all of this meant? He shook his head and marveled at the sudden welling of determination originating from within the depths of his nearly human heart. He would be the harbinger of his destiny and the foil of his fate. His brother would have no say in it, nor his mother, nor any of those who might claim him for their own. He would be his own man. He would be L'Batard's man. Come hell or high water he was resolved in it. He had things to do and a way forward. His brother's imminent arrival notwithstanding, he would not return home with his tail between his legs.

9

Les Coquelicots

Emily opened her eyes. She blinked once, twice. She was not dead. She knew this with certainty. She turned her head. Her father, asleep, breathing deeply, his chin resting on his chest, sat slumped in a chair next to her. The book he had been reading lay face down on the bed. She glanced at the title: *The God Delusion*. What must her father think? What would he say about this? Yet another miracle? Or would he measure only the probabilities? The former, she thought; her father might be a man of science but he had an illogical heart too.

She turned her head so she again faced the ceiling. She breathed in, then out: it was a technique, taught to calm her. But there it was, that anger again: She was still the same old and getting older, Emily. She recalled then applied the word she so often reserved for the denuding radiation treatments, the humiliating search for blood and bone marrow donors, and the elemental, god-awful, sickness.

"Bullcrap. It's all bullcrap," she said and almost wept.

She had been dying for the last six years with, on the average, one near-death experience a year. This, indeed, was her sixth. No tunnel of light this time; no singing angels, no ancient relatives to welcome her through the pearly gates, only nothing. It was like being asleep. She frowned, concentrating, hoping for something better. Her fingers absently traced the sharp line of bone and flesh of her chin. Nothing. She felt nothing. Perhaps she had been dead. If so, she had been cheated; she'd rather be elsewhere, anywhere but here.

Emily swore aloud, "Bullcrap!" the effort taking its toll. She felt feeble, fragile. Her head spun. She hoped she would not retch; she did not have the strength to turn to let the vomit drain away. She swallowed. She would not have that. She would not go that way. She would not drown.

Her father stirred, raising his chin, his eyes remaining closed. He lifted his hands then drew his fingers slowly down revealing a face with a pair of open, tired eyes, and a mouth firmly set, the lips pursing as he swallowed to clear a dry throat. He found the glass of water, took a sip, and then held it for her. She nearly emptied the glass. It was cold. How did he get it to be so cold?

"How do you feel?"

"Like a pile of crap," she managed, swallowing the last bit.

He did not smile. He leaned forward and grasped his daughter's hand and said very gravely, keeping her eyes to his, "We thought you had left us. I was almost certain you had."

Emily tiredly added, "Again."

This initiated a frown. "Don't talk like that..." He stood and stretched, then leaned over to kiss her. "Good to have you back," he said and kissed her cheek, forehead, nose, then lips, one after the other.

Emily smiled but weakly. Her father had seen and heard the truth and maybe had even accepted it.

He said, "I was talking to the specialist. Frankly, she was as surprised as any of us. I mean, we weren't surprised, we were hoping... and it turned out to be right. It proves there is always hope, doesn't it?"

You want me to agree, Emily thought but remained silent. There is no hope, she thought, too, again keeping her thoughts to herself. But what was taking so long, she wondered? She should have gone this time. She should have... She should have... The body sometimes does amazing things, often holding on longer than the heart can, she knew from experience. She would have gone long ago if it had only been up to her.

"Anyway," her father said — he shrugged, smiling, inferring hope when he knew there was none: "None of us know why you're here but we're glad you are." He leaned forward and brushed his lips across her forehead, his eyes staying with hers as he straightened, the truth they both knew snagged.

Emily grieved. After she had finally died her one hundred times, her father would keep on dying a thousand times more. She could not stop her tears with that thought. They would have poured out except there were none; she was completely dry. She looked away, turning her head to the side. Her body nonetheless heaved as if she possessed an endless reservoir.

Her father let his hands fall to his side. Time. It stretched out ahead of her, infinite. Time, astronomical in this hospital room, abruptly truncated in the immediate future. Only those conscious of their imminent death can understand it.

Her father kissed her again, promised to return in a few hours, and then departed, backing slowly out of the room, leaving his daughter in a preferred state, alone.

Is that true? Is that what she wanted?

Yes, of course; that is exactly what she wanted.

Time, time: tic, tock...

Emily's mind opened and shifted and, surprised, she found herself floating in space, Earth cast in all its glory below her as she slowly rotated about, the sun rising in dazzling silence. She breathed in... And out... There was air. ...That's different; everyone knows there is no air is space. Floating in orbit above the blue, blue Earth, the silence of the stars wrapped about her like a cold shroud was only in her imagination. And yet, she felt another's presence. Just there... Right there... Was that in her imagination too? She could almost touch him. Who could it be? God? No, no. Her Guardian Angel, maybe. We all need a Guardian Angel, don't we? She recalled how he had touched her shoulder, and how he had held her hand, and kissed her forehead and lips. What kind of Guardian Angel does that? She thought they were not allowed to kiss — at least not like that.

A nurse came and went, delivering Emily's sedative. With the right drugs, and just the right amount, her small world often became a confusion of place, and who was who. She would float over an emaciated body. In her drug-induced reality, in her imagination — she could not tell which, really — she would hover, weightless, watching the body — stillness itself — waiting for it to do something, anything — move, breathe — to indicate that it was still alive. It would suddenly arch its back and inhale a ragged breath before collapsing again into a pile of bone and flesh.

It was not her. There was no possible way it could be her.

Today, the nurse must have been generous and she could finally feel herself falling. It would be hours before she struck the ground and bounced back up. She closed her eyes, slipped toward nothingness but then found herself on a sculpted hill topped with a sea of heart-red poppies. She turned slowly around and around to gather in her surroundings. The distance stretched into a field of yellow and green, poppies dancing about her synchronized with the motion of golden grass swaying back and forth in an invisible wind. Blue sky, blazing sun. The wind slipped up the slope and flowed past, gently lifting her hair and the fabric of her dress. Another gust. Warm. Summer warm.

Les Coquelicots. Monet. Had she fallen into the painting, been absorbed into its myth? What a thought; what an incredible thought. What could be better but to live in a masterpiece?

And so... And so...

She ran. Down the hill. Poppies snapping by. The high grass tripping her up. She fell and rolled. The sky and green, the sky and green. The sweet scent of newly created grass. She stopped rolling and lay on her back. The sky whirled above her. If this was heaven, then let her remain. If it is only a painting, then let her remain there too.

She sat up. She brushed back her hair and straightened her dress. A bright light floated just behind the bank of willow in the distance. Flares of light stabbed out of it like a blaze from a diamond. Why was it so bright and how could it remain suspended like that? It should be moving, she thought; and, as if reading her mind, it did just that, soundlessly following the tree-line away from her.

She followed it with her eyes, slowly turning as it slowly drifted, dropped, and then followed the dazzling river caught in sunlight. A river? Where had it come from? She pushed herself upright, remaining on her knees. There it was through the long strings of hanging willow, a blue ribbon flowing toward the sea.

"Of course! *The River!*"

She laughed and climbed to feet to follow the mysterious floating sun — if that is what it was; it was so bright — as it sank beneath the tree-line but then suddenly popped up again and continued.

"Hey!" She waved.

It suddenly changed course toward her, crossing the river, through the willow branches, hugging the ground. It was pure white and outshone the sun. She waved again then turned and ran. It was tough going. The grass was high. She glanced back over her shoulder. Whatever it might be was gaining: a ball of light, a fragment ripped torn from the sun perhaps? She tripped and fell and was instantly scooped up: blue sky, tumbling sun, upside down river keeping within its bank, and she was set gently down.

She looked up shielding her eyes and caught a glimpse of him through the glare. Sunlight poured from his eyes, nose, mouth, ears; his flesh glowed. He floated off the ground as if gravity meant nothing. Grey eyes. Blonde hair pulled back off a strong face.

"Mon cher amour… ma belle petite chère," he said, as he kneeled beside her and placed his hand on her arm.

God, his voice. It was beautiful, like a symphony.

"Catherine," he said when he saw that she did not understand.

"Emily," she corrected him, still trying to make out his features through the glare surrounding him.

He smiled and brushed back her hair that had tumbled across her eyes then bowed graciously. "My mistake, mademoiselle." He spoke English but with an accent — French, possibly. He was very handsome, young; the same age as she, or nearly.

"Who are you?" she asked, continuing to shield her eyes.

"Who would you like me to be?" he gently asked, keeping the sun behind him, each word he spoke seemingly suspended in the air.

She nearly lay back in a faint. It was the sound of his voice — that is all it took.

"I don't know," she answered truthfully as she fell the last distance, and as sleep, blissful sleep, poppy sleep, overwhelmed her.

10

Singular Friends

He cast short stark shadows, the city black and white below him. The quarter moon hung above the harbor, its pale light reflecting off the waters. He lifted higher, each strobe of light accompanied by a deep rumbling sound, each one shaking the city. The moon fell back, its light now running across the chopped ocean, across the city, into the harbor. He lifted higher, now a pinpoint, and nearly inaudible. The city lights were white, orange, blue, and strung in pearls enclosed by the worn mountains, dark and folded in the night, and the silver river springing from them.

They would have witnessed him from below, no doubt pointing upward while wondering what he could be. Many hundreds of thousands would be witness to his weakness, his surrender to his memory. He could feel the air-traffic radars paint him — they would see him too. There would be a price to pay for this lapse, but so what? It was perhaps time the people woke up to the fact that their existence had nothing to do with the assumed grace of their jealous and often vengeful and imaginary gods. People are not created in the image of their God; it was the other way around.

He let his radiative intensity drop, shifting it to the high x-ray band, the emissions quickly absorbed by the atmosphere and subsequently invisible to those below. He went dark but not so dark they would not have some detectors that would see him. He lifted higher still, turning about to orient himself, and then accelerated along the vector he had selected, slowly increasing his angle of ascent. The city fell behind, the river under moonlight rising before him, followed by the empty darkness of the Adirondack's as he swept over the ancient range. The lights of Montreal, a thin line on the horizon, rising beneath him like a gossamer web, and then that city too fell behind, followed by an empty darkness punctuated only by points of moonlight reflecting off a host of small lakes in the empty tundra below him. Spreading his wings, rotating himself about, he entered polar orbit.

• •• ••• ••••••

L'Batard was the one who had informed him of her death. Until then he had had no idea she was gone. He had been sitting in the garden in Chateaux in Blois pouring over a manuscript written by an Italian nearly one hundred years previously. It was of course God-centric as was everything written and even said in those days; but it was beautiful, too, and revealed an excellent mind It was ironic that Catherine had pointed it out to him, for it was she who had stumbled upon it first. Dante's *Divine Comedy*, he recalled.

L'Batard entered the garden with his purposeful stride. He strode forward, following the twisted path. Standing before him, he waited for him to set aside the manuscript and then sat slowly down. His eyes were searching, his jaw set, and his face white. He did not have to say what he had come to say; the message was clearly stated before he spoke.

The words finally said, L'Batard standing and waiting for his response, he had imagined himself floating in an endless sea of black emptiness amidst the void between the stars filled with dark energy pushing the stars even further apart. He had imagined that if there is a beginning or an end, it must have been, and will be, empty like the way he felt at that moment.

• •• ••• ••••••

He recalled the first time he and L'Batard's paths crossed. He and Catherine turned their mounts to face him. The lead rider crested the rise followed closely by the next, followed by a gold and red standard clearing the rise swinging to and fro.

L'Batard's mission was one of mercy; his brother was dying, and would surely die without Catherine's intervention. His intent was to return her to Blois as quickly as possible. It would be a long road from that point forward; a lot of water would flow beneath the old bridge, and many lives too. It would be a one-way trip; at least for Catherine it would be. He should have scooped her up right there and then and spirited her off. But that is just hindsight. Twenty-twenty.

L'Batard raised a gloved hand and the column stopped and shuffled into order, their mounts turned outward in column defense, their lances ready. Not seeing them at first, L'Batard raised himself in the stirrups and searched the tree-line. Sighting them, he immediately swung his mount about and spurred it forward. The column followed, an escort of four riders immediately moving up paralleling him in a defensive role. When they were close enough, the guard dropped back as L'Batard continued a few more paces then stopped.

He looked down upon them, steadying his mount.

"Catherine Élise de Domremy?"

L'Batard was attired in chainmail, but his head was bare. Dark hair. Clean shaven. Grey eyes. Slender.

Catherine answered, standing straight, her head held high. "Yes, I am Catherine." Catherine had not only been beautiful and highly intelligent, but also a very proud woman, and rightfully so.

L'Batard bowed. "Lady, we have ridden a long way to find you." He then turned to face him. "Et qui sont vous, monsieur?"

He would not lie. "I am Gatc'hh'en."

First words. The first of thousands, some understood, some not.

• •• ••• •••••

It is not always wise to do what can be done, or what is easy to do; it is more important to do what is right. But is something right because someone says it is, or because it is? How does one know? Catherine learned what was right and wrong from her Book, the concept delineated by the prophets within and interpreted by the priests without, both claiming to know the mind of their God. He had read her book many times and had come to the conclusion that the definitions contained therein did not always line up with what was good for the people, and what could be construed as being right other than what is good for the people? If an action promotes the health and welfare, the mind and expression of the people, then by definition it must be right, or what does right mean? What is the notion of right for?

He often thought of L'Batard. His strength, his clarity of purpose and mind. His ability to command and direct the destiny of others. He would ask him now about Emily, if he could. "What is right?" he would ask. He would explain that, although he had given her life with one hand, he was about to take it away with the other; there would be nothing left of Mademoiselle Dupuis when he was done with her. He had originally intended to replace her body and disassemble her mind and then configure it, synapse to synapse, with his nearly perfect memories of Catherine. The wrong was this: whoever stood before him at the end of all his machinations would not be Catherine, only his recollections of her. In the end, he would not have the real Catherine back but only a facsimile: her body a perfect duplicate but her all-elusive soul a continuing mystery.

How could he explain something like that to a man like L'Batard? Even so, he was quite confident that L'Batard would never agree. He would instinctively know that it would not be right.

He recalled L'Batard again in the garden, his blue eyes locked on him. Once a soul passes on, there is no return. It is sacrilege to raise the dead. L'Batard, not being a priest, would not, could not, say anything like that, but his blue eyes would, and could.

In the end, as much as she tried, Catherine was unable to save L'Batard's brother. He died of a brain aneurysm complicated by a burst appendix. Catherine could not help him because by the time she finally arrived, exhausted after a hard week of travel, he was already dead. His mind had gone. There was no brother of L'Batard to save. But she did not know that, not for five more days after which she finally accepted it. He had tried to tell her but she would not listen.

On learning of his brother's death, L'Batard had dropped to his knees beside his dead brother and raised his hands in prayer, and quietly wept. Done, he stood and turned to Catherine. A lesser man would have blamed her but not L'Batard. He bowed to her, sweeping low, and then slowly straightening revealing his tears of loss. He was walking into the future, he said, because that is all there is. The past is the past, and he intended to let it be, and he hoped she would too. He then departed, dropping his chin into the collar of his cloak, careful to conceal the depth of his sorrow.

· ·· ··· ·····

The sun rose above the pole shattering his night, filling the darkness. He felt a different type of radar touch him; it had been designed for detecting long range intercontinental missiles. He knew they would not fire their interceptor missiles — he was going the wrong way and his profile was not ballistic but orbital. But they would wonder and take note, and there would be endless speculation. They would inevitably correlate this episode with his entry only a few days earlier, and because this time it had occurred over the Eastern Seaboard of the United States, there would be no end to it. They would not let it go.

He sighed, still wrapped in his memories of the past. He was currently two hundred and sixty kilometers above Ellesmere. He could feel the tickle of the magnetic field. It was where he had come in. He was sick and tired of playing these games. What was it to him if the people nearly panicked every time he did something they neither understood nor could imagine? If their culture took a bounce who cared? Not him. There was no point in caring. He was going home.

He dropped out of Earth's shadow into sunlight. He was fully immersed. He spread himself thin to absorb the energy. They would see him again — he would cover nearly a third of the sky at this altitude. He would appear as a curtain of energy like the Borealis, only the color of sapphire and not the mourning greens of atomic oxygen, and the autumn reds of ionized nitrogen. He shifted his color from sapphire to indigo to make his point. He let the colors wave from the horizon to the horizon holding himself in position above Ellesmere, letting the magnetic lines carry the color upward and across the globe. He would be seen across all western and eastern Canada, and along the entire Eastern Seaboard of the United States.

He followed the magnetic lines upward in a slow spiral and glanced downward. He knew he had perhaps gone too far once again when he noticed the lights below him suddenly going out. He had once again shut down their power grid. If they did not notice the odd coloration of their skies, they would most definitely note the fact their power grid had suddenly overloaded. Second time this month, in fact. Or was it the third?

He drew himself inward. It was time to leave. He had miles to go and his Singular Friend to greet. It was ironic that he should think of the ancient singularity that way; it — and it was most definitely an it — was hardly L'Batard who had been singularly a friend. It was just a thing. Something he had stumbled upon during one of his peregrinations out beyond the sun's influence where he would suspend himself, wings extended, upon the precipice of time and space that separated him from his home. Behind him would be the light and warmth of the sun, while before him stretched a vast sea of emptiness and the aching and unpassable distance between where he floated, and where he knew his home prevailed within the great arm of the galaxy. He had not understood his singular friend's potential until days later when his darkened heart — darkened by loneliness and despair — suddenly contrived a way in which it could be utilized in this mad scheme of his.

He accelerated along the magnetic lines upward in a spiral, a thousand miles above the North Atlantic, and then indistinguishable from the high-energy protons that comprised the solar wind, slipped down the magnetic tail and shot out the end, directing himself out beyond the Heliopause just a few degrees up off the ecliptic. He should just get on with it, he thought, as he increased his velocity, accelerating under the influence of the field outbound at nearly the speed of light. It was time to stop playing games.

11

First Contact

Advanced Technology Research Center, ATRC, Maikalani, Maui, Hawaii. Joseph Monserrat, Ph.D. Astronomy, Johns Hopkins University, sat with chin in hand staring at the redrawn orbit on his workstation screen.

"It has an apparent magnitude of ten point five. It's exceptionally bright, more than what can be reflected even if painted with a reflective material so I won't even guess the albedo. It seems to be internally sourcing its own light. It is very strange."

He glanced up to catch the expressions on the faces of his post-doc assistants, Kenneth Matheson, Ph.D. Astronomy University of Hawaii, and Bob King, Ph.D. Astrophysics, University of Calgary. Neither flinched at the figures.

"What could be that bright?" Monserrat asked. Neither could answer. "Bob, what do we know that could shine that brightly?" he asked again, digging.

Bob King squirmed: "Nothing I know of."

Ken Matheson responded. "According to Mauna Key, it peaks at six-hundred nanometers. It is radiating very much like the sun or a nuclear core at that temperature."

"It's hot then."

"That's crap," Bob King threw out. "But once again it might suggest it might be closer than we think. But—"he quickly qualified his response, shaking his head, "We have had a number of consecutive tracks showing it's just beyond Jupiter, so go figure."

"Do we have a mass estimate yet?" Monserrat asked looking to the two of them.

King answered. "We have over one thousand iterations which converge to a mass estimate of a good-sized mountain like McKinley — with an average diameter of forty kilometers and that's assuming a mean density similar to loosely bound regolith. It is almost twice the size of Hale-Bopp. It's moving — and this is hard to believe — at approximately five hundred kilometers per second." He grimaced, rolled his eyes then added, "That's gotta be crap."

He turned to face Monserrat, not only his friend but mentor. "Vanier has been trying to call you all morning. She says the approach to Jupiter suggests it will not impact Jupiter, or break up at all. To her, it looks more like a profile for a gravity assist — in this case, to slow down."

"No way," Monserrat lightly taunted adding a smile. "She's as bad as Ken."

They were referring to Doctor Eleanor Vanier, Ph.D., Astrodynamics, Caltech, currently at JPL as a senior member of the orbit dynamics and navigation team. She and Monserrat had known and worked together for years.

"She knows it seems ridiculous," King continued, "but she's working the numbers anyway to give us an estimate of the final velocity and direction once it does fly past Jupiter. If it's an assist, we'll find out soon enough anyway. The object should be within Jupiter's gravity-well by tonight."

"I think we should shout out what we've found right away," Matheson suggested, ensuring he was heard. "At least tell somebody in case we're scooped, and we will be scooped; there are hundreds if not thousands of amateurs looking for objects like this."

Monserrat nodded his agreement. "Go ahead. Do it now." He sat back and looked to each of them in turn. "Has anyone checked? Is there some blog out there claiming something weird going on around Jupiter?"

"We have ownership," Matheson quickly confirmed. "I did register it with the MPC the other day even though you said not to — sorry. But, yeah, to answer your question, there is some chatter out there."

"What do they know?"

"Not much — Tonight will tell, as Bob says."

"Okay." Monserrat pushed himself up from the chair and began to pace the small office, dodging around Matheson and King and the stacks of books, journals, and computer printouts. "Tell me again that we've checked everything."

King, not bothering to follow his progress, patiently explained. "We've been over it a hundred times," he said. "We have performed a hundred diagnostic tests and repeated each one a dozen times, and the results always say the cameras and associated software are fully functional. There are no hardware faults, no known software bugs; all the tests pass, one hundred percent, no deviation, every time."

"What about the raw data itself?"

"Raw data is raw data — the processing pipeline is shown to be perfect. None of the tracks have indicated any error. The iterations are highly consistent. They converge almost right away now. The object is no ghost. It is real and it's heading right for Jupiter."

Monserrat regained his chair. "Okay, fine; I'll go with that."

"I will get a select few to independently confirm what we've discovered," he went on: "Gregory at Arecibo to verify the range, if it's spinning, and, if possible, get a radar map. If it's as massive as we think, they should be able to find it with our positional data. I'll add Chavez at the LMT to see if he can get a handle on it, and also verify the attitude and range. Johansson at Mauna Key to get an optical shot in the visible and infrared. Creutzberg at Goddard to use their satellite to get a shot in ultraviolet, gamma, and x-ray. I know all of them. They'll do it without opening their mouths — at least for now."

"You can't keep them quiet for long. They have careers too," King offered.

"I know."

King shifted uneasily. "What do you think it is?"

"Some Kuiper Belt object suddenly deciding to break loose," Monserrat replied. "Or a very long periodic comet sourced as most of them are from way out there. But it is a huge one, I'll give you that, and I can't get over how bright it is — and then again the velocity is wrong. That, in particular, makes no sense. It's that that makes me think something might be wrong with our calibration of the array. Anyway, as you say, we'll know by tonight."

He had a second thought and queried Matheson. "You said before, Ken, that the object came and went. You acquired it but then lost it the next few nights but then picked it up again?"

"That's right."

"It hasn't happened since?"

"No, it hasn't. I can't explain the first occurrence, only to say there was no shift in the track during the time it apparently went dark. The fact it's coming and going may be due to the fact it's getting closer to Jupiter. It may be interacting with Jupiter's magnetic field, or it's heating up from tidal forces."

King shot back. "That's not right: Coming and going – I never heard that!"

Monserrat cut off the discussion: they didn't have the luxury of time. "If it disappears again we'll deal with it. Rerun all the scripts using the raw data. Redo all the iterations to demonstrate they continue to converge. Get all the able-bodied grad students working on it, and to speed things up you have my permission to use the entire physics cluster of workstations. I don't care what it's dedicated to or whose project it's on. If someone has a problem, send them to me."

Both men nodded and began to move.

"And don't tell them anything other than what they'll suspect, that we've discovered a new comet," Monserrat called after them. "Don't tell them how massive it is, how fast it's going, or any of that — in particular how bright it is. It will all come out eventually, but I don't want it out until we have all the data we can get."

Monserrat returned to his chair, settling in front of the keyboard. "Every workstation but this one, that is."

Mendelssohn Choir

T he universe might be put together with specific constants, but there was nothing to say he could not change those constants — at least for a short while, and at the very deepest level where space and time boil and foam. He did not by himself have sufficient strength, but if he could tap into the primordial energies of creation — and he knew he could; or at least he imagined he could — then there was a way.

While Emily healed, he had spent nearly a month to reach the cold expanse where his Singular Friend lingered, and then nearly a week more to relocate him. His diminutive friend was especially difficult to find, as minuscule and nearly invisible as he frustratingly was. But there he was, finally, drifting along, starlight bending around him while he dragged a handful of frozen still-born companions behind him — a dead giveaway.

His Singular Friend — the *Dark Horse* as he had come to think of him for who was riding who? — was on an arc that, after a correction or two, would place it in near opposition to Jupiter, and a good thing, too, for he immediately understood that he would need the massive gas-giant to help him negotiate the final transfer of his friend to Earth. He had swung about to position himself, confident, even excited as he began to accelerate his friend tangentially inward. His first attempt had been close, very close; only two corrections had been required, one a few days later, the second just a week later. The mathematics was as exact as the apple falls, as always, and what a relief that is too.

His friend's alignment had been a stroke of luck, really. It was sobering to think that if it had not been the case he might not have had sufficient resources to implement his plan in full, or even at all. Push harder, reach deeper; it had always worked for him in the past, but almost not that time. He had dug deep, as deep as he could, and after the final course adjustment, almost drained, he had been forced to recharge, immersing himself amidst the high-energy ions trapped within Jupiter's magnetic field. He had nearly wept with relief as he finally entered the field and felt the inrush of energy. It was a deep well, a very deep well, and he bathed in it, plunging deep and basking in it. Secure then, fully satiated, sober and somber, he had searched for a single word to match the singular nature of his friend and the crux of his imagined plan. Madness? Yes, of course: madness. He was quite mad.

· ·· ··· ······

It had been a quick trip from Jupiter sunward. He had followed an arc slightly inclined to the ecliptic. Earth, which he had at first seen as a little blue dot ultimately appeared as a blue and white crescent wrapped in a halo of refracted light. The crescent moon, a sliver sickle only one-eighth the size of Earth floated to his right, separated by a surprising thirty Earth diameters or so, making it appear as a binary system of equal partners except, one harbored life while the other stone-cold dead. The sun, nearly pure white, blazed to his left in a black sky.

He fell inward, accelerating, the angle between the Earth and Moon slowly narrowing as he neared, Earth becoming more central as the relative positions of the sun and Moon shifted. Music. A Mendelssohn Choir. Voices of the people. The only minds within a billion-billion miles and a billion more years that could understand this dance in all its precise glory. He extended his wings stretching them outward, bathing in the light, feathering them while he tacked, heeling over as a sailing ship would in a steady wind. He could have just as easily have propelled himself forward by his own means. It was mere self-indulgence not to.

As he neared, he tacked again — a quick spin about his central axis while drawing his wings inward to reduce his moment of inertia. Once the turn was made, he once again deployed his wings, extending them outward so that he would be seen in the early morning sky right across Western Europe and the Eastern Seaboard of North America. He didn't care. Let them guess what he might be.

· ·· ··· ·····

Understanding acquires perspective. The very small can be measured as a function of the quantization of light and matter, and the very large as a function of the decay of the universe, but everyday experience is defined by suns and planets on one end of the scale, and collections of atoms into molecules that can be held in one's hand on the other.

Understanding is acquired through experience. The first-time Catherine heard *Ave Maris Stella* and the chanson *Se La Face Ay Pale* both sung in the Rheims Cathedral she could barely speak for the entire afternoon, weeping for the joy she had felt. And the art decorating the cathedral at Rheims, and Notre Dame, was God Incarnate, so she said without thinking, for what she felt was surely blasphemy. She marveled and he had marveled as she marveled. He wondered what she would have thought if she had heard Schubert's *Ava Maria*, or viewed Botticelli's *Madonna del Magnificat*? He wished she could listen and see. Maybe she would, through Emily, he thought, and settled into the idea, dwelling on it for a moment. That, after all, was the core of his plan, was it not?

Of course, too, it had not escaped him that the years that followed close on Catherine's death were the beginning of a great shift in how the people perceived their world. He could have dissolved himself into a dew, and possibly should have, upon Catherine's death, but curiosity overwhelmed even his broken heart, and he had instead remained behind for a while, just a short while, to see what might happen. And on came the first of the great: Donatello, Raphael, Botticelli, Copernicus, Rabelais, Galileo, Bach, Vivaldi, Kepler, Milton, leading to Newton, and all standing on the shoulders of one another.

He personally met only one, just one: *Donato di Niccolo di Betto Bardi*, a sculptor of stone. It is perhaps ironic that the only hard evidence that proved that those days were real was that sculpture of him as he had been in those days of mourning. It used to be held in the bell tower of the *Catedral di Santa María Del Fiore* but was now in the *Museo del l'Opera del Duomo*; he knew because on each return he always made a point of returning to Florence just to feel the past again as much as to see himself captured in stone.

He learned through that experience, and then re-learned, that change may accumulate but the past still lingers. It is ironic perhaps, too, as much as instructive, that Donato's sculptures remain unaltered. People come and go. Buildings are erected, then torn down. But granite, marble, limestone, nearly immortal, remain either in a form purposed by the people, or in the original form born in fire or the pressures of the deep, in the folds of mountains, or cast randomly upon the plains.

• •• ••• •••••

He folded his wings at exactly the right moment, just as he caught up to Earth's Magneto-tail. He switched his polarity and ran up the lines through the plasma sheet and the South Atlantic Anomaly, picking up charged particles as he swept forward to energize himself further. Then up through the Van Allen radiation belt, and then downward through the magnetic neck to enter the Earth's atmosphere just above the magnetic north pole at the day-night terminator. The sonic boom caused by his re-entry could be heard more than forty kilometers away, to say nothing of the brilliant flash of light that preceded it, brighter than three suns. As last time and the time before, he didn't bother to slow down. He was done with that.

At five-thousand meters above the frozen surface of Ellesmere his velocity fell back to twelve times the speed of sound. He maintained that altitude and speed until he was over Montreal, at which time he increased his altitude to ten-thousand meters and dropped his speed to four times the speed of sound, his overall luminosity increasing by a factor of ten in the process. Five minutes and thirty-seconds later, he overflew New York City, then turned about, traversing the city once again before suddenly going dark. He was late — but he knew where to find her.

Lesson

This is a chicken," Catherine had once informed him holding the gangly beast gently in her arms; "It goes 'cluck'. It lays eggs which we eat." She pointed. "And that over there is a rooster — he possesses a character not unlike your own when you come think about it." She carefully set the feathered creature down and it ran off as she laughed.

"Ah…"

She pointed. "And that over there is a cat. Its purpose in life is to meow."

"A cat — got it."

"And catch mice."

"And catch mice."

"And over there is a dog — his name is Jacques. His purpose in life is to bark, and he does so brilliantly I must say. He is my dog, in fact. He comes when I call him." She canted her head to the side and smiled. "I like all my dogs to come when called."

"A dog. Jacques. He is your dog. I got it. I will not fetch for you, however."

She laughed again this time throwing her head back. "We'll see about that!"

She pointed out a host of other life, birds this time: a swallow, a robin, a red-winged blackbird, and high in the sky, a solitary hawk, dipping its wing, dropping into a spiral. She imitated the song of each one in turn, and with her hands how they flew. She was a brilliant mimic.

"I do see the pattern — honestly — and I hear and can appreciate the birdsong."

"Honestly? There is a dishonest element to all this life?" She canted her head again. "Or are you impatient with this game?"

"I didn't mean it that way."

"What do you mean, my love?"

He could not get enough of her, and her words, and explanations. He pointed. "What is that over there?"

She slowly turned to look, and then returned, her smile remaining the same. "That is a cow. It goes 'moo' — and it provides milk which we drink, or turn into butter."

"And that?" He pointed again.

She turned right about and then slowly returned. "Those are oats — I think that is what you are pointing to — which we seed in the spring and harvest in the fall, and which we eat all the next year but only if the crops of the previous year were successful. I have not introduced you to the pigs — they go, 'oink, oink'. They eat the oats too; they have beady eyes, enjoy mud, and smell horrible. I know many people who resemble pigs." She waited then added with a laugh, "Not you!"

She pointed, making him turn this time. "And that field over there is wheat which the pigs do not eat — we won't let them. We harvest wheat nearly at the same time as the oats, and make flour by grinding it, and from which we make bread, and cake." She leaned in close and whispered conspiratorially, her hair, caught in the summer breeze, tickling his cheek. "I particularly like cake, if you're interested or if you should ever wish to purchase me one."

"I see."

"It is expensive, but not exorbitantly so," she added, smiling, leaning back to study his reaction.

"What meat do you eat?"

He wanted to kiss her.

"If I cannot eat cake then I should eat meat, is that what you are suggesting?"

He laughed. "I don't know — I suppose."

"The chickens, the cows, the pigs, and the sheep — I have not introduced you to the sheep yet. They go 'baah', and we get wool from them, which we spin into yarn and make our clothing. The cattle give us our leather — such as the leather jerkin you are wearing."

"It is all fascinating. It is all very interrelated," he said.

"It is a perfect plan, barring accidents," she said. "Cold springs, dry summers, or even summers that are too wet; infestations of various insects, locust. I should introduce you to Monsieur Locust; he is anatomically interesting, as you would say."

"Monsieur Locust? He sounds like an interesting fellow, indeed." He waved his hand over the summer day in a gesture of inclusiveness. "But who are we, you and me, and all the people, in all this?"

"We are the custodians. We are made in God's image."

"God looks like you?"

"No... I am a woman."

"God is a man?"

"No... You are teasing me."

They had been sitting side by side contemplating the ripened fields separated by hedgerows beneath a blue sky, the summer sun not yet beginning to set. He had already forgotten their train of thought, distracted as he was. "We liken ourselves to be Gods?" he'd asked turning to see her reaction.

She remained staring straight ahead, her smile leaving her. "Ah..."

"Ah...?"

"That is blasphemy."

"It is a word only, and one that means absolutely nothing to me. But answer the question, please; do we, mere mortals, not liken ourselves to God more often than not?"

She turned slowly back to him. Her smile had dropped off. "You could burn for those words — many men and women have."

"Burn? They would burn you for that?"

And so they apparently do, and for much less. She told him as much as the sun slipped behind a band of dark cloud and the rain fell silently in waves along the far hills.

Standing, he reached down for her. "You talked of sin to me once before, do you remember?"

"I remember."

"If you want to know what sin is, then look to what your priests do in the name of your God," he had told her.

She accepted his offered hand and then stood, keeping close beside him without looking up. "You know nothing of this world, my love," she had said, looking toward the horizon, not smiling, avoiding eye contact.

He remembered picking up her satchel and kissing her briefly before, together, his arm around her, they headed back to their encampment. If it was true then, it is true now. He knew nothing, nothing.

14

Emily

He stood in the shadow watching her sleep. He could see that her body continued to slip down a reckless path toward dissolution; he would have to correct the misdirection of the cells that continued to betray her. She might die in another day or two if he did not. But, then again, perhaps that would be for the best — let her slip painlessly away; let nature take its course, albeit a little belatedly, thanks to his interference. It had been great conceit on his part to imagine he could easily, and without repercussions, resurrect the past: Easy in the physical mechanisms that enable it but challenging in the emotional sense, thanks to the knowing, deep down, that what he was about to do was wrong.

Emily groaned as she slowly turned and lay on her back, the sheets of the bed following the skeleton beneath. Even near death, the past lay within her, all wrapped up in the complexity of inheritance and twenty-five generations of both male and female contributors. She lifted her hand as if reaching for something beyond reach, but then without anything to grasp drew her hand back, passing it over her face, leaving it covering her eyes. She turned again with some difficulty. "Bullcrap... It's all bullcrap," he heard her say.

He called softly so as not to frighten her. "...Par ici, Mademoiselle Dupuis; je suis ici..."

She looked around her bedroom, corner to corner, still not noticing him, then threw the back the sheet and pushed herself upright. He had seen this before, how one continues even when so debilitated. She managed to stand, a little unsteady. She waited to ensure her balance — her hand on the edge of the bed, weaving a little — then stumbled the short distance to the window, passing him on the way without seeing him. He turned with her as she passed. She grasped the sill at the last moment, his hand ready to hold her upright, and looked out. The night sky glowed orange and crimson, and, where it met the city, streaked with gold.

"Damn…," she said, and very faintly smiled.

Not bullcrap, he noted.

She staggered back to her bed and fell onto it, face down in a parody of how she felt, namely worn out. She turned to lay on her back, drawing the single sheet up, then craned to again look out the window. The first stars had penetrated the unnatural color of the night sky, one at the head of the cross brighter than all the others. She was about to make a wish — silliness; raw silliness — but then abruptly changed her mind and instead closed her eyes and sighed. He understood completely. She, like he, like all those living everywhere, only fool themselves to think the stars listen. The stars never listen; they are not the listening type.

She suddenly froze, then slowly drew the single sheet up to cover herself, head to toe. Perhaps she thought he would think she was asleep, or dead.

He sat on the edge of her bed. "Catherine," he said softly. "Il est moi, votre coquelicot."

She peeked out then slowly withdrew from the protection of the sheet, keeping it to her neck. "What's a coquelicot?"

First words for her in a long time, a day or more; and the first word directed toward him, too, for that matter. She could barely speak.

He placed his hand on her shoulder, suspending it first, waiting for her to give permission. She did.

"It is a poppy."

"…You scooped me up and then set me down. The poppies were everywhere, a sea of red waving in the wind," she said in haunted amazement barely above a whisper. He had fixed her voice. It was normal now.

She would see him as Catherine had last seen him: a young man; blond hair pulled back off a strong face: grey eyes; not a threat.

"I thought you might remember."

"It was summer," she added in a hush of wonder.

"Is not life a dream?" He removed his hand from her shoulder and again let it hover, waiting for her to once again give permission. She nodded, and he placed it along the hollow curve of her cheek, cupping her face. He noted how her heart-rate dropped.

He looked into her eyes. "Do you feel better?"

"Yes… Yes, I do: Thank-you."

"I know you are not, Catherine."

She could only stare. Her lips moved but no more. "What do you want?" she finally asked.

"You, of course."

"Me?"

"Not you, exactly — but your body."

Catherine claimed he often said the most outrageous things.

Emily struggled to sit up. He helped her. The sheet covering her dropped and he quickly placed it again around her. She held it, securing it around her neck.

"Get out of here or I'll scream."

"No you won't."

She glanced at him. "Why not?"

"Because you know I am here to help you."

She stared.

"You have approximately point-zero-five-percent genetic heritage from someone I once knew," he explained.

"Who? Catherine?"

"Yes, Catherine: I intend to genetically modify you into her. You shall be the vessel through which I resurrect her."

Emily continued to stare.

"I want her back."

She looked up abruptly and frowned, but then looked quickly away, her fear crystallizing.

"In a few moments, I will introduce a set of microscopic devices into your bloodstream, one for each cell in your body. I have programmed them to implement the changes I intend to impose upon you."

She began to shake. She shook her head. "Please don't."

"My mind is quite made up."

Her frown deepened. She was about to cry

"Please try to remain calm."

"You are going to kill me."

He placed his hand on her shoulder to mitigate her fear. He said gently, to reassure her, "If we are our bodies and no more, then I will simply be giving you a new one. You will once again be healthy, wealthy, and wise; and beautiful, too, I have to add. In short, I intend to cure you of your disease. You understand that, do you not?"

He reached for the glass on her bedside table and held it as she drank. She finished, pulling on the straw until it was done.

He put the glass aside and reached for her hand and held it.

"Better?"

She nodded, looking away, then glancing back at him, then fixing on him. "I want to live."

He tried to smile. "Okay…" He then explained. "It is necessary that I rebalance your mitochondrial DNA."

"You are mad."

"That is quite likely."

"I said I would scream and I will."

"No…" He ensured she did not and gently lay her back. "I will be manipulating you at your cellular level, the mitochondria in each of your cells, and for each cell in your body. It will feel very odd... I'm afraid there might be some pain."

Her eyes remained locked on his. She was unable to move. He had ensured it.

"I must have you remain perfectly still," he added. "I will release you when I am finished." He shifted so she would see him. "Do you understand?"

He gave her enough leeway to nod, then without waiting placed his hand on her chest. Her body immediately went into spasm, locked. He lowered his hand and her body arched off the bed as if an electric current had been placed across it. She stopped breathing. He fixed that. Her heart stopped. He restarted it. He let up slightly so she could breathe and she screamed momentarily finding release. He quickly stifled her, and reasserted the pressure of his hand, and her body again arched off the bed. He removed his hand and she collapsed. It was over.

She rolled onto her side, clutching at the pillow. "Christ! You bastard!" she cried out between tears and gasping for air.

"It is strange, is it not," he quietly mused while tucking the sheets back around her, then gently combing back what little hair she had, "That I should know you so intimately, at the lowest levels — your DNA; the cells that comprise you — and yet you remain a stranger to me?"

She was still catching her breath.

"You are, I can clearly see now, not Catherine. No matter what I or the devices do, you will not be Catherine — not entirely. I know this but still I must proceed."

"It hurt like hell!" she cried out.

"I took no delight in it."

She rolled onto her back, beginning to breathe more regularly. She opened her eyes and found him. "...I feel better already."

"That is a good thing."

She drew another deep breath then settled glancing again at the window. A handful of stars punctured the grey sky. A cloud scudded past, picking up the light from the city below.

She turned back to him. "You are very odd."

He smiled.

"Are you French?" she asked and attempted to sit up. He helped her. "You sound like you might be."

"J'oublie parfois de qui je suis," he said. "You are feeling better, are you not?" he asked.

She managed to nod. She was still fearful of him. "I do... I feel weird."

"Okay..." He nodded then glanced over his shoulder. "Ah, your star is back." He stood and crossed the short distance to the window and looked out. Emily tracking him as he crossed the room. She stretched to see.

"It is called Deneb," he called back to her, and repeated the name in Arabic, emphasizing the desert intonation. "Deneb sits at the head of the Northern Cross," he explained; "Some see a swan, others the Christian Cross." He abruptly turned back to her. "Are you a Christian?" he asked.

Emily, momentarily taken aback by the sudden shift took a moment to respond. "I'm not much of anything, I'm afraid. God never listens to me — until now, perhaps," she added quickly. Recovered, returning to the subject, she motioned to the window.

"Is that how you got in?"

"It is."

"I thought I had locked it."

"I entered via the molecular structure of the glass."

"Most people would have just knocked on my front door — not that I would have answered it."

He almost smiled. "I thought I'd drop the formalities."

"My father is downstairs, you know."

"I know very well. Your father and I have met."

She was suddenly anxious again. "…How is that?"

"The hospital."

She ran her fingers along the sharp line of her chin, then remembered. "You did something…"

"I mitigated the worst of your disease — enough to get you to this point in time."

He was instantly by her side. She jolted, taken aback. "…How did you do that?" He gently lay her back placing her head on her pillow. She fell back willingly.

"There are many things I can do that you cannot — and vice-versa."

"I see."

"Do you?"

"…That you saved my life."

He again nearly smiled. "For a reason," he explained. "Please do not forget that." He suddenly switched. "Do you have a brother?"

"No…"

"I do."

"Younger or older?"

"Older."

"Does he look like you? Sound like you?"

"A little."

"I love the sound of your voice."

Emily wiped her eyes. "I'm very tired and, oh look, I'm crying! I don't know why I am crying." She tried to laugh and could not; she cried some more. "I'm such an idiot!" she laughed and cried.

He sat again on the edge of her bed. "Who wouldn't cry? Your life has been given back to you."

"I don't fear you," she said, angrily swiping at her tears.

He smiled, unable not to. "Maybe you should."

"I don't — I don't know why."

"Maybe I did something to you? A sedative perhaps?"

"I don't think so."

"How would you know?"

She extricated her hand from the tangle of the sheets and placed it on his arm. "I remember you glowed like the sun."

"I did?"

He stood up giving her hand back.

She reached for him again. "Don't go."

"We will have time to talk later: talk and talk," he said with little weight or force.

"I am twenty-three."

"I know how old you are."

"Look at me — I am hideous. There's nothing left of me. I have no hair left. It used to be blonde and curly. Some of my teeth are loose — one fell out." She opened her mouth to show him.

"All that will change."

She closed her mouth. "I am not afraid of you," she said again, with more certainty this time.

He once again ran his fingers along the curve of her face studying her.

"But I haven't told you my name." She extracted her right hand from the sheet and offered it. "I am Emily, Emily Elizabeth Dupuis." She drew her hand back when did not accept it. "...But you probably know that already."

"Vous êtes, en effet, Emily Elizabeth Dupuis. Comment pourrais-je penser autrement?" he said. He retrieved her right hand and shook it up. "I know who you are. Could you be anyone else but yourself?"

"I think that was French...," she said, blushing, laying back again, letting him continue to hold her hand. "Are you French? I..."

"You are feeling sleepy?"

"...I can't seem to keep my eyes open."

"Ah, yes, I did that; I did that to you. Dormez bien, mon amour - Bonne nuit. Fermez les yeux et dormir bien. Vous vous sentirez mieux dans la matinée." He again tucked the sheets about her then bent and kissed her: her forehead, cheek, nose, and then her lips.

She struggled to open her eyes. "Why did you do that?"

"Why, indeed," he said, and kissed her again before stepping back then departing as he had come, through the glass, silicon oxide and quartz, as if it didn't exist.

15

Valentina

More and more mysteries. More and more puzzles that, at the time, he had imagined only part of the inevitability of the pattern called life. He had rationalized that he would understand them later but there was no later. After Catherine, there had been Valentina. Not like Catherine. Not someone to love. Just a woman who had garnered his secret. In the end, Valentina, an old woman, with the wildness, her insanity whistling around her, had crawled from the burning hut that used to be her home. She had spent her entire life living within its walls and yet she had set it aflame. To his surprise, her eyes shining, her hand using the last of her strength to reach upwards, she had cried out the name of her youngest child by then deceased for twenty years. And then she was gone. Hair burnt off her body, her flesh melted, her lungs seared.

Why is it always fire?

As usual, he could think of nothing to say. As usual, he had done nothing. With no eulogy for the dead, wondering if there should be, he had only walked away knowing that she blamed him for her child's death. Not that he had made a habit of killing children; it was just that they died so easily.

But later that same night he had sat bolt upright. He could hear Catherine saying, "Turning away again, my love? Is that what you should do?" Why should he not expect that haunting? And so, he did the unforgivable. It was what the people's Satan would have done, and he did it in the name of love — not for Valentina but for Catherine. They had moved her body and placed it in the Basilica, wrapping in white linen and placing it before the altar. An old woman attended the body; she sat alone in a pew at the back in the dark shadows. Valentia's mother. He threw open the doors. He was angry. He did not know why. The dead claiming him like that.

He ascended amidst the high arches and the stained glass and the overly ornate chandeliers and transformed into a flame, bright blue, but kept himself at ambient temperature. The building could not sustain any measure of heat, and nor would the old woman; he was not there to take life, after all, but to return it. He reached down and swept away the white sheet to reveal Valentina's horribly burnt body, and then returned her life, making her whole and beautiful again. Not her, mind you, not Valentina — not the all-important soul; just Valentina's body. He could not have guessed that he would be recognized, nor the backlash that would ensue. He should have listened to his head instead of his human heart. What am I amidst all this madness? Am I not mad also? He often asked after that.

• •• ••• •••••

As unforeseen and as surprising as the unexpected might always be, the unanticipated is almost always the result of a lack of foresight. Valentina, the second Valentina, still lived: The resonance indicating her continuation had jumped out as he'd scanned for the much weaker signal from Catherine; that and L'Batard's. He had placed L'Batard's signal into the filter as well. He could not help it. They were long gone but existed still, at least their chemistry. He could not overlook that fact.

Ironically, or merely coincidently, Valentina now existed near where he had discovered Emily. He could nearly walk in his human form to where she resided if he wished; it would only require a few hours. But he did not wish; he instead flew quickly by, keeping himself invisible. He did so just to feel a connection to the past again. Not so much to soak in the irony, but more to test the unexpected coincidence of her immediate presence.

There was more to it than just that, of course. He was not a complete slave to superstition, but he did remain a slave to his delusions one of which was his supposed responsibility for what had happened to poor Valentina. The second one that is. The first Valentina had been born nearly five hundred years after Catherine and L'Batard, merely a hundred and forty-five years or so ago; the second only fifty years ago. Catherine would redefine his delusion of responsibility as nothing more, or less, than a guilty heart. He sighed thinking of it, shaking his head. There it is, that concept of right and wrong again. Would he ever be able to side-step it? Not while Catherine still spoke to him, he knew; and L'Batard, for that matter.

But what he found in the living presence of the contemporary Valentina was quite shocking; predictable perhaps, but disquieting nonetheless. She was mad, quite mad, and why wouldn't she be? He had returned her as a young woman fully formed but empty, nearly a shell. She knew nothing, her mind filled with only fragments of another past. Her mother must have taken her in and raised her as she had done once before, but this time beginning with the fully formed woman. His sin was great, then, was it not? To play God like that? Or so Catherine would intimate if she were beside him now, and with some truth too.

• •• ••• ••••••

He drifted above the mad Valentina. She was an old woman now, bent; her beautiful black hair entirely gray, awry and loose about her haggard face, not tied back as it had once been. What happens to the glow of youth? Not just the body but also the mind, and with the mind, the person? The effects of time are brought about by a breakdown of cellular tissue; an accumulation of damaging oxides in the person's cells. He would never have allowed that to happen to Catherine, nor L'Batard if he had remained by his side, and now that he was more intimately aware of time's ravages, would he allow it to happen to Emily. He could not have that. He would not have that.

He watched as Valentina navigated her way through a maze of ornamental hedge toward an old man sitting slouched on a bench, the thick briar picking at her clothing and hair. He would speak to her for no other reason than to hear her voice — the familiarity of it, proof of the past — but he would not do so in the form Valentina had once known, for who knows what that would trigger? There was only one way, a sure way without frightening her. He would instead use the old man's body, and it would not be a sin to do so since he could see the old man's soul had flown — Catherine's descriptive phrase, not his.

He entered the body. The old man's mind was a jumble; pieces and parts of memories everywhere but none connected. He searched for the reason and found it — a tumor dispersed throughout the lower part of his brain, probably not even detectable by their instrumentation. He could remove it — but was it not unlike putting his full fist in yet another pie not cooked for him, and so decided not to. There was only so much he should do. He had to draw a line somewhere.

He stood and moved each of the old man's limb, carefully, one by one. The body, old, seldom exercised, trembled, forcing him to grasp the bench with bent fingers. He slowly turned the body in Valentina's direction. He blinked — he couldn't see properly. He corrected the eyesight, but then realizing he was not about to get too far with just that correction, also fixed the old man's hearing, then the left kidney, followed by a small aneurysm on the left ventricle of his heart. He would mitigate the tumor before departing; he owed the old man that much too: a proper and appropriate payment for charges incurred. Whatever line he might draw was not here, he mused; there is always another, and then another to approach and then inevitably step over.

He called out softly, the sound issued broken, harsh. He corrected the pitch and tried again. She had always said his voice resonated like music; why disappoint her?

"Valentina?"

The neatly trimmed privet quaked then split to reveal a face, an old woman's face, scratched from the hedge, her grey hair wild about her face. The privet snapped back. Holding her breath, her eyes squeezed shut, her teeth fiercely clenched: he did not have to stand before her to know that was her stance, for he had seen her like that before. Her intent then had been murder. He wondered what her reasoning might be this time. The same insane wind blowing through? The old man on the bench, a poor proxy but nonetheless easily available?

He had seen at a glance it was true. Some things never change. More irony, then; would he ever be able to avoid it?

He was dimly aware of two men hurrying across the lawn. He noted with some surprise that one of the two was Norris, Emily's presiding physician. Another coincidence. How many could there possibly be on a day like today, the sky blue and the sun shining as it was? It was certainly unusual and unexpected that he and the good doctor should meet under conditions that were, to say the least, outside the regular stream of things. But that, of course, as he reminded himself yet again, did not suggest any hidden purpose or meaning. It was not ordained that they should meet again. It was not fate adjusting their paths. It was merely an accident of life, the complex intertwining of events that sometimes converge, often suggesting meaning where there is none.

Norris drew to a quick halt only paces away. His assistant, close behind, dropped from a run to a fast walk catching up. They apparently knew nothing of Valentina. It was he they were after — or rather the old man.

Norris suppressed his excitement. "What is your name?"

He answered truthfully. Why would he not?

"I am Gatc'hh'en."

The good doctor frowned. He had not recognized either the name, nor the sound of his voice. "What was that?" he asked, stepping closer.

He searched within the jumble of the old man's mind for a hint of a name, and extracted it from a song only a few refrains of which remained intact.

"John Schmidt – John Jacob Jingleheimer Schmidt."

That wasn't it, but it was close enough.

Norris jolted. He had recognized the sound of the voice that time but still hadn't correlated it to the scene in the hospital.

"Who?"

"John Jacob Jingleheimer Schmidt," he repeated and then, feeling frivolous, even silly, began to sing, retrieving the tune of the campfire song from the old man's memory.

"John Jacob Jingleheimer Schmidt!
That's my name too!
Whenever we go out the people laugh and shout,
'There goes John Jacob Jingleheimer Schmidt!'"

Norris' frown deepened. His assistant laughed aloud.

The word that came to his mind was fiasco. Another word: debacle.

It was time to go.

He was about to do just that when Valentina pushed herself through the privet brandishing her knife. Some aspects of human nature, many in fact, remain entirely unpredictable.

She had recognized his voice, it seemed.

"Yo! Yo! Yo sabía que vendría! Lo sabía!" she cried out.

"Valentina."

She hesitated, puzzled for a moment when she saw it was not who she had expected him to be, but then, regardless, already committed, thrust the blade upward.

There was no pain. It felt like nothing. Not like he imagined it might. It was apparent there were some things he did not understand, and perhaps never would, among them the fathomless depths of the human heart, as mad as it often could be.

He wrenched the blade free and set it carefully on the back of the bench as he watched her thrash about, held down by the two men, the good doctor and his assistant, each torn between restraining her and running to his side. He repaired John Schmidt's body enough to ensure it would not die from the wound Valentina had inflicted, then slipped away, releasing the body to collapse onto the carefully manicured lawn. If the past is unreachable, the present transient, there is always the future — such as it might be, he thought, while wondering how he could possibly have allowed himself to become so entangled once again. Damn fate. Damn his curiosity.

16

Correlation

Robert Richardson, Branch Head, Intelligence Operations Branch, Domestic Terrorism, Central Intelligence Agency convened the Monday morning session.

It was protocol. The various sections under his management gathered once a week to discuss the week's highlights: what happened where, and to whom, and did it present a threat to national security. Domestic security, international threats, economics, and trends were covered. The branch was near the top of the org chart – the meeting minutes would go to the Director, National Security Branch for review afterward.

Richardson brought the meeting to order. "Good morning, gentlemen. It's 9 AM. I expect all are in attendance." He looked about. "Who wants to go first?"

No one raised their hand. He chose at random.

"Open Source, Domestic."

A report followed. Agent James Ferris, Jim, made his report from West to East beginning with Los Angeles. Nothing going on there other than another water shortage. There was some chatter about blowing up some agricultural equipment — some water pumps - but other than that nothing new. He went on from the West, Washington, Oregon to Nevada, forgetting all about Hawaii but including Alaska

— nothing; the mid-west: nothing, except for Chicago where a package thought to hold explosives was discovered in the subway. It turned out to be false alarm. East Coast – there was an incident over NYC. A bright light hovered over the city at 3 AM. It was bright enough to cast shadows from the New World Trade Center. At least half a dozen claimed some degree of blindness from staring at it too long — but all the cases turned out to be temporary only. A deep rumbling sound accompanying it. No one could determine the cause although it was also reported by the air traffic controllers at both Kennedy and LaGuardia. It was an anomaly of some sort. No terrorist activity otherwise – at least none detected. The city is always under threat. There were more than a dozen terrorist groups that would love to blow it off the face of the map. They were keeping track of the audio from city phones, but there was nothing to report of interest; just forty different references to the dozen or so words that had some sort of inference to "terrorist"; another thirty-four similar references on Facebook; still another twelve on Twitter; and then one with the keyword "bomb" on Google — they were in the process of checking them all out. There was also a power outage that stretched all the way from Canada to Philadelphia. It only lasted a few hours. The reason for it has been blamed on — he checked his notes — on the Aurora Borealis — he had some difficulty pronouncing it. He ended, "But let's hope Congress won't repeal the Patriot Act; the phone monitoring program is an invaluable resource."

He had remained perfectly serious and poker-faced throughout.

Richardson sighed as he straightened in his chair and gathered some of his notes. He glanced up. "Thanks, Jim — and thanks for the plug. It won't be repealed, don't worry. I have the inside on it." None in the room could determine if he was intentionally sarcastic or not. He looked about the table. "Next?"

He didn't have to select. An analyst he was quite familiar with sitting in the back, hair not brushed with stray-ends flying loose about, wearing clothes he'd slept in for a week or two, made it unnecessary.

Doctor Stanislaw (Stan) Kalinowski, Ph.D., Mathematics, MIT, and a verified, card-carrying genius, and who had recently been seconded from NSA DS&T, and was a known specialist in Open Source Intelligence and Analysis, claimed the floor.

Kalinowski didn't bother to stand. "You are so full of shit, Ferris. How can you live with yourself?" Kalinowski rolled his eyes as he drew his hands through his unkempt hair, and leaned back in his chair.

Ferris, a heavy-set, dark brooding man, athletic, once assigned to Operations and not to be trifled with or insulted, straightened in his chair and glared. "Excuse me?"

Kalinowski pitched forward and pointed directly at him. "If you did your homework you would realize that fucking light over NYC was more than just a fucking anomaly." He pitched back again and again ran his fingers through his hair. "Jeesus Krist, I can't believe you suggested that!"

A ripple of embarrassed laughter swept around the table once then again. The meeting room was packed, the primary reason for which was the unstated promise of entertaining barbs and perspective offered up by Kalinowski. Richardson smiled. He had not liked Kalinowski at first but had come to respect him. As advertised, he was brilliant, although at times he could be abrasively arrogant. Richardson sat back fully prepared to enjoy himself. He had read Ferris's intelligence reports beforehand; they had mostly been appropriated from the news reports, and he agreed the bright light above the city was anything but an anomaly.

"You have the floor, Dr. Kalinowski," he announced, unnecessarily so.

Kalinowski waved to the audio-video specialist who switched Kalinowski's laptop screen to the main display screen behind Richardson. Heads turned to watch; Richardson swiveled about in his chair. Kalinowski stood and grabbed a handful of hair — then gathered his thoughts and began.

"Okay..." He played with his laptop and brought up the PowerPoint presentation he had stayed up all night to prepare. No title page; his presentation jumped to the subject without preamble: an image that all in the room were already familiar with. A ball of light approximately a meter in diameter as indicated by the scale overlaying it. It had been taken from the cockpit of a Harrier Jump Jet above Lock Ness. Amongst all the data displayed at the bottom of the image all in green, pitch, roll, yaw, and airspeed which was highlighted. It indicated four hundred and eighty kilometers per hour, or just below the speed of sound at sea level.

Kalinowski used the laser controller to switch to the next slide. It showed a very much smaller spherical object against an entirely black background. "Now look..." A third slide went up. The small spherical object was enlarged and the perspective shifted. "This is the object observed above NYC but scaled and sheared to be the same size and orientation to the sphere photographed by the Harrier. In other words, it was placed in the same range and slant angle as would be seen from the Harrier pilot who was looking slightly upward. I have removed all background detail to demonstrate that the objects are, in fact, one and the same."

Another image went up. It was a mathematical plot showing an overlay of data, one red, and the other set blue. "This plot is an overlay of the returned radar pulse from the long-range surveillance radars in the UK to the returns recorded by the Air Traffic control radar at Kennedy adjusted for range and radar signal strength. You can see again the object detected by the radars are almost identical. It shines very brightly indicating a strong return in each case. It's not hiding from anyone."

Another image flashed. "Now this will be a surprise to you, Ferris. I got this one off the front page of the New York Times — a hundred images, maybe thousands, were recorded by citizens using their cell phone; another several hundred were captured by security cameras throughout the city. I'm still working the data on that, but it appears the object was approximately two thousand feet above the city. It hovered for almost five minutes and then…" Another image went up. "This is what I wanted to show you, Ferris. It is captured by the all-sky camera at Sunnybrook which, incidentally, is strongly sensitive to not only visible light but the near ultraviolet, even x-ray. Watch this…"

The image of the bright almost light switched out and was replaced by a video also showing the bright light. It went from white to dark blue then streaked across the sky and quickly disappeared.

"I guarantee there is a correlation between this image and what was observed above New York City the other night which was not just an anomaly, not when afterward the light shifted from the visible to the deep ultraviolet and then took off at twice the speed of sound. Nine out of ten witnesses reported the sonic boom Ferris, for fuck's sake. It shook buildings as far as Princeton. Ten minutes later it was seen flying over Montreal at an altitude of 120,000 feet moving at Mach 10. Montreal is in Canada, Ferris … You know, our northern neighbor, the sovereign nation of Canada? The object then entered a polar orbit, but not before waking up a million of the good people who reside in Montreal with a tremendous sonic boom, one of the loudest ever recorded. No damage was reported. It was too high up, apparently."

Everyone in the room began to talk at once demanding to see the recording played back again. The audio-visual assistant did so, placing it in a repeating loop. Richardson managed to regain control but only after several attempts.

"Now you're going to tell us the power outage that followed had something to do with this too," Richardson suggested, settling back in his chair and smiling. He couldn't help it. It was too rich. Ferris deserved this.

"Absolutely, I am — and more than that too."

The room stilled to near perfect silence with only the soft sound of the air conditioning as he continued with his analysis. "As many of you know - it was reported in every paper, on every newscast the following morning - there was a widespread power outage which included most of Eastern Canada, as well as the Eastern Seaboard of the US as far south as Baltimore. The power grid was overwhelmed by what is called an inductive power spike. Something like that can be caused by a massive Electro Magnetic Pulse, or EMP, such as delivered by a nuclear weapon designed for such a purpose, or, and more likely in this case, by the inductive currents associated with the Aurora Borealis."

Kalinowski used his controller and the repeating video switched to a still photo of a brilliant aurora with fantastic color and intensity. "Our Canadian friends gave us this one. They have monitoring stations in the far north to track aurora activity. This one is not the largest or brightest that has ever been recorded but its close. The lower left-hand corner of the photo indicates it was provided by the National Research Council of Canada. Note the time: it is ten minutes thirty-two seconds after the object flew over Montreal."

Richardson leaned forward and studied the slide. He provided some perspective interrupting Kalinowski with a raised hand. "We concluded almost a month ago now the object the Brits were chasing, and then the French too was one of their – probably Brit – experimental aircraft that got away from them. Although everyone was shouting Aliens, and UFO's - the papers were full of it - the truth is often the most plausible; after all, what's more plausible, an alien coming down to play chicken with a squadron of fighter jets, or some top-secret aircraft going wonky as the Brits say?"

Kalinowski raised his hands in full admission. "I agree — I completely agree. At the time, I did anyway. But think of this, sir: whenever there are more than two highly unlikely events occurring within a short time period, then they are most likely correlated. The details of the 'what', and the purpose, are what's hard to determine, but that's only because we don't have enough facts. But it is almost a mathematical certainty that there is some degree of correlation; it is only the extent to which they are correlated that we don't know. At any rate, gentlemen, I can give you four such events, and I think we should scour the news agencies and social media more because there are more I am sure of it.

He continued with his analysis; some completely following him, some less so. Kalinowski switched slides. "This was a photo taken by a tourist outside of Notre Dame Cathedral — That's in Paris, France, Ferris - using his cell phone camera. A ball of light, the same one is my guess, is hovering over the cobblestone pavement. I had a hard time tracking down witnesses since they were all, mostly, tourists. But I did find and interview two witnesses, one a priest who told me that was about the time the cathedral was visited by – and he was sure about this – one of the archangels; Gabriel, he assumed - more than assumed, actually: he insisted. It is total bullshit, of course; he should be locked up in my opinion. It is interesting, though, that a second photo from the dash-cam of a taxi that was parked out front has a time-tag exactly three minutes and forty seconds after the French launched their surface to air missiles at the object. We thought initially that they shot it down but didn't want to say so, but I believe now they told the truth. Their missiles did, indeed, miss; they missed because their target disappeared from their fire control radars — but then mysteriously reappeared just over three minutes later above Paris."

Agent Ferris, elbows on the table, with his head in his hands, muttered, "That's gotta be bullshit!"

"It does sound, I know, coincidental," Kalinowski injected, "and might be. But I put it out to you, gentleman, that a similar object was witnessed in Paris immediately following the chase." He once again placed his hands in his hair and grabbed a handful. He was gathering his thoughts. "Okay... Next slide, please. This is a bit of a stretch, I know, but my French colleagues and I — who are much more open-minded about this by the way than..."

"You told them?" Richardson injected, incredulous.

Kalinowski swung around. "I had to! I couldn't get their help without it!"

"That was the trip to France and the Loire Valley I authorized last week?" Richardson asked still incredulous.

"That's it... That's it... I must go back, too... Listen," he said resuming, "My French friends did a comprehensive search of the French Social media – their Facebook pages, and Google. They searched within a one-week period after the missile launch. They found some unusual events but nothing like this." Another photo was shown. It was of poor quality; it was shot in a rush while the photographer was in motion. It was nearly a complete blur. "We'll have to get our digital photo jockeys to fix this up... I've tried to correct it as much as possible. I don't know if you can see this or not but those who were there told me that this is a little girl of about seven years' old who is suspended about two meters in midair – that's about six feet, Ferris – above a school yard. Adjacent to her is a bright light approximately — you got it — one meter in diameter. I determined that from scaling the photo and comparing to an object of known size in the background and knowing how far away it was."

"It could have been faked," Richardson suggested leaning forward in his chair studying the image carefully.

"Yeah, it could be a fake. It is certainly of poor quality, which makes one wonder. Still, there was some other shit that went down there but it was so fantastic that none of it sounds true and, indeed, does tend then to give this photograph even less credibility."

"Such as what?" someone asked.

"Witnesses — children mostly; but mom's and dad's, teachers — all said pretty much the same thing. It was even covered by the local paper who interviewed them as well. The town was pretty shaken up about it all. I have a copy of the article back in my office. I had it translated. Anyway, the little girl was not hurt; she was set gently down – and then most strangely, she was returned completed cured of some congenital sight and hearing problem she had suffered from since birth. Dozens of witnesses who know the girl and her family verified it, or so it was written in the paper, and a local doctor who knows the child well also confirmed it. The school yard has become a local tourist attraction. Some of the local Christians are praying at the site where the supposed miracle happened, making it difficult to hold school there. It has gotta be bullshit; you do have to sift through the stuff. And then once the little girl was set down, the ball of light turned into a man, a young man, early thirties blonde hair. Some said he looked like a younger version of Brad Pitt. I know that sounds like complete bullshit, but I hesitate to claim it is bullshit because it does correlate somewhat."

The room stared back at him. Kalinowski gave them the moment they needed. "And then…" He waited. "And then, the newly formed young man – aka Brad Pitt - smiled, bowed, apologized, and then disappeared. He rose straight upward until he was out of sight. Moments later there was a sonic boom."

Agent Ferris almost fell out of his chair. "That's gotta be total bullshit!" he shouted, trying to recover his balance. "I read the comic! Superman! Jesus Christ! Fuck you!"

The room laughed.

"Maybe! Maybe! But I correlated air traffic control radar images from that same time frame – and guess what? Yes, there was an anomalous track but there was no solid track, so I suppose my position on this particular on remains undetermined — I will admit that."

"This is all got to be crap, Kalinowski — sit down," Ferris mumbled from behind both of his hands that covered his face.

"I'm not done," Kalinowski stated firmly. "There is another event that follows this. That makes five correlated instances – I only needed three to pursue this as part of our in-house policy. We talked about it two weeks ago: "The Deep Scan" fiasco. We still have people working on that. We don't know what it was. I'll summarize. An orbit based high power radar radiating at 3.0 MHz at 9 Gigawatts radiated all of Europe and North America, New Zealand, and Australia. The

Western World in fact. It caused half of our personal computers including some major commercial computing enterprises to crash. We've been blaming it on the Chinese — but I don't think so."

"The Aliens again?"

"Yep — and not because he was trying to disrupt our computer networks. I don't know much about this — I'm learning — but the modulation techniques are closer to that of a medical instrument such as an MRI rather than a search radar. I think our alien friend was looking for someone: a Caucasian."

"Male or female?"

"I don't know — but I would guess female."

"Why is that?"

"The little French girl. He specifically picked out a female."

"Did they find her?"

"I think so, yes. Someone here in New York, which is correlated with the light seen over the city just yesterday. And I don't believe it is 'they;' I think it is just him. There could be more of the same but of that I have no knowledge. So far I'd say only one alien."

"Only one did all this shit?"

"I'd say so, yes."

A sobering moment settled over the room.

Richardson broke the silence. "That's why we call you a genius, Kalinowski."

"I am a genius."

The room laughed but then quickly sobered as the ramifications of what he was saying began to sink in. It required more than fifteen minutes for Richardson to regain focus. No one knew what to think. It was all probably bullshit.

17

Norris

Doctor Robert Norris slipped into the darkened room where his semi-conscious patient lay on his back: eyes closed, head on the pillow, white sheets drawn up to his chin, hands folded neatly on his chest. He'd rather not refer to his patient as "John Schmidt"; that was obviously incorrect and ridiculous too, and probably nothing other than an echo of some distant memory that had somehow risen to the surface. And yet it was the only name they had; ironically, he had been admitted as "John Doe" years ago.

"Well, at least you're still John," he said and smiled.

Norris pulled up a chair, flipped it around and sat. He had three vials and a single syringe lined up on the side table; hopefully, only one vial would be needed. "This is what you were like when you were first brought in," he said, again aloud; "At that time a bright young doctor — that would be me — administered a ten percent dopamine solution until you were semi-conscious. If you don't mind – and who knows if you would — I will try that again for old times' sake, okay?"

His patient appeared only to be asleep and yet would not wake, despite all he could do to waken him. It was a conundrum. He would have to write another paper; bring in some experts, get some recognition. He would explain that there had been no gradual advancement of awareness. One moment the patient had been semi-conscious and the next he was entirely lucid or appeared to be. The elapsed time from being propped up on the bench until spotted stumbling through his first steps in almost ten years had not been longer than one hour at most.

Norris folded back the bed sheet then lifted away the covering garment to reveal the remnants of the wound Valentina had inflicted. It was almost entirely healed. Another strange thing. Strange things add up to very strange things. An unconscious patient nourished only by intravenous supplements hardly ever recovers so well, or so completely. Nor does the body metabolize correctly when it is unconscious and laying sedate in a bed day in day out. And yet, the wound was almost perfectly healed. Just a razor-thin scar remained. The blade had entered just below the rib cage with an upward thrust. It should have killed him, and it would have had it been just a millimeter or so to the left. She would have sliced into the heart.

Norris's imagination kept returning to Valentina: Valentina, mostly gentle but decidedly insane. Valentina flashing her knife in the sun, burying it deep. And the blood. He again went back to that. As a physician, he had witnessed the outpouring of copious amounts of the red liquid, but never driven to the surface, made to swell out through a gaping wound, opened by hate emboldened by madness. It was unsettling and disturbing. Before yesterday, it had all been theoretical but today completely raw and untenable. And yet, it was not as simple as all that; not one bit. He had not only observed hate roiling within Valentina, but something more, too: Love, perhaps. And fear. Fear mitigated by love. We slaughter the ones we love rather than deal with our inner demons, but why that should be so Norris could not say.

Norris grasped the syringe and drew the liquid up out of the vial. He cleared out the air and then very carefully injected 10ccs of a twenty percent formulation of dopamine into his patient's carotid artery. It was very wrong of him to do so. Very wrong. It was unlikely to kill John Schmidt but it very well might inflict serious damage. Too much dopamine and the patient might develop a severe psychosis, or, worse, die.

Norris waited. Waiting is always the hardest part. His patient opened his mouth, the first syllable half formed. Norris administered another dose and again waited, counting the seconds up to a minute.

John Schmidt sighed. His lips moved, trying to finish the syllable. "Look at that!" he finally exclaimed in his first words since the garden. "It is very beautiful, whatever it is," he sighed, his already weak voice trailing away.

It was exactly what Norris had hoped for. He leaned forward in anticipation.

"Hey..."

"I saw a picture of it once. ...One of the Apollo's," Schmidt continued speaking as if from a dream. "...It is blue, green, brown, and silver floating in a sea of black. I see a million stars. I have never seen so many stars..."

Norris sat back, puzzled. What crap was this? One of the Apollo's? Schmidt's eyes opened and shifted about the room until they found him. "Why is it that all I can see?" Schmidt asked, clearly puzzled, almost immediately beginning to drift off again.

"I don't know," Norris answered truthfully.

Schmidt suddenly straightened, shuddered, and then bent upward in full bodily spasm. Norris grabbed hold and laid him back then jumped for the emergency button. He pressed it hard then glanced back: His patient lay with his head back, eyes closed, breathing raggedly. The involuntary contractions had passed. The strap that had secured him to the bed had held.

Norris returned to the bed and quickly noted Schmidt was still breathing — thank God. He checked the pulse — it was ruinously high. He released the hand and stepped back nervously. He quickly disposed the used syringe, and then gathered the empty vials and placed them safely in his bag. John Schmidt should be okay by morning. He'd sleep it off. He hoped.

He opened the door then stepped through. He propped it open — there was no sense in the orderly and the crash-cart team having to unlock it. He walked calmly down the length of the corridor, dodging around a corner to avoid the orderly and the crash cart with four nurses. He took the stairs up and obtained the appropriate key from the orderly on duty on that floor. Still reeling from the jolt, he had experienced in the other room one floor down and parallel to this one, he unlocked this new door. Only the mad can sometimes see the truth, he reasoned stepping inside.

• •• ••• •••••

"Valentina."

She sat in the corner hugging her knees, her gray hair falling nearly to the floor, hiding her face.

"I am Dr. Norris — you remember me, don't you?" He withdrew a photograph from the file he carried. The photo was of John Schmidt as he had been almost three years before when he had been known only as John Doe: a portrait of a man in his mid-sixties, gray hair askew, eyes vacant, drooling into his bib.

"How are you feeling?" he asked.

"I'm all right."

"If you don't mind, I have a couple of quick questions." He glanced at her chart. The sedative she had been given — phenobarbital — probably wasn't helping much with respect to her ability to concentrate.

He slipped down beside her and placed a hand on her shoulder. She might have been beautiful once.

"Are you sure you're okay?"

She angrily shrugged off his touch. "I'm fine," she repeated.

It probably was not a good idea to be alone with her; she could still be dangerous.

He pressed the photo on her.

"Can you tell me who this is?"

She glanced at it. "That's John."

Norris slowly nodded. "Okay — we agree on that. And, of course, you know him — He is often in the garden the same time as you." He waited for her to respond. "But what inspired you to attack him?" He hoped he sounded reasonable. "No need to answer if you don't wish to — I just thought I'd ask. I know you don't like to talk about these things."

The phenobarbital he had prescribed was heavy stuff — perhaps a bit more than she needed; he would adjust the dosage for tomorrow.

Valentina muttered from within the sanctuary of her hair which she had let down. It fell across her face. "You cannot dodge a blade as you can a bullet," she said.

"What was that?" He brushed her hair back just enough to reveal her in profile.

"And it doesn't matter if you're fire-proof — the blade can go right through, right into you, immortal or not," she said keeping her eyes averted, letting her hair fall again.

Norris sat back. Her thoughts seemed jumbled — But she had replied in English, which was good.

Valentina wiped her mouth with the back of her hand. "I'm glad I killed him."

It took a moment before Norris replied. He picked his words. "I can't believe no one told you: You killed no one." Valentina jolted as Norris offhandedly explained. "We whisked him off to NYP-Cornell and the surgeons patched him up. He's back here now, just one floor down, don't you know?"

Valentina squeezed her eyes shut.

Norris added, knowing the impact it would have, "He regained consciousness just a few moments ago but then slipped back. I think he's just asleep now. He's definitely on a path to recovery." He wondered how he managed to sound so ordinary, so bland given the fact he was lying.

Valentina slowly turned to him, expressionless, her eyes open.

"He is alive and well — fortunately."

"Have you ever seen a real angel, doctor?"

"Of course not."

Valentina sighed, taking a deep breath then slowly exhaling. "They are very beautiful. They take your breath away."

Norris wondered if she was being facetious. Not likely. It was beyond her, he assumed. He reasoned instead that she was having difficulty concentrating. She probably didn't know what she was saying.

"Can you tell me who you thought you saw if not John?" he asked. "Not an angel, certainly."

"You were there."

"Just — please — humor me. For the record, if not John, then who did you think he was?"

She told him — and then described him.

Norris nodded — a single nod that accompanied an avalanche of memory that flooded his mind. He excused himself politely and somehow managed to find his way to the door. He unlocked it, smiled at Valentina who was watching him closely while climbing to her feet turning to face him as if to follow him. He waved goodbye, and then closed the door, and then locked it behind him hearing her moving around within. He rested his back against the door and tried to think. He remembered everything. The hospital. Emily. *"Do no harm, doctor?"* The garden. The same young man concealed within John Schmidt. He even managed to recall his name: he had been told twice just in case he hadn't picked it up the first time. Had he detected sarcasm in the young man's voice? A certain hubris?

Norris began to walk, keeping his hand running along the wall to keep himself from wandering off. He had always known he risked madness — genetically encoded; inherited from his mother — and now here it was fully presented. Who would have thought it would come so soon, and in someone so promising — namely himself? He hadn't. Not until now, that is.

"It does, however, place John Schmidt in an entirely new light, though, doesn't it?" he asked aloud. "It certainly does," he answered, responding to the self-posed question, also aloud, not caring who might overhear.

Evolution

N ow look at this Catherine, is this not the same as you?"

Catherine rolled over in the new grass and propped herself up. She brushed her hair back off her face and looked down to see what he was holding. They lay on a blanket placed on the grass next to the Loire. Willows lining the banks. Reeds along the shore, their brown heads swaying in the light spring breeze that ruffled the smooth surface of the river. It was spring. She was nineteen, a complete miracle in body and mind.

"Let me see..."

"Does it not have the same form, the same sweep?" he had asked.

She held it between her thumb and forefinger slowly rotating it to see each side. She studied the nuance of color, the curving petals, the stamen, the stigma, and the intricacies therein. She looked up and smiled.

"...It's a flower, a buttercup. It's beautiful."

"Would it surprise you if I told you that this flower is built upon the same plan as you?"

"No, I would not be surprised at all."

He was the one surprised. He remembered how he smiled, his smile lifting her eyes to his then her smile opening to follow his.

"Why would it not be?" she had asked softly keeping her eyes on him. "God made the world. He made this flower, He made me, He made you — it is all the same plan; it is God's plan."

"I didn't mean it that way."

"How do you mean it?"

"I am referring to the building blocks upon which it is all made. The underlying pattern of life on Earth makes you and the buttercup the same because the buttercup and you are built upon the same over-arching plan."

She still held the buttercup in her hand, carefully between her thumb and forefinger. "How is that any different from what I said?" she asked after a moment. She struggled. "I mean, what you say is not literally true — this is a flower, I am a woman. We are only similar in that we are both created by God. God gave us all this to preside over." She indicated the world in full bloom surrounding them, the wildflowers, grasses, the trees, and the blue river with the sun glinting on the surface before settling back. "It is our world given to us by God."

"But I tell you that within your very core you are the same as this flower — it is the way all life in this world is put together. I have thought long and hard about it."

She carefully thought and then asked, "Are you talking bricks and mortar?"

"I am."

"Then does it matter how it is put together? Is it not sufficient to know God created it for us?"

"Ah, yes — I see."

"What do you see?"

"What I am trying to say is that God, if there is a God, has nothing to do with your existence, or the buttercup's existence."

"That is not true."

"I say it is."

She sat up and again brushed her hair back off her face. "You say the most ridiculous things, my love. You are testing me."

"I am not testing you. I am only saying what is on my mind."

"Then speak clearly."

"I thought I was."

"Are you not my Guardian Angel?"

"I like to think I am."

She turned so that she faced him fully then said in earnest, leaning forward, "You are, my love, you are — but, that being true, how can one of God's Messengers believe such nonsense?" She relaxed and smiled. "You are teasing me, I know." She twirled the buttercup between her thumb and forefinger, lifting the flower to her nose. "Cat got your tongue, my love?" she asked.

"I am not teasing you." He too indicated the spring morning surrounding them, waving his arm encompassing it all. "You, and all of this, evolved over time. The patterns within you and that flower, all that lives and is not a rock or otherwise inanimate, are imperfect. There are errors in the pattern but these errors, usually small ones, ensure that there is always change — sometimes the change is beneficial, but at other times, most often in fact, the change is quite imperfect."

He leaned forward in emphasis. "But... But — And here is the necessary part, Catherine: without change, there would be no buttercup, no trees, no grasses, no you! If that were not true, when the conditions upon which the first life ultimately formed shifted for some reason — climate, some cataclysm — life would have been unable to adapt, and it would have died out; starved to death, most likely, and this world would have been sterile again; like most worlds are, in fact."

"Most worlds? You often talk about other worlds, but there is only this world."

He leaned back. "That is not true."

"Where are the others?" She thought a moment. "Oh, you must mean all the worlds that exist between Heaven and Hell?"

"I do not. I am referring to other worlds beyond this one."

"Do you mean the moon? The stars? The sun?"

He smiled. "Yes. In particular, other planets like this planet circling their own star."

"Ah! No wonder there is no life there! They are only lights. Who can live on a pinpoint of light or circle about it? Hah Hah! I got you!"

"I'm trying not to smile," he said and then laughed.

"Shall I say what I think then?" she challenged.

"Do you not always say what you think to the detriment of those who have divergent opinions?" he had asked, still smiling, remembering that day like yesterday.

She laughed again. "Is that not the way you taught me? Is that not true?" Her laughter subsided as her smile widened. She lay back and looked up at the sky as she thought. "Okay then… I have it."

She sat up to make her point. "I believe that God made the world, and when He made it, He made it perfect; there are no errors, not even small ones. What you say is obviously a lie. You do so only to tease me. No Guardian Angel would ever say such a thing." She indicated the buttercup she had continued to hold. "Look at this again. Look! …I said look!" She continued to tease him. "There you are… looking… Very good! Now pay attention…!" She laughed and finished. "Could anything be more sublime? Could chance make this?"

He sat back, frustrated.

"And…?"

"And, there is more, much more, Catherine. The process I talk about leads to an entire range of diverse forms most beautiful. The diversity is quite remarkable. As proof, I point left and right, up and down, and all around us. It begins with a singular form of life, and through time a myriad of forms diverge from that single original form, and all because of the very slow but very real process of change introduced by the errors in the coding. And that process, my love, ultimately led to the flower you still hold in your hand and, eventually, you as well."

"And you too?"

"No, not me; I am the product of a different process. It is still evolution but self-directed. To survive, we ultimately forced change upon ourselves."

She again brushed her hair out of her eyes. He loved it when she did that.

"You say the most amazing things."

"Only what is on my mind," he said again.

"You have a most curious mind then — but then I have always known that, have I not?" She laughed and pushed him back. "I will not allow you to kiss me sir! I think you should keep your mind on the flower!"

"How changeable you are…"

"I am a woman, the ability to change is in my nature!" She laughed again. A new idea struck her. "Oh, I see the trap! I see it! Although I may be changeable, the world is not! Do not try to trick me like that again, my love!"

He laughed. "You found me out."

"I knew it!" Her smile shifted. "…But I have finally determined that this is serious: You are serious."

He smiled and nodded. "I am."

She thought, and puzzled, canting her head to the side. "What you say makes no sense, but I love you so I listen even though I know you could not possibly be right."

"I am right even so."

"It would not be good for you, my love, to tell others of your ideas; they would lock you up; or worse, they would think you mad, and then you would have to return to Heaven, and then where would I be without my Guardian Angel?"

She cupped her hand about his face and held it so he had to gaze directly at her. He covered her hands with his.

"You look so serious — you often do, much to the detriment of fun," she whispered gazing into his eyes and smiling.

He recovered her hands and kissed her open palms, left, then right, folding then together and keeping them. He smiled his concurrence. "I am too serious sometimes, I know."

"You are joking, are you not?" she asked in complete sincerity. "All of what you have just said, is a joke?"

"It is no joke. I believe in what I say. The world does not need God to be what it is."

"That will get you in big trouble, my love," she said seriously, not smiling for the first time.

He smiled for her, but only a half-smile. "Not if I'm a Guardian Angel, it won't."

She sat up straighter. "I know this is a test of some sort, but why you should be testing me here and now I don't know. I do know this: the world is as it is only because of God. The process of change, as you say, did not make the world. If it did, nothing would be right; the world would be such a mess."

"Who says it isn't — in some ways, but not all? As I have said, much of life is imperfect, and would have been much better off if it had been designed from the bottom up with its full purpose in mind."

She was almost angry now. "Oh, that too will get you burned!"

"Prove to me I have it wrong," he had asked her letting their eyes meet.

She tried to think then suddenly leaned forward, excited. "I have it! I know!"

He laughed. "What is it?"

She leaned in even further to make her point. "Gaze into my eyes, for the proof is there as it in yours."

He was so close he could have kissed her. "How can that be?"

"Look! Look!" she insisted. "Not that! …Later, maybe!" She laughed again. "You are unusually persistent today, my love!"

"I see flecks of gold in beautiful green eyes owned by the woman I love."

"Stick to the subject — Do you see the intricacy there?"

"I do."

"And how the pupils open, and then narrow? I see the world through my eyes, and when you look into them, you look into my soul, perhaps."

"Is that so?"

"It is the way with eyes — only God could make something so complex, so beautiful, and tied to the soul at the same time."

She was leaning in so close he could feel her face opening into a smile rather than see it. She knew she was right. She laughed. He kissed her before she could withdraw.

"You kissed me — I told you not to."

"That's because you kissed me first."

She laughed again. "I did not. Wishful thinking on your part."

"It seems that I am a slave to this body."

"Do you agree with me or not?"

"Not."

She leaned back, frustrated, asking while laughing, "What kind of Guardian Angel are you?" She threw her arms out wide and fell back onto their blanket and continued to laugh with her head back and the sun on her. "I surrender!"

The best thing about his memory of that day was not that he was right and she was wrong — it was the mere fact he could talk to her about such things. That and the fact the recollection reminded him how much he had loved her. More than life.

Shaming Spring

Now that his heart had shifted, and he knew that it had, there was no telling what would happen, for the uncomfortable truth was he rather liked Emily. He thought she would be empty, and why wouldn't she be? He had brought her back from death: no heartbeat, no breath of life, and nearly no brain activity. He had brought her back just in time to preserve who she was just as he had planned, and now, evidently, he was stuck with her. She was a living person in the form of a woman who was not unlike Catherine, not only physically, but also in her character. It was odd. She possessed so little of Catherine's genetic inheritance, but there was no doubt about the physical as well as the emotional similarities between the two. He had not expected that. He had not expected the effect that would have on him.

He sighed: so much for good ideas ...Once again. The culprit this time, of course, was a twist of his human heart; another heart made only of pure energy — protons, electrons coupled through a complex web of magnetic force fields — would not possibly feel the same thing. Is that not the current wisdom? That we feel what we are programmed to feel? But it should make it easier, he supposed: he would not be committing murder precisely; after all, how could he be accused of destroying a woman who was already a great deal like the one he was changing her into? That's not murder — it's something, but it's not murder. Not that he was the murdering type. He didn't like to think so.

It was that right and wrong thing again: by abandoning Catherine, he might as well abandon his Singular Friend now Jupiter-bound. He might as well allow his brother to sweep him up and take him home. Lesson over. The Rite complete. Step into the future for that is all you have. Leave the past to the past. Stop crying about it. Let the pieces he had already broken off pick themselves up and find their own way. It would no longer be his problem.

• •• ••• •••••

He stepped off the curb and propelled himself forward into the flow of human traffic. It was noon hour in Time's Square. He pushed through the crowd and stepped quickly along 5th Avenue, then a block later drew to a halt beneath the awning of an Italian restaurant — *Emilio's Ballato*. He was early. It gave him time to watch the crowds and guess at the secrets in the faces that passed. So many different countenances: hair, eyes, nose, mouth — hopes, dreams, aspirations forming a myriad of complexity that made them all the same: the same but different. In some eyes, in some mouths, in some set of shoulder and turn of the head, were people he had once known. They had long ago been recycled into dust, mortals, but here they were, with him still.

• •• ••• •••••

A black limousine, stretched with six wheels, pulled up to the curb. The door opened, and Emily's father placed a foot, black leather, to the asphalt. The repairs to his heart remained perfect and exact. He stepped out then turned immediately to reach back inside, and Emily followed, swinging her legs out then standing. His heart leapt: her physical similarity to Catherine was astounding. She kissed her father quickly then arm in arm father and daughter crossed the human river.

Gatc'hh'en opened the door leading into the restaurant: a gentleman attendant. Emily brushed past, glancing in his direction but without recognizing him: just a glance and a brief gesture as if she had sensed his presence. He had felt her bodily warmth and detected her perfume — *Shalimar Eau Légère*. His heart leaped again. Everything about Emily astounded him: her hair, her eyes, the turn of her nose, and her chin. He almost called out — but instead immersed himself in the glass of the window, allowing sunshine to pour through while watching her, but feeling guilty for his voyeurism, both the necessary and unnecessary components of it.

· ·· ··· ·····

Father and daughter sat at the back with a good view of the front window and the crowds passing by. Emily took her seat, her father helping her, adjusting her chair. She ran her fingers along the perfectly white tablecloth and lifted the thick cloth napkin, unfolded it, caressed it, then settled it across her lap. The restaurant was light and airy; warm and full of the smells of good food. The waiter — *le garçon* — or because it was, indeed, an Italian restaurant, *Il cameriere* — arrived with the wine and a basket of bread. She smeared a piece of the hot bread with butter and plunged it into her mouth, not caring how hot the bread, or how full her mouth might be. She cried with pleasure. "Oh my God! Oh, my God!" She shoved in another piece and mumbled through a mouthful, and then laughed, pieces of bread falling out, laughing while trying to catch them. "*It is so good!*" The *Il cameriere* slipped behind her and poured a small portion of wine into her glass. She took a moment to finish her mouthful of buttered bread then carefully tasted: red wine to her lips, a sip, testing the wine on the tongue, carefully swallowing, and then returning and declaring it excellent.

Emily sipped the wine again, beaming and glowing, the small amount she'd consumed already having an effect. She laughed and toasted to her renewed lease on life with the *Beaujolais Nord* — French wine in an Italian restaurant she pointed out, thinking it hilarious. Her father clinking his glass against hers, his eyes brimming, she noticing, saying nothing but her smile widening as she tipped her glass to him again and sipped again.

"You see? This is all because of you, my love! This is what you can do. Does it not bring you joy?"

He did not know what to think, or feel. But his heart hollowed as he recalled Catherine saying that to him after he cured the lepers on the outskirts of town but only because she had asked him to.

He slipped out of the window and once again stood in the street, the crowds sweeping past and glanced back to watch her order her meal. A beautiful young woman, happy, ecstatic, and full of life: short blonde hair combed back behind delicate ears; blue eyes beginning to change, and a smile to shame spring.

Emily

Emily stepped into the flow of humanity, her arms crossed like a protective shield. She felt as if she might be floating on air: Life is Heaven when you're healthy; Hell, if you're sick. She pantomimed the people, wondering what occasion there might be for them to pick up the pace, lift their faces upward, and even smile — this was New York, after all. She breathed deeply and could almost detect the sea. Her heart skipped with her feet. She stopped at the curb and waited for the light, and then pushed off dodging traffic feeling more alive by the moment.

Her mind spun with the shifting confluence of all the people, all intent on their personal journeys, the jostling and sidestepping spinning her about, creating a gentle sensation of vertigo. Unexpected images blossomed then faded raising a smile, and then a frown, and then another smile. Her lips unconsciously moved as she talked to herself, describing the images and ideas that flooded her mind spinning like an unbalanced top. One dream, one impression, after another. Pieces and parts of different scenes none of which she understood, not entirely, and not at all for many of them. None of them wrong or misplaced, just different.

Her mind and heart back-pedaled as if on a treadmill, centering her, calming her. She hadn't seen him for over month but that didn't seem to matter — her imagination just would not let him go. For the hundredth thousandth time, she wondered if he might be no more than a product of her drug-wounded imagination but then once again quickly dismissed that possibility. But it was silly, the heart often goes its own way despite one's best intentions and knowing the right and wrong of it. You can't seem to do anything about it, ever. And, of course, it didn't help that he was especially handsome.

Her feet skipped along the concrete in her spring coat, her brightly colored silk scarf, her short blonde hair combed carefully behind her ears. The real question to all this was why: Why her, of all people? How he might have cured her was hard enough to understand but the why was just a difficult. Resurrect another woman? His old lover? He had called her Catherine. Catherine must have been his lover, she told herself as a jolt of jealousy grabbed her.

She drew to a sudden halt. The crowd parted around her like a fast-moving stream over an obstruction as she stumbled across the flow, almost collapsing to the pavement. She grasped a light standard and pinched her eyes shut. She began to slip… She did slip. Her strength had suddenly gone. She closed her eyes and the world surrounding her slowly went dark.

• •• ••• •••••

Emily looked around, momentarily disoriented. She let go of the standard and turned about, and hand flew up to cover her heart.

"It's you! Again!"

"It is me, yes — again."

"I was just out for lunch with my father," she explained quickly, self-consciously straightening her coat, her scarf, and her hair. "I was just walking about getting some fresh air after the meal — I ate far too much. I'm still not used to it."

His smile had not left him. "I see you are well, almost fully recovered," he acknowledged, studying her.

"Oh... Oh... Thank you, Thank you... Look..." She pirouetted slowly about, and returning, clasped her hands as if in prayer, bowing to him. "Thank you. Thank you!" She hid her face, and despite her best intentions began to weep. She turned abruptly away from him unable to stop. "...I'm sorry. I don't know why I'm crying! You did this me! You saved me!"

He gently broke her hands apart and handed her a tissue. She wiped her eyes one at a time careful with her mascara and looked up. She had forgotten how handsome he was. "Thank you," she said again, sniffed and tried to smile. "You know you look like Brad Pitt — but a younger version," she said, wiping her eyes again.

"Who is Brad Pitt?"

"An actor."

"Ah."

"...You're dressed like a banker —. I don't think Brad would dress as a banker —. Although I don't really know him..."

"I noted many men wearing something similar. Is it not appropriate?"

"It is appropriate, it is!" she quickly insisted. "...It is just that I was expecting you to be dressed more like you were when I last saw you: old leather jacket, t-shirt, jeans, leather boots, grey wool socks — I noticed last time you wore grey wool socks."

He studied her carefully, still smiling.

She continued blushing violently. "I... I don't know who you are."

"Gatc'hh'en."

"That is not a name..."

"It is my name nonetheless."

She attempted to pronounce it and managed to get it right the third time. He nodded to indicate when she did.

"Well, that's quite a name — is it French?" she asked, wondering about him.

"No, it is an interpretation of what my name would be if you or any person here could pronounce it. It is symbolic with geometrical connotations."

"Oh… So, it is not your real name?" she asked again to confirm, hesitant, still unsure of herself, feeling more foolish by the moment.

His smile widened. "…It is, close enough."

"My doctors are absolutely shocked," Emily went on, her unsummoned words pouring out. "But pleased, too: Don't look a gift horse in the mouth, they say. Everyone is calling it a miracle — my Dad, my Mom, what friends I have left, the doctors, nurses." She opened her mouth and stepped in close. "Look at my teeth: the fillings fell out…"

He did not bother to look. "So I see…"

She stepped back and closed her mouth. "They're perfect!"

"Yes, they are."

"How can you do all this to me? Are you from the future?"

He seemed surprised. "Why would you ask that?"

"Well, only someone with an incredible technology and understanding of the human body could have cured me — that's what a doctor who came to see me said. He heard about my case and wanted to check me over. He said, too, that any technology sufficiently advanced would seem like magic to us — or a miracle; and it seems like that, too, doesn't it, he said. He was very nice and very clever."

"I'm not from the future — sorry to disappoint you."

He threaded her arm through his then propelled her along the sidewalk., she just managing to keep up.

"Where are we going?"

"A short walk to the park and then I'll take you home."

"Are we an item? I didn't know we are an item."

"I don't know what you mean by item."

"You know… *Item*."

"I'm going to take you to your home and leave you there; you are not completely recovered; you need rest — If that is what you mean."

She blushed turning an even brighter red. "Oh, sorry — of course."

He increased their pace. She fell into step. They waited for the light to change.

"Where we going again?"

"The park, a bench adjacent to the pond."

She felt yet another surge of warmth sweep up through her. The sensation was not unlike a rush of morphine. She had had the drug more than once and knew what it felt like.

They crossed the street — Columbus Circle — and entered the park. The sounds of the city faded. Sunlight pierced the upper branches. He led her to a bench. She dropped down onto the bench, self-consciously opening the distance between them and laughed. "I don't know why but I feel quite drunk. I haven't had a drink since... Since lunch!" She leaned into him quite beyond herself. "I remember everything," she said softly, her chin resting on his shoulder. She laughed quietly again and poked his chest. "You kissed me... You know very well you did."

"You are quite intoxicated."

She sat back. "You did something?"

"You are under the influence of a surge of energy that I infused into your mitochondrial DNA. It is to help you heal — and to calm you."

She leaned in again. "Does that mean if I wasn't... intoxicated? Would you kiss me again?"

He nearly smiled. "I don't know..." He turned to look at her quickly. "I would say, probably."

She leaned in closer yet. Close enough to kiss him if he would let her, or close enough for him to kiss her if he would.

"Oh? ...Probably?"

He gently extricated himself. "I have to admit you have put me off-guard," he admitted, trying not to smile. "You look and sound very much like her must be the reason."

She sat back recovered slightly. "Who? Catherine?"

"Yes."

Emily felt yet another unreasonable stab of jealousy. "You were lovers?"

Her question seemed to take him by surprise.

"What happened to her?" she asked, pressing.

"She died."

"…That's too bad."

"She was twenty-three."

"The same age as me."

"So it is."

"We've talked about that already," Emily acknowledged sitting back again. She was slowly sobering, nearly there. "I didn't tell the doctor who came to visit me — The clever one … And not bad looking, either — About the devices you put in me. I figured he'd tear me apart trying to find them. But maybe he will — He took enough of my blood so he can test it. I couldn't help that. What was I going to say?"

"You are right, maybe he will. I don't know."

She sat back fully. "You don't seem concerned."

"I'm not."

Emily considered. She straightened and smoothed her dress. She was almost back to normal. "So what's the plan?" she asked, facing him. "What's the purpose behind all this? …Is there a purpose?"

"There is not always a purpose, I agree," he said and shifted to face her directly.

"You are changing me into Catherine," she stated evenly, unflinching.

"That is it."

"My body?"

"…I did tell you."

"I guess you did."

"You need to understand that this is what I intended all along," he said just as evenly as she had. "It is the only reason I saved your life, why I entered your bedroom. It is the only reason why we are talking now."

"I thought you liked me."

"I do like you."

"I want your devices out; take them out," Emily demanded quietly. "They are what is messing with me. I'm okay now. I'm quite recovered."

"I cannot do that."

"You can deactivate them — I know you can. They belong to you after all."

"I can but I will not."

"Why not?"

"I do not wish to. It is not part of the plan — remember the plan?"

She thought. "…You are human like me — you cannot do this. You are not capable, not if you are human."

"Who says I am human?"

He was talking nonsense.

"What are you then?"

"You have seen me already. I have allowed you to do so."

She remembered. The memory had been there all along but she had pushed it away. "A sphere of light as bright as the sun?"

"Just so."

"It is not possible. I don't believe you."

"It does not matter what you believe."

"You appear so human. …But I admit you are a bit odd."

"It is to be expected, I suppose."

"You are human, I know you are; don't say you're not."

He thought and after a moment looked up. "What is it to be human? Tissue and bone?"

Emily closed her eyes and shook her head. "So you are human?" she asked again to confirm that he was. Her head was spinning. "...I thought so." She considered. "But I should admit, and I mean this in a nice way — you are very strange." She remained sitting as he stood, following him up with her eyes.

"You did not tell me you were a married man," she called up.

The jealous stab would not let her go. The barbs reached deep.

He extended his hand. "We will talk no more of this."

She accepted it and stood. "Why not?"

"I'll take you home," he said, gathering her to him "The more you rest, the easier it will be."

"But you were lovers?" she asked again, holding back, not able to get that barbed thought out of her mind.

"What do you think?"

She tried to be nonchalant. She nodded. "Okay..."

He put his arm around her and headed them out of the park. They walked slowly, he keeping his around her.

"Does that mean we will be lovers?" she asked after a moment.

He smiled but didn't answer.

"I don't feel any different — I feel wonderful. I'm not Catherine. I'm myself," she said in denial, getting back to the fact she was not Catherine and not his lover.

"I'm sure that is true."

"Will I feel the changes coming about?"

He again did not answer.

"Well?"

"When you wake in the morning — your eyes open, and you view the world — do you think you would be able to tell if you were anyone other than you? Others might be able to tell but not you perhaps."

Emily nodded and thought before reluctantly adding, "...I'm just wondering. It is funny how things could be and maybe aren't."

"What do you mean?"

"I mean, I feel weird. I don't feel myself. Did you program your devices to make me fall in love with you?" She turned to face him, stopping their progress. "That would be logical, wouldn't it? I mean, part one of the plan to change me?"

He hesitated.

She asked further, sticking with it, "If I understand you correctly, everything I think, everything I feel, could be programmed within me by your devices."

"It would be a gross violation of you."

"Please answer the question."

"Then no, if you are falling in love with me it is within you; a suggestion to do so has not been planted by me."

She slowly nodded. "I don't fear you," she said, beginning to shake. "…Oh, God, look at me, I'm shaking! Why am I shaking?"

"The devices are having an effect." He tightened his hold on her and propelled them forward again.

She seemed unable to stop thinking of Catherine, what she might look like, and what she might be like. "You were in love with her, I know," she said. "But I am not Catherine," Emily insisted again. If were not for the fact he held her upright, she would slip to the pavement.

"What is this all for?" she asked looking up and leaning into him.

"All will eventually become clear, I promise."

"You need to say more than that."

She swooned and he held her up.

"It is my human heart that is responsible for all this. I seem to have no more control over it than you over your own. We are similar in that way."

She shook her head emphatically and fell into him. "I won't be Catherine for you!

She wept and tripped, then stumbled. He scooped her up and kept her walking. She suddenly lost herself and began to uncontrollably weep. She buried her face in his shoulder.

"You are not going to hurt me? You are not going to break my heart?"

• •• ••• ••••••

He forced an electrical stimulus upon her that affected the neurotransmitters in her brain, and she calmed. She stumbled again. He held her upright. He had lied to her about planting the thought she might be in love with him. He had done so right at the beginning, in the hospital, when he thought he would be changing her completely. It was, indeed, a gross violation. He should not have done it.

He wrapped himself around her, turned dark, then ascended above the city, invisible to all those below. He took her home and put her to bed. Her eyes still open watching him, the sheets tucked up to her chin, he stepped back and entered his natural form for her to see. Her bedroom pulsed with brilliant light, the same color as sunlight in summer. He departed through the glass of her bedroom window, and a moment later all of Queens shook as he broached Mach 1.0.

21

Jupiter Analysis

I nstitute for Astronomy, Room 7-214, University of Hawaii, Manoa Valley, Hawaii. Eighteen scientists gathered about a conference table. Dr. Eleanor Vanier, Monserrat's contact at JPL, was on speaker phone, as was Dr. Phil Gregory, Ph.D., Electrical Engineering and Astronomy, University of Virginia, and Monserrat's contact at the Arecibo Radio Observatory in Puerto Rico. There was a palpable tension in the room. The word was out. The world was watching.

Joe Monserrat chaired. He got right down to it. "Okay, what do we know?"

Those gathered around the table swiveled to face the display mounted on the far wall. Dr. Robert King, on the project the longest, and an astrophysicist, explained what they knew. He remained sitting as his previously prepared PowerPoint slides were put up one by one. There was nothing beautiful about them; they listed only the facts.

"The object now formally identified as MPC-5533600 is now out of the gravity well of Jupiter. As Dr. Vanier had suggested earlier, it appears to have undergone a gravity assist as it went past Jupiter."

Two overlaying plots were shown. One of the predicted orbit before the Jupiter fly-past, the second from just the night before showing it outbound from Jupiter.

"The object dumped approximately two-hundred-fifty kilometers per second, and as this track shows" — he switched plots — "it is now inbound for Earth. The fact that it is very nearly at the velocity needed to rendezvous with Earth means that it is likely to go into orbit around Earth — What orbit, how close, the Perigee, Apogee, etcetera, we have no way of knowing at this time."

Monserrat interjected. "Just keep with the facts. That's a huge shift in velocity. How did the object stay intact?"

"I don't know. Maybe it didn't, I don't know," King stated honestly, then quickly continued to explain. "Here's why — although it was radiating in the visible as it flew past Jupiter, and before that, it has since gone dark again. It is now optically invisible — maybe it no longer exists. As you said, it could have passed its Roche limit and broken up."

"But you don't think so?"

King squirmed uncomfortably. "I don't know."

Monserrat squirmed as Bob King had, unconsciously imitating his friend and colleague. He looked across the table. "Henrik, do you want to add something?"

He was addressing Doctor Henrik Johansson, Ph.D., Astronomy, Mathematics and Physics, University of Hawaii, and Monserrat's contact at Mauna Key. He was responsible for defining the observing goals for the giant Keck telescope, and rescheduling them if need be. He was also renowned for his work on the indirect detection of Dark Matter. He and Monserrat were long-time friends.

"It went dark as you said eight hours forty-two minutes exactly after Jupiter flyby," Johansson began, keeping as precise as possible. "It was near dawn for us so we turned it over to the Australian Astronomical Observatory, the AAO, in New South Wales, and they couldn't find it either. We were on a conference call with them all day — that's two days ago — and nothing. We checked last night and there is nothing there. It's gone. It probably broke up as Bob suggests. We can't find any of the pieces, though, which doesn't necessarily mean they're not there. It just means we can't seem them; they could be too small."

"Arecibo? Phil, are you there?"

"I'm here—. Right, well, we never did find it. At least we found nothing in the error box you provided. Australia couldn't find it either." He was referring to the Parkes Radio Observatory, again in New South Wales, Australia.

Monserrat appeared grim. He had heard all of this before the meeting. He waved Bob King on.

"It's all over the news," King continued. "Maybe two hundred amateurs and non-amateurs saw the object and tracked it visually. The MPC was swamped with emails. We have an amateur photo from China that seems to show it disappear."

He displayed a set of amateur but high quality images spaced at three minute intervals. In the first two, the light from the object over-saturating the CCD, but in the third only background stars.

King waited for the group to pick up the inference. Monserrat nudged him on. "Give us the rest of it."

"I received this from Creutzberg at Goddard this morning — He couldn't make the teleconference so he just handed it over. It is not precise in that we don't have confirmation that it's still on the track it was, or even if it is still the same object. But something out there in the vicinity where it was or still is, is radiating in the x-ray, and to a lesser extent in gamma."

"What radiates like that?"

"High-speed plasma accelerated in a magnetic field."

"Jupiter then?"

"Nope, it was closer to the last sighting of the object. It seems to be in the middle of nowhere."

"Arecibo? Phil?"

"We picked it up too. It has to go through the atmosphere and it is still a long way out so the signal is weak, but we get it. Jupiter — we don't think so; it was sourced from something else, possibly something way out in interstellar space. I gave Dr. King a plot of the spectrum."

Bob King showed the slide.

"But no returned echo from the object?" Monserrat pressed.

"No, nothing: There never has been one. It's either because it's not as big as you said it might be, or it may no longer be in one piece. It must be, or was, very small."

"Henrik? Keck?"

"We couldn't make out any structure even when it was radiating and we had a really good extended look at it. That means whatever it is — or was — it is, was, less than a kilometer in diameter. That's the best we can do even with our adaptive optics at 5 AU. Very bright, though — I've never seen anything so bright at that range."

"What could that be caused by?"

"No idea — it doesn't make sense."

"How about it must have a nuclear core and we're looking right into it," Matheson quipped, unable to stop himself from putting a twist of science fiction into the dialog. He was immediately sorry he had.

Monserrat rolled his eyes. "What else does it mean?" he asked. "Eleanor?"

Dr. Eleanor Vanier took over. "It means that the density is much higher than you estimated making it much smaller but with the same mass. It is not a comet, not a KBO. It's like nothing we know of from the Kuiper Belt or Oort Cloud, which would typically have an inbound velocity of about five kilometers per second. Or, if a comet, then forty kilometers per second." She considered. "It could be from the interstellar medium. However, objects from the interstellar medium are typically much slower — two kilometers per second or so. Of course, it could have been accelerating for some time."

"How would it accelerate?"

"Just falling into the sun."

"All the way up to five-hundred kilometers per second?"

"It would take a while — thousands of years, maybe tens of thousands if it's origin is the Oort Cloud."

Monserrat sat back and sighed. "Good... Great... My phone is ringing off the hook. My email inbox is full — Thanks, Ken, for giving the MPC-my name, number, and email address. I'm not answering any questions at this time — only to say we need to get more data and confirm that the object was indeed destroyed. The fact it's trajectory shifted to intercept Earth will be a 'no comment'. If anyone has been able to figure it out, and they probably haven't — so please, Eleanor, Henrik, Phil, let's keep that quiet until we all do our homework."

Everyone agreed. Monserrat adjourned the meeting. The conference call was disconnected and there was a mad rush back to their workstations to work out the potential scenarios and to go over the data again. What they needed was more observing time. They didn't have to worry. It took precedence over everything else. The world was waking up.

22

Emily

Emily wore emerald stud earrings that matched her eyes, and a string of pearls about her long neck. Her blonde hair brushed back behind her ears and held in place by a barrette made of pink pearls, crystals and garnet. The pearls had been handed down by her Grandmother and were very special to her; the barrette she had purchased just recently, loving the rich color, thinking it went with her hair.

She slipped across the living room and quietly opened the French doors leading outside, closing them quietly behind her. The scent of a mid-spring garden after the recent rain filled the air. She had the presence of mind to grab a shawl on the way out and now wrapped it about her shoulders as she kicked off her inside shoes and stepped onto the wet grass: cool, nearly freezing. The sensation calmed her, putting out the embers. She had no way of knowing why she felt as she did, only that when all was said and done, he had better not break her heart.

She glanced back and noted her reflection in the glass: a young woman floating in mid-air: slender body, full breasts; blond hair the color of the sun cut stylishly short; emerald-green eyes, very clear, shining, levelled on her own; milk-white skin, nose tipped up, sensitive lips in a cautious smile — cautious because her world had been placed upside down, albeit for the better: infinitely better.

"Thank you," she said.

There was a photograph somewhere, lost in an album, stored in an unmarked box in the attic. The photo, taken years ago before Emily had been born, was of her mother standing in this same garden wrapped in a similar shawl. Her mother's hair had been cut fashionably short as was hers; she wore earrings, small studs that flashed, as she did, and her mother had a delicate neck like her neck. She was young and beautiful: Happy — Happy then, and happy now, too. Not in the same way, but happy; even wiser. She was more like her mother now.

Emily addressed her reflection, searching for more solid ground. "I don't know who I am half the time." Then still searching: "But I have never been well enough to know, have I?"

She crossed the patio to the arbor overladen with spring roses, and bent to take up the emerging aroma from a few nascent buds, and just one rose just beginning to open. Her mother's roses. She ran her finger tips along the soft petals. It was good to be alive. She answered the question she had inwardly posed days earlier, speaking aloud to the hushed night, phrasing her response less like an answer than the way she felt. "When close, I can feel his warmth. I can smell him — summer hay."

Straightening, she turned and found herself facing her father. She immediately smiled and he smiled back as he stepped down from the patio. He was wearing his favorite slippers; they were going to get wet.

"Who were you talking to?" he asked.

"Just me, myself, and I."

"You know, for moment I didn't think it was you standing there. It was dark, and I couldn't see you properly." He wrapped his arm about her and gently began to turn her back toward the house. "But come on in, Emily; it's wet, you'll get a chill. I have just had a call that you should know about."

Emily resisted and held him back. "I'm okay."

"No, no, you're not — come on in. I have just had a call from a man named Kalinowski. That's why I came out to find you. There is something you need to know."

Emily, still resisting, held her ground. "Oh?"

"There you go being stubborn again — You are becoming more and more like your mother every day."

Emily smiled with him. "No, it's only me: it's just me and me and me," she gently chided.

Her father laughed. "I know, you've always been your own self, and that is a good thing. No one should be anything other than themselves, should they?"

"What's it all about then?" Emily asked. "Why would I be interested in your phone call?"

"It's nothing — believe me, it's nothing." Her father shuffled, and turned his collar up. "It's chilly out here…" He smiled again. "He says he works for the FBI, the CIA, and the NS; all three, he claims. I like him — He sounds like a nice guy: a regular guy. He made it a joke. Anyway, I have a meeting with him tomorrow morning downtown. I didn't want to, but I said I would go in the end." Her father had it memorized: "The FBI Building, 10AM Wednesday, Room 15-245. Apparently, someone on his team noticed the photos your mother posted on Facebook: the before and after pictures of your miracle cure. He wants to know all about it, and more about you, and me. He's just the curious sort, he says. Maybe they have a van parked outside to whiz you away, I don't know: put you in a lab, poke and prod you, and all that."

Emily laughed. "That's silly."

"I guess."

"But why would they care?" Emily implored more seriously. "A so-called miracle cure is not usually a matter of national security. I would think I'd get a call from the Mayo Clinic rather than the CIA or the FBI."

"Of course, that's right — Do you want to come with me and explain it? He'd probably appreciate it and I'd like your company."

Emily leaned back, surprised. "No!"

Her father smiled again. "Would another time would be better? I can call him back?"

"No time would be better — Let him get a warrant and then maybe I will."

"Then tomorrow is good, then?"

Emily shook her head, drawing out her response, laughing, "*Noooo...!*"

Her father laughed with her. "Why are you being so stubborn? You are just like your mother again!"

She stepped back, shrugged, and threw her head back, returning a loose lock of her hair behind her ear. "It is the new me, I guess."

"The happy you."

"Do you want the old, more somber, Emily back? It can be arranged, you know?" She laughed again.

"No, I like what you've become — I have never seen you so healthy, or beautiful. This is what you're supposed to look like, I guess: It is the healthy, real you. It's been so long."

Emily studied her father still smiling. "What happened to you and mom, anyway?"

"You know, or you should know — Francis wanted her own life; she didn't want to be just 'Mrs. Marcel Dupuis.' She has a mind of her own your mom, just like you seem to have now. Can't say I blame her, or you either." He kissed Emily's cheek, and turned her back toward the house. "Let's go in; the grass has ruined my slippers. And I know you're freezing; I can feel you shaking."

"I can't imagine why felt compelled to step outside in them — they're your favorite," Emily gently admonished falling in next to him. She was freezing; her feet were like ice, and she was beginning to shake. The devices he had planted in her must be working overtime again, she reasoned.

"Leave them by the fire, and they'll be okay," she said, nodding, her mind elsewhere.

"So you say."

Emily closed the French doors behind them. She latched them shut and locked them. She looked up to once again catch her image in the glass: blonde hair, barrette, small ears, a pair of green eyes staring back, and a half smile. She absently traced the edge of her chin with the tip of her finger. Catherine's eyes or her eyes? Catherine's smile or her own? There was no answer for it.

Norris

The hollow sound of echoing footsteps bounced along the corridor and off the steel doors at the far end of the hallway. They ricocheted off the polished floor, reflected again and again, not losing their intensity, challenging Norris's courage. He led two men dressed in identically gray suits and an orderly dressed in impeccable white up to the last door. Norris himself was dressed in jeans and a T-shirt covered by an unbuttoned lab coat. He nodded to the orderly who removed a set of keys from his belt, fumbled with them, then stepped up to the door and peered inside. John Schmidt was lying on his back on a narrow bed staring up at the ceiling. He appeared to be either asleep or unconscious. The orderly inserted the selected key and cracked the door open, then stepped aside to allow the others access.

"Is your patient dangerous?" one of the two well-dressed men asked as he entered the small room.

"Not at all."

The safety precautions belied this. Norris knew they did. He also knew that the two men would interpret from the inflection of his voice, the casual, knowing way he shrugged, that the patient just might be dangerous.

He glanced at the man who had introduced himself with a smile and a quick flash of a gold and blue metal badge — FBI "Special Agent" it said. He had introduced himself as Special Agent Marlon J. Hines. The other, clearly an acolyte, had identified himself as Special Agent Glen L. Wetmore and similarly, if not identically, had flashed his badge to identify himself. Hines was middle-aged, large framed, tending towards heaviness, with suspicious and mostly intelligent but cold eyes. Wetmore was half his age, powerfully built, athletic, shorter, same eyes. Without knowing a thing about them, Norris detested them both intensely.

They filed into the room, Norris following the orderly and the security men close on Norris's heals, so close that Norris could detect a trace of his after-shave: *Neroli Portofino*. For some reason this annoyed him. He didn't think that would be allowed. How could one sneak up on one's enemies smelling like the Italian Riviera?

Hines indicated his patient. "What's the matter with him?"

"He's unconscious."

Norris watched the muscles in the younger man's jaw ripple.

"I can see that, doctor. Can you wake him up?"

"I wish I could."

They shuffled around the bed staring down at the unconscious form. Wetmore glanced in his direction then circled the bed a second time. The directed glance increased Norris' dislike for the man grew exponentially.

"Is this some kind of joke?" Wetmore asked, finally turning to him.

"Not at all — As I told you both earlier, except for a brief moment about a month ago, he has been more or less in this state for the last eight years."

He was not about to tell them about the other day when John, or whomever, had sat upright. He was still absorbing that incident himself. The right and wrong of it. The lucid and the delusional aspects of it.

"Eight years!" Wetmore shook his head mumbling something deprecatory not meant to be heard but nonetheless clearly understood.

"You mentioned earlier that your patient might be of interest to us. Why is that?" Hines asked Norris, covering for his associate.

"The unexplained is always of interest I would think."

"So this patient who was unconscious for eight years suddenly regains consciousness — and another patient slips a butcher knife into him within seconds of his awakening?" Hines prompted with his summary of events.

"Yes, that's right."

"And where is she?"

"You know about Valentina?"

"It was covered in the New York Times, Dr. Norris — we read the paper; even the third section."

"No one mentioned her name in the article — I should know, I was interviewed for it. She's not responsible for her actions; she is mentally ill."

"So we hear… We do our homework." Agent Hines reached into his folder and handed him a large-framed photograph. "Have you ever met this woman, or have had any association with her?"

Norris studied the photo. "No, I don't think so," he answered honestly.

"You were one of her attending physicians, Dr. Norris. We checked — another homework assignment." He sneered or nearly did. "It was at NYP Weill-Cornell right downtown about two months ago," the agent prompted keeping his measured smile.

Norris studied the photograph more closely, turning it about in his hands. He still could not recognize the woman. She was beautiful. He tried to think. He would recall someone as beautiful as her. He looked up and asked for her name. They gave it to him. He was shocked.

"Emily?" He examined the photograph again; he still could not recognize her. "Yes, of course. I know her. I know her father —

Marcel. I rather like him. Very much under control, and, unlike so many others, so very understanding of what can and cannot be done."

"But Emily…"

"But's that not Emily," he interrupted the agent impatiently waving the suggestion off. He tapped the photo. "This woman is most definitely not Mr. Dupuis' daughter. The Emily Dupuis I know is far too ill to be her. In fact, I would not all be surprised to learn that Emily is deceased."

"She was that ill?"

"She was," Norris confirmed. "There was no hope. It is often difficult to say how long someone in her state would have had, but it couldn't have been more than a few days, a week at most."

The agent pointed again to the photograph. "Could the woman in this photo be a sister or a cousin of Miss Dupuis?"

"How should I know?"

"Guess."

He studied the photo again. "Perhaps a sister or a cousin; her mother, perhaps her mother in younger days, I don't know. There are some similarities."

"I see. You should know that her father assures us his daughter is very much alive and this is her. He claims a miracle cure." The agent studied Norris carefully, looking for something, a reaction. He pointed again to the photo. "Look at her. She's beautiful. Have you ever heard of such a thing as a miracle cure?"

Dr. Norris shook his head. It was a ridiculous suggestion. "It's not possible," he said. "There is no such things as miracles but it is true there are things we do not understand."

"Do you have any theories of who she might be that you might want to share?"

"She's not Emily Dupuis, that's all I know. I have no idea why a man like Marcel Dupuis would say otherwise. He didn't call or otherwise inform me about his daughter's change of fortune — not that he would, we're not friends; but he is a good man, as I said."

Special Agent Hines retrieved the photo. He glanced at his partner who nodded then entered a brief note in his notebook already opened and ready for the note.

"I hope I have not put Marcel into any sort of trouble," Norris cautiously added, feeling more nervous by the moment. "He seemed like a good man, and an honest man," he also added, covering for a man he barely knew.

"Did you know that Dr. Marcel Dupuis is a senior diplomat with the United Nations?" Wetmore emphasized the word 'doctor.' "His official title is-," Wetmore referred to his notes: "Co-chair Counter-Terrorism Committee."

Norris was surprised — but it was not wholly unlikely; the man he had known had seemed highly competent. He said so. "It really doesn't surprise me, no."

Agent Hines considered. He nodded to Wetmore who continued. "We need to understand the complete picture. When was the last time you saw Emily Elizabeth Dupuis? Exactly when, please," Wetmore prompted.

Norris was taken aback. So, this was what it had been about all along? They weren't interested in his John Schmidt or Valentina, or even him. They were interested solely in Emily. "Dr. Dupuis called me in to see her," he began then hesitated before proceeding. "He was quite in a panic. He had imagined she'd expired but when I arrived double quick the electronic monitors we had on her indicated just the opposite." Norris hedged. "She was maybe better than I knew, I don't know." He added sarcastically, "Maybe the so-called miracle cure happened before I arrived? Who would think?"

"That was the very last time?"

"I was off duty after that — and have not seen either since. That's the way it often works, I'm afraid; hospital care can be somewhat impersonal."

Hines produced a composite sketch of the man recently described to them by Emily's father — they had not informed Norris that they had interviewed him a few days previously; they were just about to but were waiting to test his reaction with the sketch. Norris gingerly accepted the sketch. He glanced at it then handed it back.

"Do you recognize that man?" Hines asked.

"I don't think so."

"Look again. You didn't look very carefully."

Norris accepted it back and studied it.

"Are you feel alright, doctor? You look pale."

"I'm fine —. I've changed my mind; I do recognize him."

"Would you like to sit down, doctor?"

"Yeah, fine." Norris sat down on the edge of the bed. He was as white as the bed sheets covering John Schmidt who still lay back as if sound asleep oblivious to all.

"What do you know about him?" Hines asked.

"Nothing — I know nothing of him. He is as much a mystery to me as he is no doubt to you."

"He spoke to Miss Dupuis?"

Norris hid his hands to conceal the fact they were trembling. He glanced up avoiding eye contact. "I don't know. But I believe she must have been unconscious the entire time — I just don't know. Why don't you ask her? If she's still alive, it shouldn't be a problem."

"But he was with her when you entered the room?"

"Yes, that's right — I remember now." Norris looked about the room, to his patient and then back to the agents. "How do you know all that?"

"Dr. Dupuis — we interviewed him just a few days ago. He called us; we didn't have to call him. The composite sketch comes from his recollection. It took a while to get it out of him but he was ultimately quite cooperative and very helpful. We will want to talk with you too in more detail sooner than later to see if your recollection lines up with his as much as where it might not. Someone will call you and set up a time — possibly tomorrow if that's all right?"

Norris swallowed.

"Is that all right?" Agent Hines asked again.

"That's fine."

"We have an office downtown. It shouldn't be too much out of your way."

"I didn't do anything."

"I didn't say you did — but you were a witness."

"Yes, but what does that mean? A witness to what?"

The agent studied Norris for a moment before continuing. He ignored his questions. "So, going back: the man in question, a young man, good looking, hair pulled back, ponytail, grey eyes, a normal enough young man as Dr. Dupuis described him — was with her when you entered the room? He could have spoken to her before you and Dr. Dupuis entered? It was possible."

"I suppose so."

"What else happened?"

"Nothing, nothing! I can't remember. It is strange that I can't seem to — I don't know why that could be," he lied. He'd be damned if he'd tell them anything more. Let them figure it out for themselves. He'd call Marcel and they'd talk about it, figure it out. Get their stories straight.

"What exactly was he doing when you entered her room?" Hines prompted.

"He was standing by her side, his hand on her chest as if measuring her heart rate. He looked up as we came in."

"Anything else?"

"No."

"Anything unusual happen or was there anything unusual about him? Did you think he was some sort of pervert? His hand on her chest like that?"

"No, and no. There was nothing sexual about the way his hand was placed on her chest. I place my hand on women's chests all the time, to check the heart, lumps in the breasts, lymphadenopathy, skin rashes etcetera." He indicated his stethoscope then motioned toward the sketch. "The likeness is completely accurate. He was young, good-looking. Not a large person. But seemingly very fit. He left immediately as we entered. I think he was French."

Agent Hines, moderately surprised, made a careful entry in his notebook.

"How do you know he was French?" he casually asked.

"His accent."

"I thought you said he didn't say anything?"

"I might have been mistaken." Norris ran his hand through his hair. He was perspiring profusely. "I'm sorry, I can't seem to think right now."

"What did he say doctor? Try to recall."

Norris attempted to sound like the young man he had found hovering over Emily, forcing and exaggerating the French accent getting both his accent and the intonation wrong in the process, missing the sarcasm completely. "Do no harm; is that not your credo as well?" Neither agent smiled at his attempt to mimic him. He felt like a fool.

Hines supplemented his notes. "Well, that's something." He seemed satisfied. It must have been important, Norris thought.

"What did Dr. Dupuis do upon entering the room?" Hines asked, for some reason deciding not to pursue the subject of what the alien might have said any further; apparently, it would keep.

"He went immediately to his daughter's side."

"At what point did the suspect leave the room?"

"At that time — just then — as soon as we entered. He said what he said and then departed, rather quickly. He's a suspect? A suspect for what?"

"By what means did the suspect leave the room?" Hines insisted.

"What means?" Norris asked. "What you do mean? He presumably departed as he arrived, through the doorway. How else?"

"But no one else saw him but you and Dr. Dupuis — and there was no record on the security cameras either of him arriving or leaving the building. We checked."

"We haven't checked everyone or every possible access," Wetmore quietly corrected him.

"Quite right," Hines replied. "We will interview everyone. We thought we'd start at the top, doctor. That would be you."

A quick entry and the notebook was flipped closed and returned to the agent's pocket. The agents again exchanged glances. Agent Hines said, "Thank you again, Dr. Norris." A short silence lingered as all three studied the prostate form of the body lying on his back staring sightlessly up at the ceiling. "We'll be in touch — you can be assured of that," Hines added. "Don't leave town, as they say." He smiled. It was a professional smile and not intended to mean anything.

Norris shuddered. "Do you want to see Valentina now?" he asked timidly, feeling more a fool by the moment.

The agents were putting away their notebooks. As their jackets opened, he could see their badge, and their weapon, a 9mm Luger, attached to their belt. "No, I don't think so — later perhaps," Hines replied.

Norris knew they wouldn't bother. The so-called investigation into the stabbing had been a ruse. He stepped nervously towards the door and motioned the orderly standing outside to open it. "Sure," he said.

"And I'm glad to see you had the sense to keep your patient locked up. I hope you continue that policy, doctor," Hines added.

Norris felt the back of his neck grow warmer. He felt incredibly stupid, found out. He turned to face the agent.

"We don't want him wandering about now, do we?" Wetmore added, poker-faced.

Norris hated him all the more. He could barely contain how he felt and wondered if it showed. "No, we don't," he answered with as much dignity as he could manage.

He was damned if he was going to tell them anything. Besides, how could he? It was all so incredible. They would at first think him mad. Later, though; later, after he had figured it all out for himself, they would thank him.

They exited the patient's room following the orderly who had been standing by, Norris all the while highly conscious of John Schmidt — that is Mister John Schmidt to you, Doctor! — lying on the bed, eyes closed, breathing regularly. Was Schmidt conscious or unconscious, he wondered? Deaf or completely tuned into the conversation that had just occurred? The answer: Possibly. Maybe. Maybe. Possibly. There might be absolutely nothing wrong with him at all — or he might be exactly as he appeared to be. Norris resisted the temptation to turn back to see. He let the door latch shut behind him and followed the agents out.

Interrogation

Emily's father, Doctor Marcel François Dupuis, Ph.D.,
International Studies, Princeton, 1980, and a serving member
of the United Nations Committee on Counter-Terrorism, was
escorted into a paneled, windowless, room. The door latched shut
behind him then sealed with a hiss of air. Five men sat at a large oval
table; two he had met at a cocktail party over a year ago. Of course,
they were both senior government officials; of course, it was now
obvious which department they represented, not that that was much of
a surprise. The other two were the FBI agents who days before had
interviewed Norris at Spring Grove, but Emily's father did not know
that, and nor did he know them. The fifth seemed out of place. He had
long hair untidily tied back, wrinkled clothing, and a favorite leather
jacket two or three sizes too big for him. He guessed it was
Kalinowski because he knew Kalinowski to be a scientist; who else
wouldn't care what they looked like — or, from another perspective,
were arrogant enough to feel they could dress any way they might
choose? Even so, names were secondary; he knew this was not about
people but facts: who knew what, and when, what they feared, and
why.

This was his second interview. The first, less than a week
previously, had only collated facts and resulted mostly in the

composite sketch he had helped them build. The agents who had interviewed him then were not present on this occasion. It was not a good sign; it meant they were too junior to be present. Of course, on this occasion too they had once again asked Emily to accompany him but she had continued to insist that she would not. They did not seem to be particularly bothered by that and he wondered why.

Richardson, his first name Bob, steel-gray hair, unlike the others impeccably dressed, sat across the table with a welcoming smile. He was one of the two Emily's father knew. He stood as Marcel entered and reached across the table to shake his hand. Firm shake, friendly smile. He was introduced to Ferris, first name Jim, younger, bigger frame, and not nearly so well dressed. He had narrow eyes and a bald head and wore his suit like a uniform. Undoubtedly ex-military: Army, he'd guess. He sat as a close ally to Richardson immediately to his right. The two other agents, apparently junior, not by age but by position and level of authority, sat side by side at the far end of the table. They did not even bother to look up as they were introduced, merely signaling with a nod and a wave that they were the one's so named: Agents Hines and Wetmore. The fifth, Kalinowski — yes, it was him — stood to greet him. He then sat, apparently bored: another affectation of a scientist. Still, the fact he was a scientist meant, at least in part, he might be impartial, and that was a good thing.

Richardson opened in a smooth and friendly manner. "Good that you could drop everything like this for us, Marcel. Please..." He indicated the chair across the table from him. "Take a seat."

Emily's father felt a rush of trepidation. Was Richardson a friend? They had met before. They had got along previously. He had rather liked him. But this was not then.

"We have a few more questions, Dr. Dupuis," Kalinowski stated from across the room not looking up while rifling through a pile of notes. Richardson, seated, calmly reasserted himself, motioning Kalinowski to wait. He apparently knew Kalinowski well; his interruption didn't seem to bother him.

Richardson spoke from prepared notes carefully ordered and laid out on the reflecting surface of the table. The notes were filled with text in point form. He was no ally. This was all business.

Richardson peered over the rim of his glasses. "Please don't think this is the Inquisition, Marcel — if I may address you as such. I hope you see what we're hoping to accomplish here in the next hour or so as only a friendly chat."

"I do, Bob."

"And thanks again for taking the time."

"No problem."

Richardson smiled and nodded in a friendly way. "I would not ask you to drop everything for something trivial. I hope you know."

"I understand. The times we live in, and so on."

"Precisely."

Richardson referred to his notes. He again looked up. "It is crazy, isn't it?" he mused. "All these unusual happenings all over the world? UFO's, worldwide crashing of computer networks, power grid collapses. It's crazy. Wild." He had not made it sound as if it was crazy; he had stated it as if was all a matter of fact, and something to be cataloged and then understood.

"Yes, I can only agree."

"What do you think is happening?"

"I have no idea."

Kalinowski twisted impatiently in his seat. He raised his hand halfway, about to make a point, but then withdrew it when he saw it was not yet his time to speak. There was something likeable about Kalinowski. It was difficult to pinpoint; perhaps it was because he was obviously not one of the others.

Richardson formally opened the meeting. Emily's father had thought it had already begun. "I declare the meeting open. Start recording. We are gathered at 26 Federal Plaza, New York, Room 23-245. The time is 14:23 local time, 19 June 2017. Richardson, Robert, Branch Head, Intelligence Operations Branch, Domestic Terrorism,

Central Intelligence Agency chairing." Richardson listed the FBI agents in attendance — it was their building after all. Then Kalinowski, identifying him as seconded from the NSA, and giving him the title of Scientific Investigator, Grade 4. He identified CIA Special Agent Ferris, the other CIA agent in attendance then carefully and accurately identified Emily's father, all for the record.

Richardson sat back and smiled. "You realize why we asked you here, of course?" he asked, beginning a smile. He waited for Emily's father to indicate he did, and then continued. "It's the same old thing — routine questions that popped out when we reviewed the notes and recordings of your previous interview. Thank you very much for that, by the way. It's just what we were talking about. Weird stuff, huh?"

Emily's father nodded slowly.

Richardson again focused on his notes, reading them to the end. He looked up when done. He shrugged and almost apologized. "None of this makes any sense, does it?" he asked reasonably enough. "All we are trying to do is make some sense of it."

"I can understand that."

"You have not done anything wrong," he reiterated.

"I know."

They had said the same thing over and over at their previous meeting.

"Or your daughter for that matter," Richardson added studying him carefully.

"I know that too — but I must insist that she's not involved in this at any level. She has been very ill and is just recovering. She was not conscious through any of it as I stated earlier." He glanced at Ferris. He did not like him. "I signed the very same document at that time, in case you're wondering." He was referring to a document he had signed earlier; it was verbatim to the one he had just signed. Bureaucratic duplication is a curse.

Richardson continued to smile. He was about to say something more but then another thought crossed his mind. He switched and admonished himself. "Oh, I forgot myself... How is your lovely daughter, Marcel? And how have you been doing since we last met? It was that seminar on Mid-East trade, I believe?"

Marcel swallowed. "Yes, that was it. I did not think you had forgotten."

"Quite right. I never forget." Richardson smiled again but thinly. "I merely suffer from an occasional lapse in manners. Please forgive me."

"There's nothing to forgive."

"And how is your daughter? I remember you were concerned about her health. Better now, is she?"

"I won't say cured — that's saying, and hoping, for a bit more than even I can dream of — but she is certainly feeling much better, thank you."

"Her name is Emily. Isn't that right?"

"Yes."

"Same last name as your own?"

"Correct."

"Okay," Richardson acknowledged, then returned to his notes, fitting his eyeglasses. His smile dropped away as he read. He looked up after only a moment of reading. "Now this is the Top Secret part — I've been authorized to let you in on an incident that occurred just a few days ago, nearly a week actually. An unidentified object entered Earth's atmosphere high up in Northern Canada. It was traveling at Mach 10 on an arc that would take it directly to New York — that is to say this city, right here. It required four minutes twenty-six seconds to reach the Adirondacks in northern New York State at which time it disappeared from our radars. At last contact, it was traveling at Mach 4 at one hundred thousand feet and still on track for the city. Notwithstanding the fact it violated the airspace of two sovereign countries, if it were carrying a weapon payload there would be absolutely nothing we could have done to stop it."

Emily's father spread his hands, impeccably manicured, the palms profusely sweating, onto the table top. He could not think of how that could have anything to do with him or Emily.

"You see how seriously we are now taking this?" Richardson said. "The military — Airforce mostly, and NORAD — is involved up to their eyes in this."

"I do — but I'm still not certain that the man Norris and I saw has anything to do with all that and everything else that's happened. Why would he, if he's the one causing so much havoc, be interested in my daughter?"

Kalinowski, leaning back in his chair, pitched forward. "Precisely! That's it, isn't it?" He turned to Richardson and nearly begged. "Can we get on with this? Can we?" Richardson nodded, indicating it was finally his turn. Kalinowski sighed with relief and climbed to his feet. He walked around the table, then sat on the edge of the table facing Emily's father. He gathered his thoughts, sighed again, and then smiled turning to Marcel. He seemed almost friendly.

"This meeting was really my idea," he offered in a tone that suggested the others in the room were superfluous. "I'm sorry, too, that I was not at the other meeting where you were interviewed but it was unavoidable," he added offhandedly.

"There's no apology necessary."

"I was in France as it turned out."

"On vacation?"

"No — on business." Kalinowski leaned forward then confidentially whispered, "I'm not one of these guys — you can probably tell."

"You're still being paid by them."

"I'm a scientist."

"I thought as much."

"And I have to tell you that all this..." Kalinowski waved his hand about the room; "and all that..." He expansively indicated the outside world. "Has everything to do with your daughter, and don't think it doesn't." He turned back to Emily's father and waited for his reaction.

"I cannot believe that. I do not know how it can," Emily's father responded.

Kalinowski recoiled as if surprised. "Oh." He was entirely facetious. He thought a moment then suddenly asked, quickly shifting, "What do you think of Dr. Norris, in a professional sense?"

"I don't like my daughter being targeted like this. I can assure you it is unwarranted. She is completely innocent of whatever you might think she is involved with," Marcel Dupuis insisted.

Kalinowski threw his hands up as if he'd been caught out. "Oh, right... Whatever you say... Sure... Good... And I think you're right too — but please answer the question. What do you think of Dr. Norris's capability as a medical doctor? Do you believe him to be competent?"

"Yes, he's an excellent doctor. His bedside manner could be improved but he is otherwise highly professional, very competent. A bit cold perhaps."

"You trust his judgment, at least professionally?"

"I do."

"He says that your daughter Emily should not be in the state she is currently."

"What state is that?"

"Alive."

"What?"

"The FBI — Special Agents Hines and Wetmore sitting right there — interviewed him earlier in the week," Kalinowski explained. "We asked Dr. Norris down here just the other day. I'm sorry to say I missed that interview too, but I did review the recording of it on the flight back. He says she should not be alive. Norris's story corroborates yours very well by the way on all the other issues."

It took a moment for Emily's father to catch up. "It should," he said, faltering a bit. "We experienced the same thing,".

"Of course, and I know you said this during your previous interview, you both did, but it seems a bit of a stretch that as you and Norris entered the room, the alien, or whoever, after travelling halfway across the galaxy, so to speak, quickly departed as if embarrassed to be caught in the act."

"What's so odd about that? That's what I would do."

"Well I wouldn't — and not because I have any alien blood in me — if, indeed, he has any blood in his veins, or even if he has veins or even a body. No, if I was in the middle of doing something that I had very carefully planned, and had gone to a lot of trouble to make happen, and then was interrupted by the two of you — I don't know, I think I might have zapped you with my phasor or something instead of apologizing and leaving her to you two."

"It was nothing like that."

"And you are sure that nothing else happened?"

"No, I'm sure. I went out because I thought my daughter had passed on." He lost his voice for a moment. "I returned with Dr. Norris and there the young man was leaning over her. He then left. That's it. He then left."

"You mean dead? You thought your daughter was dead?"

"Yes."

"I see." Kalinowski brushed the notion aside then returned to his line of questioning. "Another thing that bothers us is how did he, the young man, the alien, whomever, depart — that is, by what route and by what means did he exit the room and the building?"

"What do you mean? He departed as he presumably entered, through the only way in or out; through the door."

"Norris called you right after we interviewed him at the Psychiatric Hospital. I thought that odd."

"Why should that be odd?"

"The two of you getting your story straight perhaps?"

"That would be ridiculous — and you've been monitoring my phone. I thought I was not under suspicion."

"You're not under suspicion," Richardson quickly injected.

"The two of you are friends?" Kalinowski continued, drawing Emily's father back.

"No."

"We checked and checked, you know. We asked almost everyone who had on duty that day in the hospital and no one saw him other than you two. That's not all that unusual; people come and go all the time. But the interesting part is, nor did the security cameras on each floor and in the elevators and the foyer pick up anyone like you described an hour before or after the time you said he left."

"I don't understand that."

"We don't either."

Kalinowski thought a moment. He leaned back and looked up at the ceiling then returned with a thought. "I had to look this up — survival rates for your daughter's type of leukemia vary considerably, but given she has had two previous remissions, her survival rate from that point forward was less than one percent over a one-month period."

Richardson leaned forward to finalize the point for Kalinowski. "Marcel, my friend, I'm sorry, but we have checked, and checked, and have gathered third and even fourth opinions…"

"You are not my friend."

"That may be. But the filing cabinets at New York Presbyterian are chock full of your daughter's medical records, and I am sincere when I say that all the medical experts we have consulted have indicated that your daughter could not possibly be in the state she is in now. She should be dead, or at the very least still hovering near death. It is, in their professional opinions, impossible that she should exhibit the picture of health she currently enjoys. She is now a very beautiful young woman rather than deceased, it would seem."

"They ran tests that showed she was fine. It was their own damn tests!"

"They, Dr. Norris included, cannot explain the results of those tests, other than to think it is not the same woman being tested each time — that's their argument at any rate."

Marcel Dupuis blinked. "She is obviously not dead." It was all he could think of to say but he had sounded false even to himself.

FBI Special Agent Hines withdrew a full-color photograph from a folder he had laid out before him even before the meeting began and handed it to Kalinowski who turned it right side up and handed it to Marcel.

"That is your daughter?" Kalinowski asked sitting back.

Emily's father drew the photograph toward him. It was, indeed, Emily; it had been taken only days before. He recognized what she was wearing: her mother's sweater and the emerald earrings. He pushed the photo back and nodded. "Yes, that's my daughter. Just a day or two ago. I recognize what she's wearing. Who took the photograph? You are having her followed?"

Richardson again quickly explained. "I'm afraid we are — that, I know for a fact since I authorized it — and the tapping of your phone I have to admit to that too. Once again, I am sorry for the misdirection but this is serious stuff and we can't let it go. I hope you understand."

Emily's father nodded. He reminded himself again that neither he nor Emily had done anything wrong.

Kalinowski pressed. "Only one daughter?"

"Yes."

"No closely related cousins, or anyone like that?"

"No." He did not care for resonance within his own voice; it revealed too much of the real anxiety he felt. "I swear it's my daughter!" he said, this time sounding strident. He flushed red, flustered.

"You wouldn't mind then if we arranged to test that theory?" Kalinowski asked.

"Not at all, be my guest," Emily's father snapped. He quickly corrected himself and again stammered. "Emily should be the one to give permission. She needs to agree."

"Of course," Richardson called out not looking up. He was taking copious notes.

It suddenly struck Emily's father that they already had tested her. "You already know!" he cried out. He jumped to his feet enraged. Neither Richardson nor any of the other agents had given anything away. He had gathered the truth from Kalinowski. He pounded the table. "What!" he demanded. "What? How dare you!" He almost reached out and grabbed Kalinowski but held himself back — that would have been a mistake.

The agents remained calmly sitting studying him. Kalinowski was the only one who appeared to be taken aback. It was clear the reaction he had achieved was stronger than he had thought it might be.

"Of course you know," Emily's father added, his voice shaking. He was about to pound the table again but again held back. He clenched his fist and bit his lip. He knew how he appeared. Standing straight, facing them, feeling like a fool.

He didn't have to wait long for the answer. "A very close relative. A second cousin. But not your daughter," Kalinowski quietly explained.

Emily's father fell back into his chair. He covered his face and let out a howl. It was impossible. He dropped his hands after a moment and pushed back from the table. He imagined he might be sick.

"I hope you'll be okay," Richardson offered as he recovered. "Don't feel bad — believe me, feeling stressed enough to be sick happens more times than you might think. You are under a lot of stress and we understand that."

Marcel lifted his head up and sat back. He was shaking, unable to control it. Richardson was watching him carefully. Was that a smile, Emily's father wondered. It was. The bastard. "I'm okay — I'm in shock," Emily's father said. "But you have to know your findings are impossible."

Kalinowski interrupted. "It is your daughter — or at least, she is in part."

Richardson sat back surprised as Kalinowski jumped to explain. "It's like this: Your daughter has been genetically modified and is in the process of being modified further. We have taken three consecutive samples of your daughter's DNA, without her permission I have to admit, and each one shows a different woman," he explained. "Or I should say the samples indicate different women but who are very closely related. Or, and this is my theory, the same woman who is being continuously changed into who, we don't know. Or how, for that matter; we have no idea how he could be doing it."

Richardson fell back with surprise while Agent Ferris blew up. "That's got to be crap, Kalinowski!" Ferris shot out. "What's more believable? Someone pays big bucks to turn their life around or an alien from another planet is genetically changing a random woman for an unknown reason! I've never heard such bullshit!" Richardson silenced him with a quick hand placed on his arm as Kalinowski gritted his teeth.

"You and I just don't get along, do we, Ferris?" Kalinowski shot back.

Richardson turned on Kalinowski. He was furious. "That's not what you briefed us with before the meeting. What the hell is this?"

"I've just heard about it myself, sir. I just read the report."

"I'm adjourning the meeting," Richardson stated flatly. "It's adjourned until we clear this up. You just don't introduce new information like that without informing us beforehand. It's protocol." He moved to stand, clearly still angry. "And who approved taking all that DNA and the testing?"

Kalinowski begged. "I am sorry, sir, I really am; and I know I should have about all that sir. But there was no time before the meeting — I just flew in from Paris very late last night. You will want to hear this, sir — really."

Richardson see-sawed. "If you want to keep your job, young man," he said, "I'd be very careful what you say next." He glanced at Ferris beside him, and then at the two FBI agents, Hines and Wetmore, who remained poker-faced and waiting for what would happen next.

"Yes, sir," Kalinowski confirmed. He shuffled around the table back to his seat and slowly began to collect his papers. "Okay... I'll shut up," he acknowledged.

Richardson, still standing, seethed. He watched Kalinowski take his time sorting his papers and then stack them. The air conditioner hissed. The meeting hung suspended.

"Are we still being recorded?" Richardson asked turning to the FBI agents.

Agent Hines promptly responded. "Yes sir."

Richardson made up his mind. He motioned to Kalinowski. "Okay, if you've got something else we should hear it. Let's put whatever you've got on the record." He pointed aiming at him. "But don't fuck with me like that again, Dr. Kalinowski. If you have shattering information like that, you let me know about it before the meeting. We can always delay the meeting. Do you understand?"

"Yes, sir. ...Sorry, sir."

Richardson turned to Emily's father. "I'm sorry, Dr. Dupuis; unusual and somewhat immediately important circumstances motivate me to continue." He turned to Ferris with the same exasperation. "Your criminal conspiracy theory is a good one, Jim, but there's a lot of stuff going on here we have to follow through with. My call, not yours." He opened his notebook and nodded to Kalinowski. "Go on." He then sat, white of face, still visibly angry.

Kalinowski made his way back to the table's edge. He again leaned back, not quite as confident as he had been previously and continued. "The alien stopped off a Blois, France, where the old French court used to hang out in their Chateaux but I think that whatever the connection is, it predates the construction of the Chateaux by hundreds of years, and I have some proof of that. But that's not what I have to tell you."

Agent Ferris leaned back in his chair and rolled his eyes. "Fuck this," he muttered. He placed his hands on his bald head and squeezed his eyes shut. The others in the room shifted their attention from Ferris back to Kalinowski.

Kalinowski pressed on. "As the little girl — her name is Jacinth Anna LeBlanc, and she is seven years old — was held suspended about two meters above everyone's head as he checked her over..."

Agent Ferris could not contain himself. "Oh, for Christ's sake! This is ridiculous!"

FBI Agents Hines and Wetmore could not refrain from laughing; only Richardson and Emily's father remained deadpanned. Richardson, exasperated, once again waved Kalinowski on. "Keep going Dr. Kalinowski, but try to keep to the point."

"Yes sir..." Kalinowski gathered his thoughts then addressed both Richardson and Ferris, focusing on being precise. "I'm referring to the little girl the so-named alien supposedly picked up and rotated through the air and set carefully down again. That little girl, and that alien. I hope it's clear of whom I'm speaking." He glanced at Richardson who impatiently waved him on yet again.

"I had the French test her," Kalinowski explained, "since I couldn't very well, could I? Anyway..." He gathered his thoughts, still unsteady. "Anyway, it turns out that little Jacinth and Emily have a common ancestor twenty or so generations removed. It took me a month to get that bit of information but when I finally received it just before walking in here, I damn near fell over."

It was the first Emily's father had heard any of this. It was the first Richardson or anyone else in the room had heard anything of this. Richardson again began to boil. "There you go again — and you're talking with the French again!" He apparently didn't know what else to say. He was nearly speechless. But it was too late to stop the meeting now.

"Yes sir — it couldn't be helped, sir. It is all part of the analysis."

Richardson angrily waved him on.

Kalinowski returned to Emily's father and addressed him directly. "It means she and your daughter had a common ancestor approximately 600 years back. He rejected seven-year-old Jacinth but did not reject your daughter presumably because, again in my opinion, he preferred someone older. But it is also possible he rejected the little girl simply because she is a little girl and he didn't want to hurt her. He subsequently went out of his way — far, far out of his way — to find your daughter by bombarding the Earth with a high-power MRI scan, and when he found her he must have thought she was a perfect choice for him. She was dead, or nearly so. Whatever he had planned for her would be better than what her options otherwise might be. In short, he gave her back her life only to perhaps take it away again as he slowly changes her into whoever, or whatever. But even so, it is still a good deal for your daughter. I mean, the alternative for her was not great."

"Changes her into what? Another one of him?" Richardson asked, still exasperated and yet now fully engaged.

"No. No, I don't think so. His species — for all he can do — is nothing like us. If he's even alive as we know it — he might be a machine — We get that from the way he flies about: no living being could do that. No, he's changing her for some other reason which I don't know. Perhaps into someone he knew back then. It is all crazy stuff but it is the best theory I've got."

"Back when?"

"Well, twenty generations ago — it would have had to be in the early 1400's approximately."

"What went on then?"

"It was the end of the Hundred Years' War. England occupied France. There was a collusion between the English and the so-called

Burgundians. The town of Blois is close to the city of Orleans where the French defeated the English with the help of Joan of Arc. The general was le Comte de Dunois who some called Le Batard de Orleans, and who was a cousin of the future French King Charles VII sitting in exile in Bourges, France. Joan of Arc was instrumental in that victory as, of course, was the Comte."

"Joan of Arc? He's not trying to revive Joan of Arc?" Robertson stuttered, startled.

"No, sir; no — the French immediately jumped on that too; they know Joan of Arc's lineage pretty well, and whoever our alien friend is trying to revive it is not Joan of Arc. Young Jacinth may not be directly related to Joan of Arc but she has a number of similar alleles that indicate her ancestors came from the same part of France as Joan, namely the upper reaches of the Loire Valley, near the village of Domremy." Kalinowski expressed his admiration. "Those French — they are good at this sort of thing."

"You have the entire French Secret Service working this? With all the other internal security issues they have to deal with?" Richardson asked, clearly exasperated by Kalinowski's revelation, albeit inferred; no other organization within France would have the authority to assign that many resources. Agent Ferris fought for control while Hines and Wetmore recoiled in disbelief. Richardson gave them a look that immediately settled them and turned back to Kalinowski. "We'll be talking after this, Dr. Kalinowski. Who the hell is paying for it, that's what I want to know!" He had by now lost most of his polish.

"Yes sir... But what else was I supposed to do?" Kalinowski pleaded. "I just couldn't ask them for all this help without telling them something!" He seemed to know he was in trouble and that his career might never recover.

"How much do they know and who's paying for it?" Robertson bluntly asked, still exasperated.

"They know everything — but they're really excited about it — and they're funding it," Kalinowski answered holding himself back.

"I bet."

"They are helping us out, sir. They have a large team of people scanning the historical documents looking for some weird thing that might have happened way back then."

Agent Ferris blew up. "I mean I can't fucking believe it! The French! For Christ's sake!"

"They are on our team, aren't they?" Kalinowski angrily shot back. The Brits are involved in this too — I couldn't very well leave them out, could I? They're almost as excited as the French."

"Yes, but —," Richardson began, then dropped his head into his hands and gave up, shaking his head.

"You gotta know I could not have made this leap without them!" Kalinowski responded with feeling.

"Where's the Brits in all of this?" Richardson asked, beleaguered.

"They've been sharing their radar data of the object and the video recordings with the French. They've set up a good-sized team as well."

Richardson closed his eyes and sighed. When he opened them, he was calmer.

"They did give us the data from their Harriers," Kalinowski reminded him.

Richardson nodded. He then motioned to Kalinowski. "You may sit unless, of course, you have something else you'd like to reveal?"

Kalinowski feinted an apology. "No, I don't think so — I think I've said enough, really."

Agents Hines and Wetmore laughed aloud.

"What are we going to do about this? What can we do?" Richardson asked, ignoring them, his anger building again.

Ferris lifted his head up out of the cradle of his hands and suggested, "If this Emily is so important to this guy — whoever he is; he's no friggin' alien I can tell you that; I've never heard anything so fucking ridiculous! We should bring her in. It will force him to come to us."

Kalinowski, half way around the table, jumped back into the fray. "You gotta be fucking kidding me!" He swung on Richardson and pleaded. "I beg you, sir! Do not, do not, fuck with this guy! If we pick her up, keep her in isolation, or whatever, he's likely to get very, I would say extremely, fucking pissed, and you do not — repeat, you do not want this guy pissed with us! I'm not sure he'd take out the entire Eastern Seaboard, but he'd take all of us out with no trouble at all, that's for sure. And then he'd get her back if we didn't kill her — and if we killed her, accidentally or otherwise, then I would then say, yes, say goodbye to the Eastern Seaboard of the continental United States! He's gone to a lot of trouble to do what he's doing. Don't fuck with him! Please! I beg you!"

Agent Ferris lay face down on the table mumbling to himself while Agents Hines and Wetmore were barely able to contain themselves. Richardson, beat red, pointed toward Emily's father but addressed Kalinowski. "We are talking about this man's daughter!" he pointed out. "He's in the room — you've noticed that, right?" He managed not to shout, but he was clearly angry. "There's a Need to Know in this situation, and he now knows far too much for his own good!"

Kalinowski stepped back, flushed. He nervously ran his fingers through his thick mane of hair then, apologizing under his breath, he then slowly retreated to his chair.

Richardson turned to Emily's father still recovering from what he had heard. "I'm very sorry for this Dr. Dupuis," he said in apology. "Our agents are not normally like this. It is just that this is such an unusual situation."

Emily's father regained his self-presence. He didn't know quite what to say. "It all seems quite incredible. I can hardly believe it," he did manage to say.

Richardson was calmer. "You know, of course, you cannot discuss anything you have heard here with anyone, not even your daughter. She might not even be your daughter. She might be a good facsimile and not your daughter at all. She might have been once, but not now. I would be very careful."

"She is my daughter," he emphasized: "She is. ...I don't have to be careful."

"That's up to you."

Richardson waited a moment then turned to the others to announce his decision. "I'm pushing this upward. I'm sure this meeting will be reconvened sometime soon with a lot more players. It's certainly beyond my pay scale."

"I want my daughter protected."

"We will keep on doing what we're doing and that is keeping a close watch on her," Richardson stated. He turned to the others. "In the meantime, I don't want any move on the alien — that is if you can locate him — without direction and written permission from me until someone higher up the food change takes over this mess. Is that clear?"

It evidently was.

The meeting was adjourned. "New York City Offices. Richardson, Robert. The time is 16:23 hours EST, 19 June 2017. Stop recording."

Nerves

Institute for Astronomy, Room 7-214, University of Hawaii, Manoa Valley, Hawaii. Three men and one woman sat around the great oak table: Monserrat, King, Matheson, and Dr. Eleanor Vanier, who had flown in from the coast, Pasadena. They were staring at their hands. No one could think of what to say.

Eleanor broke the silence. She spoke carefully and precisely careful to keep only to the what was known. "The object has been observed by almost every ground and space-based asset we have. It has been radiating, incredibly brightly, as it decelerated and made its course adjustments. It is an incredible feat. The amount of energy required is, to coin a phrase, astronomical."

Monserrat immediately jumped in, glad to be finally moving forward. "How much is that? Can you give us a reference point?"

"It is able to source more than an average nuclear plant, and continuously, so it seems. How all that energy is converted into something useful we don't know; it is quite astonishing."

"What about it going bright and then dark?"

"The object goes bright then dark, but it always makes the course corrections while bright. It is confusing why that would be. It suggests it is expending more energy during those maneuvers, some of which is radiated in the visible."

"X-ray, gamma?"

"Those wavelengths as well — But similar to the sun the spectrum peaks at six hundred nanometers, just as we saw earlier; nothing has changed in that regard." She gathered her thoughts. "I know they may not be necessarily everyone's conclusion, but I believe that there is almost no doubt that this thing, this mountain of an object — literally the mass of a good size mountain in the Rockies — is intelligently controlled. There is no natural way for it to have accomplished what has been accomplished, the course corrections and so on."

Monserrat sighed. He was nervous and agitated. "Well now the entire world knows so we don't have to hide the facts any longer. Still, I don't like it. I wish there was a more natural explanation, as you say."

"There isn't; it fits the facts — as incredible as they are."

Bob King glanced up, frowned and squirmed sympathetically. "You are front and center on this one, my friend."

Monserrat nodded. "I'm not alone. They're assembling a big team as we speak. Fortunately, it is a bit above my pay scale. It is being organized out of Caltech by Trevino." He was referring to Doctor Jose M. Trevino, Ph.D. Astrophysics, Princeton. "We're going there from here," Monserrat continued. He motioned to Eleanor. "...Sorry to drag you out here just to drag you back, Eleanor."

"Anytime — you know I love Hawaii. Plus, I owe you for that incident during the Shanghai conference last year. That Professor so and so was a bit insufferable. I barely escaped with my dignity intact, or his for that matter."

Monserrat smiled. "You're free and clear of him now." He went on. "There are a lot of questions. That's all this thing is, in fact: a huge set of questions. But the big one is, is it going to impact Earth? Is Earth a target? Everyone is asking — What do we say?"

Eleanor again responded. It was why Monserrat had invited her to his meeting and she knew it. She answered directly. "My report to the committee that is just forming under Dr. Trevino is that it will not."

"But if it did?"

"If it did, the impact would be approximately forty-four times greater than the famous — the infamous, I should say — K-T extinction event that presumably wiped out the dinosaurs. Although I hear that may no longer be the case. Science? What can you do? You can hardly depend on it to reach the same conclusions twice." She smiled, completely facetious.

She quickly continued as the others smiled. "But I believe that is certainly not the intent — although that is merely a matter of faith, I suppose. I feel that the course maneuvers are too precise and too exact to be used in such a blunt way. If they wanted to destroy us, there are much easier ways requiring far less energy. They could bombard the entire planet with lethal doses of gamma radiation for example. No, I believe the intent is to enter orbit, but what kind of orbit I do not know, somewhere between the Earth and the Moon is the best guess currently."

"If it is as massive as we say it is, why can't we see it? Have we figured that out yet?" King asked.

Everyone shrugged. Nope.

Monserrat, following Bob King's lead, asked, "Can we confirm that when it goes bright it still has no discernible dimension or structure? ...Anyone?"

"It has been suggested that it might be a Black Hole," King offered; "That's what Trevino is suggesting, and that's what the news media is glomming onto. It's a farce and likely wrong: A black hole typically has a mass greater than our sun and this thing is not that massive, plus there has been no gravitational lensing effects detected. It's been viewed for many hours now looking just for that."

"I have something — and this is going to be new to you," Eleanor said, containing herself. "My team at JPL has been working this day and night. I have everyone working on it. It is very exciting, really." She caught her breath and continued, uncharacteristically flushed almost as if embarrassed. "The object, when it is in its free inertial state — that is, coasting — indicates a mass of approximately ten-million-billion kilograms, but while implementing the maneuvers themselves its behavior indicates an object much less massive, closer to a thousand billion kilograms. Still a big number, but much, much smaller than the first number. No one knows why, but it would seem the alien can mask a portion of the object's inertial mass and corresponding inertial components such as its angular momentum. It means they most likely have control over, and can manipulate, gravity."

She sat back to let her theory sink in. It was incredible news, and enormous in its implications. "There are a lot of excited people out there in the big wide world of science," she finished, barely able to contain her own excitement.

She smiled at each in turn, but then became reflective. She sighed and added, "I have to admit I did let some of this slip out a bit before now. I called Jacobski at Caltech. It turned out the great Ramanujan was in town." She was referring to Doctor Jacob Jacobski, Ph.D., and Doctor Srinivasa (Srin) Ramanujan, Ph.D., both at Lunar and Planetary Laboratory, University of Arizona, Tucson, Arizona.

"The two of them rushed right over and we sat up all night talking about it. I showed them the data and he—. Well, I can't really say what Ramanujan said, but let's just say he's very excited. I have been asked to turn our observations and our preliminary models over to a team of research astrophysicists, theorists, who are currently gathering at Caltech. Why Caltech? Because of the JPL supercomputer cluster nearby, which is now dedicated to them — mostly, except for what I need. As a reward, I get to present to their team — that's the day after tomorrow."

She glanced at Monserrat. She looked stressed. "I wanted you as a sounding board. It was worth the flight. I also got to think a lot while I was in the air. I am having a hard time absorbing this. And it seems as if I'm getting a little too wrapped up in it. I feel that way."

"We all are," Monserrat admitted. "You'll be joining us at the conference center in Pasadena?" he asked.

Eleanor sighed then shrugged and shook her head. "I don't know... My team and I could be seconded to their team. Ramanujan made some noise to that effect, and he's in charge of the science effort, as you'd expect. When the object enters Earth orbit, you'll want to be at the JPL OOC instead of at the conference center, Joe. The conference doesn't ramp up for a few days after."

"You're right — Is there any way I can get a copy of your results before then?"

She shifted uneasily. "I don't see why not — as long as you don't publish before me."

Monserrat smiled. "I would never."

He turned to Bob King. "I also want the two of us to review all the visual data from Keck and James Webb, and anything else that's out there that can provide any insight. I've arranged to have the entire Physics and Astronomy departments working on this, including all post-docs and any decent grad students we can get. It wasn't hard to do given the current climate. I'm organizing it, but I want you to collate the information, Bob. It all goes through you, and only you, to me. I present at Pasadena."

Dr. King acknowledged.

Monserrat turned to Matheson. "My instructions from Trevino, the committee chair, is to continue normal operations of Pan-STARRS. That and all the other NEO assets are to continue to search for any and all incoming objects as they were designed to do, in case this is not the only object incoming. Like Bob, your team reports to you and only you, and you report whatever you might find directly to me, and only to me. Is that clear?"

Dr. Matheson nodded his agreement. He didn't look up. He was very pale.

"Do you have any other thoughts, Ken?" Monserrat asked, seeing he might.

Matheson twisted awkwardly. He knew he would be walking on thin ice but said what was on his mind anyway, turning to Eleanor for support. "You've seen the news lately, right? I mean, not just this but the other news about aliens? It's everywhere. The New York Times is carrying it and so is CNN. There have been signs of aliens, or an alien, in Europe playing chicken with fighter planes, and now over New York. That bright light over the city two days ago? You saw that story?" Both Bob King and Eleanor had; Monserrat had missed it. "Anyway," Matheson continued, "maybe this is the mother-ship coming in. That's what some are saying."

"Do you believe that, Ken?" Eleanor asked him quietly before Monserrat could respond.

"I suppose I do."

"Why don't they communicate with us then?" she asked reasonably.

"I don't know — maybe they have nothing to say?"

She sat back and considered. She glanced at Monserrat. "That's disturbing, but I think that is exactly it."

"None of that speculation leaves this university," Monserrat stated bluntly, furiously taking notes, trying to ignore the chatter and speculation. "Facts only," he emphasized, pushing through and sitting back. "Tell everyone that might be involved that no one talks to the press or anyone in the public but those assigned to do so. No Facebook updates, Tweets, nothing on this subject. Whoever does and gets caught will lose his or her job. I have talked with the Chancellor of the University and they will soon be coming out with a statement to that effect. All news releases will go through the Chancellor's office, and only through that office — that's the plan. Is that clear?"

It was, perfectly.

"Good. I declare this meeting closed — Closed for good." Monserrat slammed his notebook shut. "This matter is officially out of our hands — at least the decision-making part is. We still have a lot of science to do. Trevino and Ramanujan will tell us what to do — More Ramanujan than Trevino, I hope."

He motioned to Bob King and Eleanor. "Bob, I'll see you in Pasadena tomorrow." He turned to Eleanor. "Eleanor, I know you're flying out later today, and I just want to say good luck. A lot of this will be on your plate from now on. I wish I could be in the Ops Center with you when the object enters orbit — if that's what it's going to do. But it wasn't possible: standing room only, it seems. You'll be there with Ramanujan, I know. We couldn't be in better hands, in my opinion."

Eleanor smiled and nodded her appreciation.

A slow but orderly retreat out the door followed: notes, binders, laptops gathered and put away. Eleanor tagged Monserrat in the outside hallway. He had been walking slowly, waiting for her to catch up.

"I'm truly sorry I couldn't get you into the OOC, Joseph," she said, paralleling him. "It should be exciting. But you're needed at the conference — Tell them what you know. They will want to know."

"It's okay."

She could see what he was thinking. "It's not the end of the world, you know?" she said and smiled.

Monserrat stopped short. He waited a moment catching her eye with a puzzled look then threw back his head and laughed.

Bath

Emily lay back in the warm bath to study her glistening body. Her new body, pink and unblemished — perfect, absolutely perfect — floating amidst the bubbles like a newly formed island of flesh. She slowly and exactly traced its length using a single finger. She began at the tip of her nose, plunging over the ledge of her chin, then along the length of her neck, between her perfectly shaped breasts, along her ribcage and the basin of her stomach; and then further into darker water along the gentle contour of her hip, then down along her inner thigh until both hands rested on her thighs, the tips of her fingers reaching almost to her knees.

She submerged herself wholly and then sat up, tipping her head back to let the water drain off then drew her hands over her face then along the length of her neck, then again over her breasts. She slipped beneath a second time then repeating a third time. She finally sat upright bathwater coursing over her breasts, along her shoulders and arms, down her back the stream originating from her wet hair. She could feel none of the devices; if they were there — and why would she assume they were not — they were silent guardians. Guardians — yes, that was the right word; they were not only changing her but also keeping her healthy — and more, too: better, smarter; and, it could not be a coincidence, but also at peace: A lovely peace.

She leaned across for a towel and then stood, the bath water cascading along the length of her body mottled and pink from the warm bath. She wrapped it about her and stepped out onto the bathmat, reaching for another. She dried her face, then worked her hair. She knew with certainty that he had cured her, there was no other reasonable explanation. But a major question remained: Why? She was certain it was more than just a selfish need on his part to resurrect his past love, since he in no way seemed selfish or self-centered. There had to be more to it than that. But what, exactly, she didn't know.

When all of this had begun, she had had nothing; she was nearly dead. Or, if she believed her father, she had been dead. Her man from the stars, if that is who he was and not just her Guardian Angel, had given back her life. It was not so bad since she rather liked her new body. What woman wouldn't? But she could read his heart and knew his experiment — or whatever it might be undertaking, whatever he might call it — was getting out of control, and she was the reason. She smiled wistfully thinking about it. All lovers can read each other, can they not? If not, they cannot possibly be lovers. They might be something, but not lovers.

She again wiped the surface of the mirror: thin face; wet blond hair cut to her shoulder. Small ears cupped like seashells nearly hidden in her wet hair. She was beautiful. Perfect. Perfect in youth, perfect in health. And, more important, she was still Emily; she was not Catherine — at least as far as she knew, for how much of us are our body and how much our mind? Do any of us know who we truly are within? When you wake in the morning, do you know who you are, or do you know only what you have become? Isn't that what he had said?

Emily continued to study her image in the mirror now streaked. Her eyes had been blue before, but now they were green and strikingly so. Her face had narrowed: she now possessed a smaller nose, wider lips, a more sensitive face, sad but without a sad smile. "I'm not you," she said gazing into her eyes, not entirely certain whose eyes they were. "I am Emily. You will just have to get used to that fact, Catherine. I am not you."

Once she had been sure she was not changing her into Catherine — at least not inwardly where it counted — she had wanted to know more about her. What woman wouldn't want to know the details of their competition? The had met several times to discuss it, he ostensibly to check her health, she to learn more. Catherine had been young; the same age as her, in fact. French. Beautiful. She had been a great healer. She had asked if she was a nurse, a physician, a midwife, and he had said, yes, all of them and more. The only thing she could not cure was death itself, since once the body has slipped deep enough into death, the soul flown, there is nothing anyone can do, he'd carefully explained, watching for her reaction as he did so.

She had been surprised by his reference to the soul and asked him if he believed in it. He'd said that Catherine talked incessantly of her soul, and it was clear enough what she meant, although he remained unclear if the soul was something real or imagined. He'd quietly asked her what she believed, and she had answered she didn't know, but she didn't think so. She had been close to death many times and had felt nothing. When the body goes you go with it.

"How did she die?" she had asked, quickly changing the subject

"They burned her."

"Who were they?"

"The priests."

"They burned her at the stake?"

"Yes, that is it."

"In France?"

"Yes."

So, it had been a long time ago.

"What was her crime?"

"There was no crime."

She had wondered why his sorrow wouldn't go away; time usually heals all wounds and it had been a long time ago. He must have loved her greatly. That is what this was all about then, wasn't it? Of course, it was.

She had then asked him of his clearest memory of her.

"How do you mean?" he'd asked.

"How do you envision her when you go to sleep at night?" It was quite a question; asking it, she wished she hadn't.

"Ah …"

"Ah, yes…," she'd replied, echoing him. She loved that affectation of his: that soft, drawn out, 'Ah…' "But tell me, I want to know," she had prompted, surprising herself yet again by her effrontery. She was getting used to having him around.

He hesitated as if unwilling to give up the memory, but then finally said, his eyes drawing distant as he recalled, "I remember her in the summer. We were beneath an elm. I remember because … she had told me it was an elm; I had never identified an elm before, or had at least named it, I should say. Anyway, it was summer. Do you know what summers in France are like?" he'd asked momentarily coming back to her.

"No, not really; but I can imagine not too much different than it is here."

"That is not true. The air is always sweeter, and the wind softer." He again returned to his memory. "I remember her hair caught in sunlight, and her eyes were cast downward watching me slowly turn an Iris about in my hand. She had just handed it to me. An Iris is a flower, if you don't know."

"I do know. I am from here, remember?"

Emily could picture it all in her mind. It was as if she had lived it.

"Look, my love," Catherine had said, handing him the wild Iris, delicate in form, purple and veined with beautiful whorls and folding petals. It was summer beneath an old elm, a light breeze bending the grass, sifting through the leaves above their heads. Her hair caught in sunlight, drawn back behind her eyes. They sat close together, their lunch spread out before them. Golden silk threads drifting about her face.

"God made this flower as He made you and me," she had said, smiling, feeling the warm summer sun on her bare arms, and face. Emily smiled, thinking of it. It was not a memory. He was not playing with her mind. She was certain of it. But why it should feel so real she didn't know. Nothing to be afraid of.

• •• ••• ••••••

She entered her bedroom, dropping the towel and began to dress. She slipped on her panties then fitted her bra. Her arms behind her back, her head lowered, her hair falling around her face. She turned to the mirror and brushed her hair back. She combed it down. It reached as far as her shoulders. She would have to do something about that — perhaps she should brush it to the side. She did so as an experiment. It looked right. She would have to pin it to keep it in place. She looked about for a barrette amongst her jewelry and found exactly what she wanted: pink pearls with purple amethyst. She fitted it then inspected the result.

"You look good — French," she said, and smiled.

• •• ••• ••••••

He had called her on her cell phone — of all things. It had shown an unknown number. She had hesitated not expecting anyone to call but then answered. Her heart leapt when she'd heard his voice. It was a very clear connection. She imagined his face, the half-smile, and his gray eyes. Her heart pounded furiously. Where the heck had he been? Almost a month had gone by. That's twice in a row he'd been away like that. Where was he going? What was he doing?

"Hello?"

"It's me," he'd said.

"I know it's you."

"How do you know?"

"I just do." She wondered if he could detect her smile - she knew he would.

"How are you feeling?" he'd asked, his smile opening on the other end, she could tell.

But she had had to find a place to sit; her knees were wobbly. "I'm good. I'm feeling really good, thank you." She immediately cringed then kicked herself. How would he interpret that? Thank you for my life, sir. Thank you for this body, too. Thank you very much. What a fool she would have proved herself to be, if she had said all that.

"Are you sure?" he'd asked, surprising her; he was always so certain of everything; he would know before calling.

"Of course I'm sure."

"No dizziness? Nothing unusual?"

"No, no, nothing like that."

He wanted them to meet in Central Park after dinner, the same bench if she could find it just to be sure.

"I can find it… What did you say your name was again?" she'd asked. She couldn't believe how forward she had become. It was not like her.

"I didn't say — I just said it was me."

"Oh yes, you… and that park bench — what time?"

He told her then laughed. It sounded odd hearing him laugh over the phone, yet quite normal at the same time.

"Why were you away for so long this time?" she bluntly asked, her face splitting into a smile but already returning to her central question.

"Promises to keep and miles to go," he'd answered, he, too, smiling, she could tell.

"Ah…," she'd said, teasing him again.

"Ah, indeed."

He might as well have been standing immediately in front of her; she could see an image of him clearly in her mind. He was very handsome with his blond hair pulled back and gray clear eyes.

"See you," he finished.

"See you."

He broke the connection.

She put on what little makeup she needed, her heart rate again picking up in anticipation of seeing him again. She pulled up her new dress, fitting the straps over her shoulders. She had found it in *Macy's* just the other day. It was a single piece spring dress, light, colorful, patterned in purple iris's. She smoothed it over her flat stomach and over her hips and looked at herself in the full-length mirror.

"Okay…"

With the cab waiting, she would be there almost instantly with no time even to get nervous. "It's bullcrap — I'm twenty-three years old and I don't get nervous," she said once again glancing at the mirror. She smiled and went to the door picking up her purse on the way, looking forward to the warm summer evening with him.

Central Park

Emily took the metro and got off at Columbus Circle, Central Park, West. She slipped into the park and followed the shaded walkway between the elm and chestnut until she reached the line of maple by the pond, and there saw him sitting on the bench with his arm stretched along the back and his legs out in front. She had not seen him for almost six weeks and she once again wondered where he'd been, but seeing him now she thought only how much she was looking forward to seeing him again.

She tapped his shoulder, making him turn, then returned his smile, brushing past him, barely glancing at him as she sat, holding her head high.

"I wondered if you'd come," he said smiling, taking her hand.

She answered lightly. "Why wouldn't I?"

"I don't know… I can think of several reasons."

"Can your eyes ascertain any difficulty within my person?" she demanded to know, suppressing her smile.

"They cannot."

"Are your devices working correctly?"

"They are indeed."

"That confirms it then — I am fine." She stood to go. "I will go now — that is all you wanted to know, wasn't it?"

"No, not all —. Please sit."

"Why should I?"

He gently drew her back down. "No reason."

"I presume I look more like Catherine? You must be very pleased to see her again. It gets better every time, does it not — for you?"

He studied her, keeping his half smile.

"Who am I, exactly?" she quickly asked, caught up in an unexpected shrift of jealousy.

He thought about it a moment then shrugged. "I do not know."

She said, keeping her voice light, amazing herself by speaking effortlessly in French, "Vous chicaner, monsieur, et détourner trop. Je pense que vous savez ce que je demandais."

He smiled his surprise. "Je ne vous trompais - ce qui est très grave. Je suis sérieux," he replied.

A gaggle of geese with their young in tow cut the still gray surface of the pond immediately in front of them, their gentle honking drawing her attention away from him.

"I wish I could trust you completely," Emily said.

"You can."

"You did this…," she said indicating her new body with a flourish of her hand.

"The devices I implanted did."

"You put them in me, and you take responsibility for that."

"So I did, and so I do."

"I feel wonderful."

"So I gather." He smiled.

She looked away again, the conflicting nature of her frustration growing. She nodded again, thinking. She finally said, "Okay…," nodding again, still uncertain. She gathered her thoughts watching the geese glide along the shore then climb up onto the bank. "Okay…"

She then turned to him and smiled and waited keeping her half-smile.

"Better?" he asked.

"I suppose... I'm not entirely certain."

She glanced over her shoulder and caught sight of a man and woman following the path adjacent to them, the woman pushing a buggy. She turned further: two joggers on the far side of the pond jogging in opposite directions but destined and meet close to where they sat. She looked opposite: another couple on a blanket preparing a picnic, and an all-terrain vehicle heading slowly toward them with two park maintenance workers sitting inside.

He stood drawing her up with him. "Where are we going?" He wrapped his arm around her and propelled her forward. "Where are we going?" she asked again: "You've seen them, too, obviously."

The vehicle paralleled them moving slowly. The man and woman with the buggy were nearly on them. One of the joggers turned the corner while the other was quickly approached from behind. The all-terrain vehicle suddenly cut them off. The couple on the blanket jumped to their feet. The woman with the buggy stopped and the man with her reached into it. The joggers made the corner.

They all suddenly collapsed. The baby-buggy tipped over, dumping its contents: HK MP5 submachine guns. The picnickers fell to the grass and rolled onto their backs revealing the barely concealed weapons. The maintenance men lay across the path, their Glock 17's still in their holsters. The joggers dropped in mid-stride, landing hard, their skittering loose along the asphalt.

Only one remained standing. He had been standing next to a tree watching. He turned to go but then was drawn back. His body was not his own. He walked stiffly up to them, ramrod-straight, his eyes roving wild in his head.

"What is your name?"

He was suddenly released. "Stan - Stan Kalinowski. ...I know you're pissed — I'd be pissed."

"Pissed? I do not know the meaning."

"Angry," Emily interpreted.

"Ah."

"What did you do them? Kalinowski asked, looking about with consternation.

"Their blood has been solidified; theirs joints calcified. They cannot breathe. I have stopped their hearts from beating but they are wide awake experiencing their last moments. You should know I intend to do the same to you in a moment."

Emily interjected, "Gatc'hh'en, please…"

Kalinowski stepped back but suddenly froze. He was caught.

"I have also incapacitated your four snipers," Gatc'hh'en continued evenly; "The additional five in the blue van, plus all those in the building only a few blocks from here, ninth floor, who are monitoring this."

Emily placed her hand on Gatc'hh'en's arm. "Please stop…," she implored. "They're only doing their job."

He abruptly turned to her. "You decide, then."

She was taken aback. "…Decide what?"

"Tell me what I should do."

She could see he was angry. "...Decide what?"

"I await — they await; they have moments only. This one included." He indicated Kalinowski with a quick nod.

"Let them go!" Emily cried, her hands flying up to her face in alarm when she finally understood.

The agents collectively rolled onto their backs as Kalinowski immediately dropped to the pavement. He hit hard.

Emily dropped her face into her hands and wept. "Oh, God!"

Gatc'hh'en steadied her then kneeled next to Kalinowski. "Do we agree we want to avoid confusion?" he asked quietly.

"I do…," Kalinowski managed to say barely conscious.

"Then, understand this: If you, or if any of your compatriots make any further moves against Emily, I will bombard the entire planet with high energy protons, enough to kill every living thing."

Kalinowski nodded.

"I wish to hear you say that you understand."

"I understand."

"Good."

Gatc'hh'en placed his hand on Kalinowski's shoulder. "Do not worry, you will be feeling better soon as will your friends and colleagues. In a few hours, you will all be as right as rain, I promise."

He stood and placed his arm around Emily and drew her along the path. "They will be fine," he told her as they moved away taking their time.

Emily could barely walk. She was shaking violently. If were not for the fact he was holding her up she would fall. "Kalinowski is the one I told you about," she said. "He's the one who called my Dad and interviewed him along with his buddies. He's not a bad guy, my dad says, despite everything."

"I remember."

The world was sinking around her. "I heard what you said, and you will do no such thing — about the bombardment, I mean."

"I have a mind to do whatever I like."

She stumbled along. "Don't pretend you are anything but who you are, my love — and don't joke when it is so serious."

"I'm not joking."

"You could have killed them. What then?"

"What then?" He stopped their progress and turned her to him. "What do you mean?"

"If I had told you to kill them, would you have?" she quietly asked not meeting his gaze but standing her ground.

"You would never have allowed me to hurt them in any way," he answered: "That would not be you."

"...But if I had said nothing, would you have?"

He waited for her to look up. "I would be nothing but a machine without you," he said, and then propelled her along the path again.

A painful constriction in her throat followed by a sudden welling of tears, and, blinded, she lost her footing. He held her upright and kept her moving.

"This was a test, wasn't it?" Emily asked, unable to see. "That's why you called — you set this up, or at least allowed it to happen."

She raggedly wept her denial to what she now knew to be true. She had lost. She had lost.

"I am not Catherine! I am not!" she cried out.

She hid her face against his shoulder, and despite her tears scolded him now lost to the new person she had become.

"Never pretend you are God, my love! Never pretend to have the right to do what you threatened to do even if you can do it! You are not God!" she wept.

"I know."

Norris

John Schmidt slept. He slept and slept, the outside world, the real world, ignored, unwanted, shut out. What was it like in there; what was within that sleeping carcass, what sentience, what cognition, what being, what malice, what love? Norris had no idea. He sat on the edge of the bed and stared - not at the sleeping face amazingly alive and fresh, neither shrunken nor diminished, but at the floor. The waxed polish, the stain, and spots along the wooden baseboard splashed up by the cleaners. His shoes, the laces of his shoes, the angle-iron making up the hospital bed, and then, finally, like a contradiction, an antithesis, the bleached white sheets tucked beneath the mattress caressing the steel.

Norris addressed the body laid out before him. "I know you are in there. What is it like to possess a body that is not your own? What is it like to be flesh and blood for a change?" We destroy what we fear or worship it, he thought, but despite that newly-minted understanding could not help prevent himself from saying, "I won't worship you. You are flesh and blood, not a spirit, nor a god."

The body breathed. Norris followed the rising and falling sheets beneath which lay a chest, and then a heart. "But I fear you — a man should always fear his God; don't you think? And love him too? I suppose I should be grateful for this life. If I lost it, I know you would give it back to me. You are, after all, a medical practitioner of unparalleled ability, not unlike Christ, don't you think? Changing water into wine? Healing the sick, the mad, and the lepers? Raising the dead?"

Not the face, not the body, but the spirit of the body. He was aware of the contradictions but could not remove their place of honor from within the intricate folds of his mind. He feared he might be mad; voices spoke to him as clearly during the day as at night. Pointing like a ghost from a Dickens' novel, they revealed events that had occurred as well as some that had not. Were the images, the dreams, the memories, meant as parody? It might be the carcass saying, "See? See what you might have done?"

Norris considered. He felt calm, perfectly calm. He said to John Schmidt, "I remember you stopping my heart and restarting it. I remember you allowing me to breathe again. I remember you in the garden, the same voice, with the same tone and arrogance. In particular, I remember your eyes as you decided whether or not to allow me to live. Are you about to do that again? Are you? Are you?"

Norris sat back. He felt good. Good. Even calm. But what to do? What to do? How to cure oneself? Physician, heal thyself? Do I need to be cured, he asked? Am I healable even? He asked all these questions and more, with each one leading him to the same conclusion. This was no God laying before him, and no devil either. "The problem, methinks, is within me," he said aloud, hearing the truth in the returned echo. An imbalance of dopamine — the same 3, 4-dihydroxyphenethylamine he had injected into John Schmidt — could be the underlying mechanism of his madness. We are all chemicals in the end.

He could still inject a small amount into himself to see what might happen; but, no, he had tried that already with mixed, mostly negative, results. His natural neurotransmitters, the endogenous chemicals that transmit signals across a synapse from one neuron to another, were failing him for some reason. He was going slowly insane and the catalyst, if not the cause, was the body lying on the bed. It was false reasoning and he knew that too and yet he could not see his way around it. How could it be that John Schmidt could be possessed by a creature who came and went as he pleased? Well, that's what he is, isn't he; a creature? He is certainly not human. He is beyond human; more powerful.

Norris' imagination shifted, then jumped. Everyone knew who the agents were, masquerading as they were pushing their empty gurneys about, just as everyone knew who they were watching. They were primarily interested in the good doctor, of course — that would be himself — and not John Schmidt, or Valentina. The interview the other day had not gone well. They had not accused him of anything, not directly; but nor had they completely accepted his side of things. He had managed to speak to Emily's father, Monsieur Dupuis, before then and without them knowing — at least they had not questioned him about it if they had known. But, then again, they were tricky, weren't they?

He and Marcel had met secretly, not trusting their phones. No, they had decided, speaking confidentially next to a busy intersection, the sound of the traffic muting their conversation, that they could not tell the authorities, the bastard agents, how the alien had stopped their hearts and then restarted them. Nor could they tell them how he had disappeared through the sealed glass of the window instead of through the door. Not even aliens from far-off worlds — if that's what he was and where he came from — could do that. They would think them mad. He laughed inwardly recalling how he had arrived at his present state of mind. Well, were they not mad? Had he already not arrived at that same conclusion?

"What do you think he did to her?" Marcel had asked, unshaven and wretched, staring sightless at the traffic. It was unthinkable for him to believe that Emily could be involved in all this. He loved his daughter so.

Norris had tried to explain — he rather liked the old guy; he was
rather an upstanding chap — that there hadn't been enough time for
whoever — the alien, whatever — to do anything; and, besides, a
monitor doesn't lie: the measured heart rate is the heart rate.

They had both agreed that Emily must have been alive when
Marcel left the room — she was certainly alive when they returned.
He concluded he must have misread the monitor, seeing in it what he
feared instead of what it told him. It was good reasoning. Solid.
Marcel, good chap, almost accepted it. "I know she was dead; I know
it. I could feel it. What did he do to her? Is she really Emily?" he kept
asking again and again each time in greater anguish.

"But why, but why?" Norris had insisted in turn. "You have known
Emily all your life; you watched her be born. What would she
possibly be to him, and he to her?" He had shaken his head adamantly
and insisted, holding him by the shoulders, *"No, no, c'est ne pas
possible!"*

The agents who had chaired his second interview were from a
different gaggle, more polished, more focused and, likely the same
who had interviewed Marcel earlier. Like Marcel, they had questioned
him endlessly on Emily's condition both before and after the so-called
alien appeared — if, indeed, there is an alien and it is not you, Dr.
Norris, they had suggested, carefully monitoring his reaction.

But he had kept his cool. "Do I look like an alien?" he had shot
back. "Can I sift myself through glass?" he'd asked, or at least wished
he had. He had instead stared them down. He had told them only what
he and Marcel had agreed upon and would say, and had not said,
anything more than that. He had argued that if the alien — whoever he
was, whatever he was to them, and why was he so important anyway?
— had done something to her before they walked in, he, Norris, most
certainly would have been able to tell.

It was, of course, a lie; he did not know if *The Whomever* had, or
had not, said something, or did something to her, how could he? It was
just that there was no evidence to suggest that he had — other than the

fact Emily was mysteriously alive and wonderfully healthy. But what was more reasonable to believe, he had asked; that an alien from the dark reaches of outer space should somehow decide to save the life of some random woman, or the admittedly unexplainable remission of her disease? He had justly chastised them. "Use your heads, gentlemen; Occam's Razor applies in this case as in most other," he had said to their blank stares in return. "Among competing hypothesis the one with the fewest assumptions should be selected."

Their questioning went on for hours and not for just the few minutes they had promised. What's the matter, you didn't watch the air show the other night, they'd asked? The skies were ablaze. Have you not watched television? We're being visited — it's the most exciting thing in the world, if you believe it. Did he believe it? He couldn't say. Well, he wouldn't say — and, yes, he had watched the CNN coverage; it was over-reported as usual. They had finally let him go, not happy with him at all he could tell. They knew he was lying, at least in part. Don't leave town, Dr. Norris. Well, where would he go? Mars?

• •• ••• •••••

A nearly inaudible knock on the door made Norris jump. He glanced about, behind him and to each side, momentarily confused but then quickly regained his composure when he understood the source. He unlocked then threw open the door. Valentina stood framed in the brighter lights of the corridor.

"Who let you out?

She peered past him towards the still form on the bed before answering. She glanced at him and said, "You did - my door was unlocked." She brushed past him into the room to stand at the foot of the bed. She seemed unusually composed, he thought.

He closed the door then locked it again. His heart was pounding. He slowly turned to her. "Are you okay?" He was the bastion of reasonableness, was he not?

She nodded.

He stepped around her to the side of the bed and stood over the prostrate John Schmidt, without taking his eyes off her. "Try to relax," he said.

She only glanced at him as before, again focusing on the body on the bed.

He had a sudden idea. He cast back the sheets and lifted the gown to reveal John Schmidt in full nakedness. He indicated. "Here's the scar," he said then stepped aside to let her see. "Another millimeter and his sleep would have been eternal."

"That's not him — I told you it wouldn't be," she stated, embarrassed.

"Valentina…"

"I said that's not him!" she repeated then turned away.

He gently drew her back. "Look harder. Look beyond the body lying there. Do you see who you saw before?"

She shook her head adamantly. She was stubborn, that one — he'd have to work on that… There is a drug for everything.

A wave of dizziness suddenly engulfed him. "I said it's not him," he heard her say again as he grabbed the bed for support. "Valentina…," he began and looked up.

Valentina suddenly jolted. She doubled over, then reflexively straightened; then cried out and dropped to her knees. He watched it happen; there was nothing he could do. He called out and stumbled to her side, barely making it. She pitched over and hit the floor. He couldn't hold her. She screamed and began to writhe across the tiles. "

"Valentina…"

She screamed again, her body twisting.

"Valentina…!"

He crawled to her side then rolled her onto her back. She screamed, pulling at her hair twisting and scrambling across the floor away from him, tearing herself from his grasp. He looked up for the emergency button – found it, drew himself up, and threw himself at it as she again screamed aloud and twisted over the tiles in agony. He hit the button and then collapsed, hitting the floor hard. She was just beyond his reach. She straightened in another paroxysm of pain then doubled over, straightened and then suddenly released.

"Valentina!"

She threw head back and cried, "It hurts! God, it hurts! Let it end! Let it end! I want to die; I want to die!"

She collapsed again.

"Valentina…," he called out softly.

She was still, like death.

"Valentina?" he called again.

She lifted her head slowly and sat upright. She ran her fingers through her hair, gathering a handful and drawing it over her shoulder. She drew more around in panic. She climbed to her feet and stood, her dark hair falling around her.

"Lo hizo otra vez! Oh, Dios mio, ioh, Dios mio!"

"Valentina?"

She stared at him in complete shock.

"Valentina?" he whispered. He could not believe his eyes.

"Dr. Norris?" she croaked, her voice changed.

He could neither confirm nor deny. He no longer knew who he was or what was happening.

"Dr. Norris?"

"I am here."

She stepped tentatively toward him. "It is me, Valentina!"

"I see you — at least I see someone."

She lifted her hands and examined each side, completely incredulous. "What do you see?" she asked looking up to him for confirmation, her eyes wide with wonder. He wouldn't say. He couldn't say. It was clearly impossible.

She searched about for a mirror and, finding it, gazed into it, lifting her new hands to her young face. "Yo no merezco ste regalo! Yo soy un pecador! Oh, Dios, yo no merezco esto regalo!" she cried softly, weeping, laughing and praying. She turned to Norris and said in complete wonder, "Not even God would do this for an old soulless beast like me! Who would or could do such a thing? Do you think it was him?"

She threw herself at Norris, laughing and crying. "It is a miracle! It is a miracle!" She kissed his face, over and over, peppering him with her kisses. He could barely breathe.

"Valentina! It wasn't me! It wasn't me!" he tried to explain.

She laughed in response, throwing herself into the air, landing lightly, then spinning back to him, her head back, her back arched, palms open, like a dancer.

She slowly bowed then straightened and asked, "Do you see?"

"I see…"

She beckoned him. "Come! Come!" waving the tips of her fingers. He reached for her hand. She offered it, then withdrew it, only to offer it again, laughing.

"Ahora, ahora, ahora! Otra vez no!" I know what you want! Don't you think we should dance a little first?" She laughed.

He found he couldn't answer. He couldn't speak. She laughed again and accepted his hand. "There… you are very frightened," she said, and drew him to her.

"What's happening?" he managed to ask.

"I don't know," she said, laughing. She offered her other hand and he grasped it. They were posed as dancers. "I hear music," she said; "Don't you?"

He concentrated. He did hear it. The Bolero. "I do — I hear it now."

She pressed her body to his, her arms wrapped around his neck, her head back, her long dark hair hanging down.

"Valentina…"

"*Shhhh…*"

He held her as he was expected to. She rubbed her thigh against his and snuggled closer.

"Valentina..."

"We are animals, are we not?" she whispered in his ear.

"I don't know, I don't know," he answered also whispering and in her ear. Was it mescaline? Was that what she had slipped into his wine? Or was it the air in the room? Carbon Monoxide poisoning?

Wine? He didn't have any wine.

She led him by his hand. Laughing, playful, she drew him into the light of the courtyard, then further, past the fountain. They picked their way through the courtyard then into the midst of the dancers where she let him go, then turned back to accept him in her arms, her skirt swirling. She laughed, unwinding to the end of their tethered arms, throwing her head back her dark hair flying, then sweeping back into his embrace. "You love me? Tell me you love me!" she whispered in his ear, her breath hot and sweet, and her eyes shining and dancing as her body danced, teasing him.

"Valentina... please don't do this," Norris begged.

"Why ever not?"

"I..."

"Dance with me, Dr. Norris — don't just stand there!" She leaned in close. "May I call you Robert?"

Norris nodded and swallowed.

Valentina laughed "You have no choice, do you, my darling Robert? You are like me; you have no choice!" She laughed again.

Norris danced, slowly, reluctantly; and then finally, surrendering, he danced like he had never danced before, irrevocably intoxicated, swept along, his head back, his eyes glazed, rough laughter pouring out. Valentina raised her face to his and he spun her about then received her back in his arms, enveloping her mouth with his.

"Mas vino para un soldado!" he cried out in Spanish. He held the bottle to his lip letting the intoxicating contents pour down his throat then spill across his shirt.

218 · JOHN TALISKER

She was in his arms again. "Kiss me, Robert! Kiss me again! I beg you!" He kissed her. "Ah, the wine! It is a Rioja!" she laughed. "Give me more!"

• •• ••• •••••

The dance suddenly ended. Norris stood alone in the middle of the room breathing raggedly, his arms wrapped about nothing.

"Have you ever thought," the young man from the hospital and who had stood over Emily asked, indicating the body lying on the bed as it had always lain, "What you are made of?"

The sound of his voice was like a clear note played on a *Viola da Braccio*.

Norris slowly turned toward him. "You!" It was him; there was no doubt: blonde hair tied behind his head, gray eyes.

Whoever he was, whatever he might be, smiled ever so slightly and then bowed, keeping the smile as he straightened.

"Yes, me."

"What do you want? I protected you! I told them nothing!" Norris cried spiraling toward panic.

"It is time for you to know the truth, perhaps," the alien added quietly, even gently. "I have responsibility not only for John Schmidt but for you as well. There is no end to it, it seems."

Yes, alien, for who else could he be?

"What happened to Valentina?" Norris asked. He stumbled to regain his balance and looked about in near panic.

"Nothing happened to Valentina. She is where she has always been, upstairs asleep. I have settled her mind. I should do the same for you."

Norris recoiled. "Don't you touch me!"

The young man lowered his hand. "I will not, then."

Norris's legs trembled. They were barely keeping him upright. He felt he was a dead man. He considered begging for his life but then decided not to — what would be the point? Let him die now. He was more than ready.

The young man hesitated, thought a moment, then lifted his hand and the sheet and garment covering John Schmidt was suddenly thrown aside leaving the body naked. "What you see before you is made from the same stuff this planet is made of, as are all living things," he carefully explained as if speaking to a student who was not quite understanding the lesson. "It is composed of oxygen, carbon, hydrogen, nitrogen, calcium, fifty-seven percent water, and no more."

Dr. Norris nodded. It was very true. He was a doctor; he had already passed that test.

"Do you believe that?"

"I do."

"Do you know it all?"

Norris shook his head to the negative.

"Then listen and learn if you can."

The young man moved his hand and the body dissolved into a puddle. Gross liquid absorbed into the fabric of the mattress, the excess spilling over the edge to splatter on the floor. Only a small pile of mud remained.

"Do you see?"

Dr. Norris nodded. He thought he might be sick.

"Is that not what we place within our graves?" the young man asked.

Norris nodded. Of, course.

"But in the end, are we not more than that?"

Norris could not answer. We are not more than that, he thought. How could we be?

"Watch again."

The young man again moved his hand and the body reformed, the liquid rising from the floor, the mud extending outward until the body was once again whole and breathing again. The body sat up and rubbed its eyes, and then smiled.

"It is a mystery, is it not? If we are merely living beings, then where and from whence comes the soul? A grand illusion, perhaps."

Norris could not answer.

"Or perhaps not."

Norris still could not answer.

The alien shrugged and explained. "I corrected his tumor. To do so, I had to dissemble him and then put him back together without the offending neoplasia that disrupted his mental state, and I had to do it quickly or, too long in a dissociated state, he most surely would die." He stared hard at the good doctor. "Do not tamper with, or otherwise inject your chemicals into, this man again, doctor, unless you intend to cure him. Do no harm, doctor, remember? You are no more God than I am."

• •• ••• ••••

The unequivocal statement of who was responsible for what was said in an empty and dark room. The only light came from the emergency lighting. The door was open and the fire alarm was ringing. Norris could hear running feet drawing nearer: the orderly and the agents they had posted to watch over him: The Calvary in the nick of time.

The nightmare continued; not even the orderly or the agents could stop it from unfolding.

Wouldn't they be surprised?

"Hey!" John Schmidt exclaimed, rubbing his eyes.

"Hey," Norris rejoined, still in shock.

"Hey, who are you?" John Schmidt asked, blinking in the dim light, finding Norris.

"I'm Dr. Norris, your attending physician," he managed to say, his heart pounding; he thought to grasp it and put it back.

Schmidt looked about the small room still trying to orient himself.

"You have been admitted to a hospital," Norris explained before being asked.

Schmidt swiveled back to him. "What?"

"A hospital. You've been admitted."

"I have?"

"Indeed, you have."

"What's that noise?"

"The fire alarm."

"Is there a fire?"

"No — false alarm; it will be turned off in a moment."

Schmidt seemed to consider. He looked around then returning shrugged. "Got anything to eat? I'm hungry — starving."

The orderly burst into the room followed by two more who he knew were agents dressed as orderlies. The agents had their weapons drawn. Norris ignored them and responded to John Schmidt.

"I'll see what I can do."

"Are you all right, Dr. Norris?" the orderly inquired looking about the room, notably anxious. The agents lowered their weapons when they saw there was no immediate threat.

"Who are they?" Schmidt asked, surprised by their sudden and abrupt appearance.

One of the agents spoke into a concealed mic within the folds of his coat. "False alarm — turn the damn thing off." They were abruptly dropped into silence.

Norris forced himself to remain calm. "Never mind them," he said. "But who are you?" he asked, addressing Schmidt.

"You don't know?" Schmidt asked, as if everyone should know who he was.

"No, I'm sorry, we don't. You were admitted comatose: No identification."

John Schmidt appeared indignant. "Well!"

"What is your name? Tell us and we'll know."

"John Jacob...," Schmidt began without thinking, but then frowned. "I don't think that's really it — that's just what popped into my head." He seemed amazed. He considered then shrugged and then smiled. "I'm sure it will come to me sooner or later after I've eaten something — Why do you think that is, Doc?"

Norris shook his head. He once again thought he might be sick. "I have no idea.

Body and Soul

It is strange, is it not, that a person should be both body and soul without differentiation? He could hear and see Catherine in Emily and not just in Emily's appearance, her tonal expression, her idioms of speech, her quick smile, her quick mind, and the little games they once played together. In the early days, he had imagined the people, the way they expressed themselves, what they did and didn't do, to be a product of their genetic inheritance with each individual, sans free will, doing nothing more than blindly obeying a set of genetically encoded rules expressed in their genes. Did that not make them anything other than machines? Just like him? In their case, machines built upon a unique arrangement of amino acids mediated by electrostatic fields, and fed by sugars derived from the energy of their sun? If they are not more than their bodies, then they are biological machines, no more, no less, clear and simple.

"Take one more step along the evolutionary ladder, my love, and you will be me," he thought as he dropped his human hands to his side.

Although he had never stated it plainly, he had always thought Catherine's concept of the soul no more than superstition; at best, a contrivance created to rationalize her mortality — and his mortality, too, for that matter. Catherine's soul, as challenging as it was for her to describe, was everything to her; it remained incorruptible and pure while her body — the bodies of all people, his human body included if he let it follow its natural curve — was inevitably corrupted with death. But where is the much-vaunted soul when the old drool into their bibs, he should have asked her somewhere along the line but never had. Has not the soul flown in such a case? And if flown, to where did it fly, and thinking that it comes and goes, from whence did it come? You do not require the concept of the soul to explain your existence, he would explain to her while adding, "Are we not, all, living beings and no more?" Then waiting before concluding, she looking off into the distance, his smile not yet seen, he would add, "…Some of us that is." He would smile but she would laugh, his argument, if indeed it was an argument and not just a way of explaining one's self to another whom you love, thereby nullified.

The worst of it, the very worst of it, was Emily, of course. Even if he successfully accomplished the orbital transfer, but then failed to open the secrets of his Singular Friend, what would become of her? What would the people do to her when they discovered what he had turned her into?

• •• ••• ••••••

He fell along a mighty curve alone in the empty silence of space, the crescent Earth dominating the blackness, the waxing Moon a brilliant cousin. It was clear what his brother would say. He would say, "Do what you need to do and finish what you started Gatc'hh'en, my brother," and that would be the right thing for a brother to say. And what would L'Batard say? L'Batard, whose heart had soared above all of those he had known? He'd say — he was certain he would say: *"Parfois, un homme doit aller au-delà lui-même pour être un homme."*

"Sometimes a man must reach beyond himself to be a man."

The Moon floated in the star-studded black, a tiny sliver of white-gold falling into the blue of crescent Earth. His friend was surprisingly difficult to maneuver. Yet another miscalculation on his part. How many more must he suffer before he failed entirely?

His friend was small enough to wrap himself around it, but that alone was insufficient to reduce their combined angular momentum. The energy equivalence was nearly too much. He had only one choice, and one choice only other than a disaster which of course could take many forms, and that involved skimming his Singular Friend through Earth's atmosphere in such a way that his friend would rapidly decelerate and then veer sharply toward the Moon. He would then, using whatever resources he might have left to him at that point, ride his friend in a tight arc toward the point where the greater effects of gravity were balanced. The greatest risk was to the Moon. If he could not negotiate the transfer, he would be forced to let go and his Singular Friend would impact the surface, the resulting collision creating an enormous crater larger even than Copernicus. Of course, there was also the possibility he might not even be able to negotiate the Earth flyby, in which case — well, in which case failure would include his own death because he could not allow that transfer to fail. His gut wrenched thinking how Emily would look up, along with the billions of others, to see the end approaching but only she suspecting that he was the cause of it.

The great crescent of the blue and white Earth with sunlight glinting off the North Pacific filled nearly half of the way forward, with the moon, waxing, suspended in the distance. The sun radiated shards of bright crystals of fire to split open the blackness. He unfolded his wings, reached back, and enfolded them about the mountainous singularity he had carried so far and with so much effort. He could feel its unforgiving and ancient presence buttressed within him. How dare he play with such a thing? Hubris? Yes, Catherine and Emily were both right about that; it was all hubris, and, of course vanity. It was wholly ironic.

He turned himself about and began the exchange. He would be seen in broad daylight ten times brighter than the sun to those below. No one could look upon him without blinding themselves. He should have warned them about that, he supposed. He took a deep breath. This was it. There was no turning back.

Orbit Injection

leanor Roberta Vanier sat back and watched the plot. The object, or the Bright Maneuverable Object as it was called now, or simply BMO, was being monitored with every telescope, radar, radiation detector available, a great portion of the data being fed directly to the Object Operations Center, OOC, at the Jet Propulsion Laboratory, Pasadena, California.

Jose Manuel Trevino, the appointed head of the hastily convened committee to study all aspects of the encounter with the alien, or aliens, or whomever, or whatever, was driving humanity to distraction pointed over Eleanor's shoulder at the plot. "It's still coming right at us."

She gritted her teeth. "I can see that — it would. It has one hell of a lot of momentum to dump to make orbit." She had answered him a little impatiently. She couldn't help it. Trevino was an anchor around her neck. If she had her way, she'd only report to Ramanujan and Ramanujan only; he was the true lead on this. She squirmed in her seat.

"What orbit?" Trevino asked impatiently.

She nervously chewed her finger and again squirmed in her chair. She was trying hard to remain calm "We don't know yet." She twisted around in her chair to face him. She had lost some of her self-confidence. "If this thing begins to radiate as it did during the Jupiter flyby, it will be extremely, even dangerously, bright. Has everyone been warned?"

"Yes, of course, Dr. Vanier. It's been done. Don't worry about that."

She nodded and rotated back to her computer screen which showed the real-time Sun-Earth-Moon configuration as a three-dimensional plot, with the object falling inward at an astounding and troubling rate, much faster than a spacecraft or any device made by man. The current trajectory, highlighted in red, indicated it would impact Earth somewhere mid-latitude while the projected trajectory highlighted in yellow showed it just grazing past. If it hit Earth it would be the end of everything. It would be the greatest extinction event since the meteor impact that had wiped out the Dinosaurs. The projected trajectory would require the object to perform a course correction, a correction that had not as yet occurred.

The optical track consoles suddenly lit up and the console operator broke in on the com. "We have confirmation from Haleakala, Maui. It's gone bright." He shared the video feed with the large monitor on the wall. It showed a very small but very bright object. It seemed far away but closing fast. "We have a full lock," he announced. "We'll be able to track it all the way in."

"It's begun then," Eleanor said tense but completely focused. "And it's right here above the West Coast. If we went outside, we'd see it."

She pointed to the plot. It showed the object veering slightly, very slightly. "It's moving, it's moving…," she said, tracking it.

"It's still coming right at us," Trevino interjected, on edge.

"I can see that."

Ramanujan nudged him from behind. "Let Ellie do her job."

Trevino nodded biting his lip.

Visual optics broke in again. "Haleakala reports a second object. I have audio only. It's Matheson… He says it's closing with the first and brighter object. We should see it… now!"

The room turned about to face the monitor which clearly showed a second object quickly closing with the first. The image bloomed at impact and then went dark but then gradually recovered showing only one much brighter object.

"What the hell?" someone echoed.

A sudden power glitch caused the lights to go out. The large screen monitor had switched off as the power had gone down, but the computers at each console stayed up. Emergency lighting snapped on.

"Ops Control, this is Engineering. The power grid is down; we're on backup generators."

"Roger that, Engineering."

The main monitor followed by the lights immediately switched back on.

Visual Optics broke in again. "Haleakala reports the second object merged with the first. The combined object is a thousand times brighter than previously, and ten thousand times brighter than the sun. It's fantastic! Are you getting this Pasadena? Is everything working there?"

Eleanor excitedly pointed at the plot. "It's moving! It's moving! It's on track! It's going to make the flyby! It's good! It's good!" She threw down her headset and jumped up. "Let's go!" She pushed herself through the crowd, towing Ramanujan behind her. She opened the big double doors. The hallway was flooded by stark-white light, surreal in the way it washed away all color, replacing it with its own overwhelming brightness. She shielded her eyes and stepped into it, fumbling with a pair of dark glasses in her pocket.

"I wasn't about to miss this — no way!" She put them on and cautiously tipped her head back. "Good God!" Ramanujan stood beside her, shielding their eyes. "Damn!" The hallway soon filled as the Operations Center emptied, all wearing the same glasses. Eleanor placed her hand on Ramanujan's sleeve. "It is just like you said, Ram — they, or whomever, are converting momentum into light and heat."

The object suddenly split in two. Part of it accelerated away sunward while the remainder continued along its track less than half as bright as it had been before. The sunward-bound object quickly disappeared while the second dimmed and then faded until extinguished. The elapsed time of the event was exactly four minutes and ten-seconds someone noted.

The control room was again quickly filled. Eleanor squared herself in front of her monitor, Ramanujan and Trevino joining her. As the data came in, she made her report. "It's heading toward the moon. It will be there in about two hours. "Why the moon… Why the moon?" she mused. She twisted about to find Ramanujan. "I think I know where it's going!" She turned back to her console and made some quick entries. "My God, if I'm right…" She made a few quick entries and the plot quickly updated showing how the calculated course almost exactly overlay what was being observed. She sat back and laughed.

"Damn! I'm right!"

Precession

Without his brother's help two things could have happened. First, his Singular Friend could have impacted Earth mid-latitude and everyone, Emily, Catherine, L'Batard, and himself included, would now be dead; burned to a crisp. Second, he and his singular companion would have ended up in a highly elliptical orbit around the sun, and he would be dead. It would only be a point of mild interest when the former rider, still locked in a horrid embrace with his Dark Horse of a friend, swept past yet again months later, colder than space.

It was not an error on his part to refer to those long gone as if their lives too had been somehow at risk. Does not destroying the present not also remove the past, to say nothing of the future?

He had not told Emily of this; he barely could think of it himself, but It was a fact, though, too, that after Catherine, feeling empty and abandoned, all seemingly lost, he had in a moment of great despair placed himself into orbit about the people's sun and allowed himself to disperse. He had spread himself as thin as possible until his thoughts, too, thinned, and became empty, leaving the ache of love and loss mercifully behind. But as luck would have it, as his remnants drifted along under the influence of gravity, the solar wind, and the energy of the sun, the pieces ultimately precessed so that he was once again oriented facing the sun, and through the revitalizing energy imbued upon him, re-collated and ultimately regained consciousness. It was not a trick; it was not something programmed into him — although he sometimes wondered about that — it had been just luck. That is how it is with luck, is it not? We, each of us, owe our living days to luck?

But he was having difficulty rationalizing what had happened. Without his brother's help, the situation would have devolved into a complete fiasco. As soon as he had wrapped himself about his Singular Friend, the Dark Horse — quite an excellent pedigree too; very ancient and well-founded — he had known he was in trouble. He had pushed and pulled, the blue Earth growing larger, then filling his view, his arc changing slightly but not nearly enough, his sense of panic growing. The first indication his brother was about to intervene was not until he had swept up beside him; he had said nothing, not so much as a nod, before merging with him making the two of them far more powerful that just two alone. Merging is what lovers do, man and wife, mothers and fathers with their children; sisters with their sisters, brothers with sisters, and now, apparently, brothers with brothers.

His very earliest memories were a result of merging with his mother. He remembered her saying as he slowly gained consciousness for the first time, "Here, my love, I give you these," and she had shown him the images from the distant past, their history as she understood it, and their love for one another. In the end, their sun blown to pieces, their new bodies more like machines than a living being, the only thing that that had saved them was the unplanned and circumstantial merging process: man and woman, or man and man, or woman and woman — never one, always two or more — to imbue the sentience and intelligence of the mechanism with love for one another. It did not mean there had been no discontent but at least it had meant they were whole. In retrospect, then, he should have expected his brother to help; after all, that's what brothers do, don't they?

• •• ••• •••••

The Moon floated in a sea of black, closer than Earth, and ringed by a halo of silver, nearly eclipsing the flashing sun. The people's spacecraft tumbled out of control nearby, the sun alternatively flashing off their panels of gold as they rotated slowly about. His Singular Friend, nearly invisible, hovered amongst them. With any luck, he would break that barrier, and in so doing release energies found only in the heart of stars as well at the beginning of time. With any luck, he would tear space apart to recreate it. What would he do then? Well, of course, he would sweep down through a hole in time and space with the newly minted and transformed Emily by his side and surprise them all. There would be no more of this… This emptiness.

Isn't that what he wanted? More than anything?

Yes, of course.

First, though, he needed to rest.

Failure and Truth

It was no good. He could not source sufficient energy to spin his Singular Friend up anymore, to say nothing of the catalytic changes necessary to convert its captured mass into energy. It was simply too massive a body, and too contained within its boundary.

He pulled back. His friend was dull red and spinning like a mad top. It should be white, pure white, and spinning much faster. He backed away from it further. The remnants of the JWST tumbled against the stars behind him. He turned toward the sun, a beacon of brilliance a half degree wide, and spread his wings. Earth appeared as a silver and blue crescent, the entire globe revealed by a halo of sunlight refracted through the atmosphere. The crescent moon was almost as large, the unilluminated portion revealed by Earthshine, a soft darkness, blue-grey. But no matter how long he remained reopening his conduit to the sun, or how often he diverted himself back to the sun's corona to recharge his internal cells, he still would not be powerful enough. There was only so much energy he could source either from the sun or from within. Without help, he was about to fail at this too.

He reconnected with Earth's magnetic field — weak at this distance — and fell inward, picking up speed, putting his friend the Dark Horse and the wreck of a half dozen satellites including JWST behind him. Closer to Earth, a bright flash suddenly appeared over the night side — it would have blinded his human self. It originated over the mid-Pacific. He immediately ascertained that it was a nuclear explosion; for some reason, it had been detonated in low Earth orbit. Another blast quickly followed, followed by two more. A surge of high-energy protons swept past him, ricocheting back and forth from one magnetic pole to the other breaking the resonance of the field. The sky glowed blue and green, jumping in curtains of ionized oxygen and nitrogen. It was beautiful. He spread his wings further to absorb the additional energy and rotated slowly about to bask in it.

It was a desperate thing for them to do — the EMP would kill most, if not all, of their low Earth satellites; perhaps a few polar-orbiting military satellites might survive. He slowed but continued to cross the field lines, heading downward across them, Earth looming larger. There was another blast quickly followed by two more just like the last time but at a higher latitude. It was a signal. They were sending him a signal.

He slowed further. The upper atmosphere was a riot of color, intense green mixed with blood-red, tied with strings of blue He thought of Emily. It would be nearly dawn in the city; her sky would be like nothing she had ever seen. It would be a riot of color, but a false color, a color neither she nor anyone would have seen at dawn before. Green, blood red. What desperation had driven them to do this? What had he done?

He slowed further, switching his polarity and then going dark. No more games. They deserved better than games. He dropped his speed to be the same as the rotating Earth and fell into the Earth's gravity-well, straight down. He dropped through curtains of ionized atmosphere, the ions already combining, the brilliant colors diminishing. He hit the ionosphere, then the troposphere, the first clouds, and, still accelerating downward, slowed by spreading himself outward, and he flew. He levelled out at ten thousand meters, running dark. The Midwest United States, hollowed in the night with only pinpoints of light to mark where the solid ground would be, swept past beneath him. He was ten minutes from New York and Emily.

• •• ••• •••••

He found her by the large picture window looking toward the sun rising over the city, the surrounding sky painted in the abstract. She turned to face him as he entered. She wore a single piece dress tied at her waist. She had purchased it in the shopping plaza attached to the hotel; at *Remy*'s she had said. It was patterned in buttercups; thin green stems, golden cups, leaning in a warm summer breeze. She had put it on knowing he was coming, he knew. It was to be a surprise.

He kissed her, once, twice, forehead, lips, then stepped back, keeping her hands in his. He saw the changes in her. She was already beyond who Catherine had been.

"I saw you coming," she said, looking up, smiling, and canting her head to the side exactly as Catherine would have. But unlike Catherine, she was beginning to radiate.

"You did?" he asked.

"Yes, you flew out of the sun as you normally do," she said softly. She stepped in close and smiled, turning her head to let strands of her hair brush against his cheek, knowing it would tickle, and to make him smile. "Just a tiny ball of light."

He slowly nodded. He could not say what he felt; he felt too much – too much like a failure. But he was not there to discuss that. He had come to confess his guilt, and why not? It was just one more failing in a long and growing list. He had been taught better than that. Redeem thyself…

She spoke carefully, smiling up. "You should be more careful — if I saw you, so will they."

He knew they had. He had let them. He had flown in dark but once over the city he had wanted to shout out his presence and damn them all.

"I am angry," he said, avoiding the truth.

"What are you angry about?"

"I have failed."

"You have not failed — how can you say such a thing? You and whatever you were dragging with you successfully entered orbit — it was in the news. Everyone saw it. You have created quite a stir, my love. Many are afraid. I'm not."

"Arra'll'en helped me."

"Ah! Your brother!"

"I was not strong enough alone."

Her smile widened. "I had almost forgotten about him!"

"Why are they detonating nuclear weapons?" he asked.

Emily hesitated, caught off guard by his sudden shift. She bowed, her smile dropping off. "They are trying to gain the alien's attention — have they?"

"What do they want?"

"They want you to stop whatever it is you are doing. They want to you to explain yourself."

"I will not."

"Why not?"

"I am angry, as I've said."

She again reached for his hands. She held them in hers and gently said, "At the world? With everyone on it? Talk with them, my love, and let them know you do not intend to harm them."

"How do you know I do not?"

She smiled knowing he never would. "Give me some credit; I do know you."

He saw that she knew. "I am angry at myself — because I do not have sufficient strength, as I said."

"Strength of character, or physically?"

He looked at her carefully but didn't respond.

"Look what you did to me?" she added calmly, laying her hand across her breast. "Is all of what you did to me for nothing?"

"It will not be my only sin," he said.

She drew him to her, and looking up into his eyes, and in emphasis said, "You know nothing of sin. Look what you've started — the whole world is turned upside down. I've been turned upside down."

"Do you think I do not know that?"

"What alternatives do you have?"

"I can leave it as it is and then my brother and I will go."

"You will abandon me?"

He stared at her unmoving.

"Why did you change me into Catherine? I am Catherine, am I not?"

"As much as I can make you."

"But why?"

"I am weak."

"You are not — not in that way. There is another reason."

"I am not strong enough then."

"That is not true."

"I have another confession to make just to prove to you how weak I can be, and how deceitful too. If you think you love me, you do not. I placed a suggestion in your mind to make you believe you did. I did so right at the beginning while you were in the hospital and I didn't know you."

She closed her eyes.

"I lied. Two sins then. I should have walked a higher path."

She opened her eyes and then asked, "Where is your brother in all this?"

"I lied to you. I manipulated your mind to make you believe you loved me."

"Where is your brother in all this?"

"He is watching, waiting to escort me home with my tail between my legs, I should not doubt."

"You are too hard on yourself, Gatc'hh'en."

"I'm not hard enough. You do not understand, all of this has been quite a joke."

"A joke?" She indicated the apartment, and then with another sweep of her arm, the world outside. "All that?" She turned to face him and again spread her hand across her breast. "Me?"

"I do not mean it that way. I mean my life. What have I done with it? Catherine died because of my neglect. I played with her and you like musical instruments with no consideration of the people you are. I violated your mind and your heart. I moved an ancient body with the intent to extract its inner energy and all in the name of hubris and vanity. I thought I could do anything but the truth is I can do nothing. Nothing worked out. Nothing. I am a failure. I have failed my Rite."

"Call your brother. He will help you."

"I will not."

"He is your brother."

"What is that supposed to mean?"

"He is your brother. Brother's help their brothers — that's what brothers do."

He heard it echoed and hesitated. "I cannot."

She gently turned him about to face her and placed her hands on his shoulders. "Look at me."

He looked at her then shifted off.

"So, you are going to leave things as they are?" she asked, turning his face back to hers, reaching up and drawing it to her with the tips of her fingers. "Let your brother escort you home? Let Humanity pick up the pieces? What will you say to me then when you look at me and remember all we have gone through? Will we talk about your failures?"

He could not answer. The changes within her were remarkable he was thinking. Tell her about that too? Or did she know? It was possible.

"You note I include myself in this. I will not leave you, or allow to leave me for that matter," she added firmly.

"Emily...," he said softly. He strongly suspected she was not Catherine: her body, yes; her soul, no.

"Ask him. He will help you, I know."

"How do you know?"

"If he is anything like you then he will — and he must be like you in some way or he wouldn't be as patient as he obviously is. I believe he understands you and I suspect he is waiting for you to call him. What else would he be doing? He helped you once he will again."

She suddenly stepped into him and kissed him. "I do not know what you are trying to do," she said. "But you have given me this life so I can only imagine that what you are planning must be just as great, probably almost impossible. Even so, you cannot fail. Call him."

• •• ••• •••••

He ascended above the city, a small pinpoint amidst the tall buildings and then made himself visible. A flash brighter than five suns: and again, and again, radiating from the infra-red, through visible, then ultra-violet, to gamma rays — all frequencies — the city below him consecutively painted in black shadow and harsh white, each flash resonating with a deep rumbling sound. He lifted higher so as not to irradiate the inhabitants. He cut through the morning cloud, the flashing light and sound swallowed but still seen along the outer edges, the sound and brightness diminishing as he rose higher. A moment later a sonic boom shook the city to its roots.

Almost everyone in the city below him would take note, he knew; the spectacle he had made of himself was, after all, somewhat difficult to ignore. And yet, it was all unnecessary; his brother could be contacted much more readily, and with no fanfare. He had radiated and sounded out as he had because of how he felt. He had not expected Emily to support him so full-heartedly. He had expected a slap, a turning away, outrage and indignation, but instead she had only shown how much she loved him. Her reaction was most unexpected. His heart soared as it fell. What if he failed? What if he really and truly failed?

Over the Atlantic, the grey ocean wind-whipped and tossed, stretching to the horizon, he received a message coded, again, only for him.

No excuses this time, brother. You know where to find me.

Arra'll'en.

Love and Loss

Time is nonlinear. He could only move forward within it caught up as he was within its stream. It did not matter how quickly or slowly, or what accelerated frame he might be in, it always flowed forward. He could neither see nor feel the nonlinearities but he could capture time, replay it in different forms, and rewind it, then replay it, all in his mind. The sad part was, indeed the horrifying part, was that he could not ever go back in time to make things right. If he could, then none of what had transpired; Catherine's death, his sin, would not have been necessary, none of it. What a farce all this... this... this traipsing about would only have been. If he only could have reached back to correct each small mistake along the way. But that is never the way it is, is it?

It was clear what he would have done if he could. He would tell Catherine it was all his fault. And it most definitely was. It had seemed such a simple and necessary thing at the time, his act of revenge against the priest who had assaulted her. The priest, so certain of his right to do so, had slapped her hard across her face. And for what? Heresy? Blasphemy? Healing the sick when only God could do that? For that, for the slap, and because he would not allow anyone to touch Catherine like that, he had destroyed the priest's mind.

He had merely whispered into his ear using the scripture of the priest's own prophets to ignite the fire that would consume him.

"And I saw a great white throne, and him that sat upon it, from whose face the earth and the heaven fled away; and there was found no place for them... And whosoever was not found written in the book of life was cast into the lake of fire..."

The guards came, the priest having summoned them; but they had taken the priest away instead, the priest foaming at the mouth begging for forgiveness from his suddenly recalcitrant God, while Catherine wept and begged him to make the priest right again.

Revenge always leads to revenge, violence to more violence. He should have swept Catherine up and out, giving the self-righteous but unharmed priest good reason to believe the devil was amongst them. Later, he and Catherine would laugh about it. She would retain her powers to heal. She would not ever be ill. She would never grow old.

• •• ••• ••••••

He used to dream of Catherine and a dark wood in which he was lost. All around was the same: green canopy and rigid upright trunks and a forest floor strewn with dead leaves and skeletal branches. He would cup his hands around his human mouth and call out her name. The brown leaves danced *The Dance Macabre* as the green foliage trembled and flew about as if bending to a high wind. In the depth of his nightmare, he felt more than he could speak, knowing he had killed her as surely as if he had lit the tinder that had then leapt into the flame that had at first burned away her hair, then seared her lungs, then scorched her flesh.

En fin de compte, mon amour, vous allez créer une grande lumière, et dans cette lumière, vous trouverez Dieu, et pour la première fois vous vous connaîtrez pour qui vous êtes vraiment.

Ainsi dit sainte Catherine.

"In the end, my love, you shall create a great light, and in this light, you shall find God, and for the first time you shall know yourself for who you truly are."

So sayeth Saint Catherine.

What grotesque irony. Catherine often referred to her light as something that existed in its purest form only in the presence of her God. He knew what light was: it was a small part of the continuum of energy and matter that made up the world; more specifically, radiant energy. It was also perhaps another slice of perjurious irony that the essence of light as he understood it also included truth and beauty, for is not beauty always true and pure?

He had never fully understood Catherine's concept of light in connection with her God: in who, and what, her God might be, and could be, including her belief in Heaven, Purgatory, and Hell. Still, he sensed that she did not live just for the love of her God, but for all things she loved. She had, for instance, loved him she had once said like she loved the rebirth of spring. The glorious colors of sunrise and sunsets; warm summer days; blue skies, the Golden sun, the red and golds of the fall leaves, and the near perfect silence hanging over the valley in winter. And she had loved him, he knew, not only because she had told him so, or the number times she had. Wrapping herself around him, she had often peppered him with kisses, and laughing while falling onto the grass with him in her arms. Sex? Yes. Passion? Yes. Animal thrust and desire? Yes. Are we not all evolved from animals? Yes. Is that all we are? No.

He had often wondered what she had taught him and why it was he missed her so. People die all the time. Her death was just one of many, he had once tried to rationalize hoping to lessen the pain through false reasoning. It had taken him hundreds of years before he finally understood the truth: she had taught him that we live for what and who we love or we do not live at all — or wish we did not.

246 · JOHN TALISKER

Of course, that begs the question of why he continued to live long after she was gone. Perhaps he should have given up his life then. It would have been noble, and right, perhaps, to end. Again, he did not know if that was true, or right to even contemplate. It is a sin to take one's own life, Catherine had once told him, and he could see the truth in that for, after all, what is even a thousand years to live when one is free of pain or any anguish whatsoever for all eternity after death?

· ·· ··· ·····

He and Catherine had once sat together in L'Batard's garden in the old Castle of Blois. The guards having passed through the gate were stepping towards them, their knobbed boots sounding hollow on the stone path. Catherine, turning in his arms, kissed his cheek and whispered in his ear. "It is time I left you now, my love." He kissed her once then let her go. She stood, straightening, wrapping her winter cloak about her and then looked down at him with a sad smile. "Give me three months, my love; and in the spring, come visit," she had said, her beautiful face outlined by the trellised roses of autumn and the gray sky beyond.

"Do you promise to remain at Claix?" he'd asked, standing with her.

"No... but I will let you know wherever I am so you can always find me again, and I you."

"Will you become a nun?"

She laughed. "That is not my calling," she said and then kissed him again.

"Here, my love, take this." She handed him her necklace, ninety-two percent silver, the remaining almost all copper.

"Thank you; I will keep it for you."

"Keep it warm. Around your neck, as I wore it."

"I will."

He had not — but he had kept it close and still had it somewhere.

She suddenly threw herself against him peppering him with kisses. Holding off, leaning back to take him in again while holding on as if drowning, she had said, "Let your light burn brightly, my love!" and then she had let him go. And then she was gone with L'Batard's guards falling in to conceal her forever from his vision.

No, not gone. She lived for a while longer. He, of course, if he had wanted could have hovered somewhere near, protecting her. But although the words had never been spoken, at least not explicitly, he knew that she would not want him to watch over her like a guardian angel, a guardian angel who might, just might because he loved her, inadvertently tip the scales of her fate that only she should control. And so like an innocent while he was anything but he had naively withdrawn respecting her privacy.

So, what did he do while his love succumbed to her final light? This, of course, was inexcusable, and it was his sin. He shut down. He turned himself off. He waited for the spring, inwardly acknowledging their agreement, while knowing that the spring was only a short arc along the orbit. While his love died in fiery agony, he lingered, luxuriating, self-absorbed in the intricate details of a winter garden and the impressive array of books arraigned in the library at Blois. Oh, how content he had been. He had been like a child sucking its thumb safely asleep in its crib, and yet he was not a child. If only he had raised an eye, thought for one moment, if only...

· ·· ··· ·····

Once Catherine had passed beyond, her soul departed, the untamed, un-conjured reality of her un-claimable, she became completely and forever beyond his reach. He had wanted to scream, to rant, and to tear out his heart; he had wanted to tear Earth from its orbit, knowing that the heaven of hers was unreachable and not even real.

Of course, again, he had done nothing. He had been too empty to do anything, not even seek revenge.

• •• ••• ••••••

Time leaves ghosts behind. Images. He made a point of pulling them all together, having to know the last moments of the woman he loved. He asked himself if he was no better than a voyeur, a semi-interested spectator, and Catherine no more than a mere abstraction. The idea terrified him, sickened him. She was, and remains, far more to him than that, for to relegate her to such an abstraction would be to minimize his own reality to near nothingness.

In a replay, summing the currents of the past he could not affect but could reconstruct, he watched what had unfolded from the first moments she had stepped across the threshold at Claix to the very end. He heard her prayers and knew of her disenchantment with the stifling atmosphere of the small village. He knew that out of frustration she withdrew to a convent. And then disillusioned again, she made her way to Paris in the company of a small troop of nuns. They were intent on lifting the poor from their seas of despair; intent on healing their diseases, finding them food, showing them through example and love the way of their God. He was immediately afraid for her sake. If time could have allowed it, he would have swept down and picked her up off her feet and placed her down in the safety of Blois chastising her roundly. But what good would that have done? Catherine would have only turned around and continued. That was the way she was.

He rushed the scene forward and watched the priest stalk her in the streets. The priest's habit was torn and filthy. The look of death was in his eyes. He had not bathed and had barely eaten since the moment he had been shown the imagined face of his God he so carefully, so insolently, worshiped.

It was wrong of him to twist the priest's mind. He should not play with the minds of people. If there was a lesson to be had in any of this, it was that. Catherine had tried to tell him.

"Oh, Lady! Wait! Do not run from me!" the priest had cried.

"I do not run."

"Thank you, Lady! Oh, thank you!"

"Why do you touch me so?" Catherine asked, turning to face him. The priest had thrown himself onto the cobbled, rubbish strewn stones of the street, his fingers delicately, hesitantly, caressing the leather of her shoes. She had not yet recognized him.

"Oh Lady, forgive me for I have sinned!" he cried.

A crowd was forming. They were mumbling among themselves in wonder, some in fear. "Stand up," Catherine gently ordered. She lifted him to his feet - then she recognized him; then she knew fear.

He was mad.

"Oh, Lady! Lady!" He breathed, swooning, returning to prostrate himself on the filthy street. "My very soul has been stolen from me! I am like clay; I am as nothing; I am like the walking dead!" He threw his arms about her legs almost toppling her. "Give me release! Oh, please, Lady; give me release!"

The front rows of the crowd stepped back, pushing the ones behind, spreading their fear - and curiosity - like fire through dried wood on a windless day.

Catherine struggled, finally releasing herself from his grip. Standing clear, she addressed him again. "You have a great sickness of the heart, sir."

Nameless faces chanted, "Il est possédé! Il dispose d'un démon! Le diable a lui!" as they packed in tighter. Those gathered behind were jumping up or climbing up onto the shoulders of those in the front for a better view.

The priest clamored over the stones to her feet. "Cure me! Help me! Release me with your touch, oh Lady!"

Catherine hesitated. Then she made the greatest mistake of her life. If he had just thought. If he had not been... so remote and distracted, he could have stopped her. He had had the means, he just... had not. She reached down and touched the priest. She held her hand on his forehead and the priest screamed. He flew into convulsions. Catherine jumped back, then remained paralyzed, her hands reaching for the priest, her eyes searching those assembled around her for assistance. But fear-struck, they scrambled back almost causing a stampede until they saw they were in no danger. They then turned back to watch the spectacle, those that were closest quickly crossing themselves.

The priest bled from self-inflicted gashes on his forehead. He beat his head against the stones. He foamed at the mouth, arching his body, screaming in agony. Near the end, tiring slowly but inevitably, his eyes glazed over. Mind gone, soul gone, with the last of his strength he turned to Catherine, unseeing. "*I have seen Hell!*" he cried. Then he died, eyes open, spittle trickling from this mouth, his bladder letting go.

It did not take long after that. In Paris, at that time, the Church was attempting to secure its position against the secular forces of the corrupt monarchy and the English rulers. Heretics could be burned at the stake but only with implicit approval from the crown. A priest had been possessed. His dying words had condemned her. There were witnesses, a multitude of them. Most important, someone had associated Catherine with the House of Orleans and L'Batard.

And so, subsequently, on the twenty-first of March 1421, after a perfunctory trial, without even a confession, or a preliminary round of torture, Catherine was first stripped, then all her hair cut off to reveal the mark of Satan, a mole on her shoulder. It was proof that she was Satan's mistress and she was subsequently burned at the stake for the entertainment of the restless Parisians as much as for revenging the dead priest. They piled the brush up about her and then ignited it so that she died within a wall of flame. She died of asphyxiation as the flames scorched her throat and air passages making it impossible for her to breathe.

He remembered this part very clearly; he did not need to reconstruct this. He remembered it. He had awoken with a start at her last dying scream. He knew she had been burned; and burned, he knew she was beyond reconstitution. He knew that she was dead and dead forever just as he knew that her last thoughts had been of him.

• •• ••• •••••

That was not all.

Far from it.

Time did not have to show him this; he recalled it well enough.

Back in Blois, the garden gate slowly opened. L'Batard stepped through, carefully closing it behind him before turning to him. He was dressed in his daily attire of leather and a simple brown tunic, his head uncovered. It had been the first day of April then; just it was the first day of April now. Time moves forward only but often repetitiously loops back on itself if only in the heart.

"I hear you are ill," L'Batard said, calling from the gate. "I hear you do not speak." He waited and then said evenly, "I have heard from Paris." L'Batard waited for a response but not getting one stepped out following the path through the garden, first drawn away, but then turning back toward him. He entered the alcove and sat on the stone bench opposite, his eyes gray like the morning that promised rain. "The fair lady Catherine is dead," he said. "She was caught in Paris before *the Cathédrale du Notre Dame*, tried for heresy, and burned."

Yes, that was the truth.

L'Batard's breathing was deep and irregular as he too fought for control. "Claix was too small for her," he said evenly. "You should have known that about her."

Yes, he should have known.

"I saw how the two of you embraced when she departed," L'Batard added. "Why were you not by her side? Were you not her Guardian Angel?"

He would not answer.

"You were her Protector, were you not?"

He remained silent. He could not answer. There were no words to say what he felt.

L'Batard did not press him any further. He stood to go, turned away, then turned back. "You should remain here," he said, dropping his eyes, full of pity, on him.

"I cannot."

"You should remain until your heart does not sit so low."

"I cannot."

L'Batard tried to draw him back but he would not be drawn. He shrugged off L'Batard's hand and stepped out, one pace... a million paces already between them. He walked out of the garden, following the path L'Batard had taken, and at the gate, carefully opened it, stepped through and did not bother to close it behind him. He walked across the courtyard and shed his cloak. He was dimly aware of L'Batard following, but keeping back. Knights, men at arms, boys from the stable, women from the kitchen and nursery, all turning to watch as he openly wept, tears mixing with the rain that suddenly came thundering down. He shed the remainder of his garments as the rain soaked him. The gate swung open, the guards stepping back, commanded by L'Batard to do so. He walked through, naked in his humanity, colder than the sea, and he entered the forest that came close in to the road leading from Blois.

34

Brothers

Brother and brother met half way across *Le Pont Jacques-Gabriel* with the beautiful and bountiful Loire running fast beneath the ancient stone arches. The *Cathedral du Blois*, constructed out of river stone two-hundred-fifty years after the death of L'Batard, towered above the town just to their right; the high turrets of the *Chateau du Blois*, rebuilt many times since those days, to their left. Despite the worldwide turmoil, people flowed around them as traffic rushed about spinning off into the fan of narrow streets that fed the town. The larger world existed beyond their borders; this was the heart of France.

He could see his brother's features clearly through the façade, the camouflage only superficial. "L'Batard."

"I did not know what form to take," Arra'll'en stated evenly, L'Batard's eyes tracking him. He was very powerful, his brother; much more than he had imagined.

"You have been looking into my past, reading my mind," Gatc'hh'en replied; "Or have you been watching me all this while?"

"I have not been reading your mind, brother; it is quite unethical to do so. But, yes, we have been monitoring your progress from a distance — not me, specifically, but others."

"And L'Batard? I take that as an affront, and an invasion."

His brother bowed. "I am sorry you see it that way. I perceived an image of this body — L'Batard, you say — when you and I merged. You have a very clear mind, brother. You are much more intelligent than me. More honest, too, I have to say."

"Honest, brother? You are dishonest?"

Arra'll'en answered flatly, without inflection. "No... I am just weaker." He carefully picked his words. "What you are attempting is all very impressive, brother, if not a bit overly dramatic, and dangerous, too, I must say. But wherever did you find an object like that?"

"Drifting far out beyond the influence of the sun, looking toward our home, wondering where you all were, why you had not come to repatriate me."

"Ah, I'm sorry — But more to the point, a minor slip and this world will be turned into a cinder. Why would you risk your people like that? Of course, you can do whatever you wish; it is not up to me to judge."

Gatc'hh'en stared back.

"And the female person — Emily, I believe her name is — what you are attempting there is a bit shaky as well, is it not? I'm not sure our Mother would approve. Playing with evolution to say nothing of her heart, and all for one who is long dead. Her name was Catherine, was it not, and you want her back? I can understand that, I really can."

Not expecting an answer, Arra'll'en turned to stare into the distance toward the Old City, L'Batard's grey eyes taking it all in. "So this is where you traipsed on your hunt for truth, is it?" he mused. "I can see your ghost is everywhere." He examined L'Batard's hands, turning them back to front. "I like this body," he mused further. "The chemistry is peculiar but the biology undeniably successful. It is quite exceptional to have people evolve within it." He looked up and held Gatc'hh'en's eyes to his. "I, too, have undergone *The Rite*, brother, so I know none of this is easy."

Gatc'hh'en continued to stare, expressionless. "How is our mother?" he asked finally.

"She is well. She sends her regards."

"Father?"

"The same."

"Why was I not repatriated? I thought you might all be dead."

"I'm sorry if you thought that. But no one came because it was felt you had not reached the point where you could, or should, be brought home. You were not ready — apparently. But don't ask me — I'm not one who is qualified to judge."

"I have learned so much here. I nearly died here."

"We know. You almost killed yourself, if that is what you mean. We watched you do that. Of course, you would not be permitted to disperse yourself like that. Mother almost tore this star system apart when she heard about it. She was quite angry, and not just with you. Need I remind you only the old and feeble do that, Gatc'hh'en — that and the desperately mad?"

It required a moment for Gatc'hh'en to respond. "I cannot imagine how you stand before me now or say such things."

"To be honest, Mother sent me," Arra'll'en quickly stated, less careful with his words, throwing them out as they entered his mind. "She has been quite beyond herself with all this." He hesitated, uncertain. "I am to blame."

"What is that, brother?"

"I am to blame — That is, it is me our mother blames. You see, I stole one of the Tunnels. The other two were dedicated to heading me off. There was no way to repatriate you. Someone would have come sooner if it was not for that, I am sure. You may blame me, brother. Go ahead."

"So now you tell the truth?"

"Now I tell the truth. I do not know how it momentarily evaded me."

"Do you speak lightly? Is this a joke?"

"No joke."

"Have you no shame?"

Arra'll'en held his ground. "It is true, I have none."

"…Why did you steal a Tunnel? I cannot imagine you doing so. I cannot imagine you standing before me if having done so."

"Because my people, those that I lived amongst and became — at least in my heart I became — you must know what I mean, brother — were threatened by an outside force that entered their solar system looking to harvest them. I would not have my people exterminated for no reason other than the vanity of those that thought they could claim living people for their own purpose. You would do the same, would you not, if these people were threatened by some external force? *Human Beings* you call them – an interesting description with its emphasis on *being*. I see it now."

Gatc'hh'en wrestled with the emotions surging through him.

"I saved them," Arra'll'en continued, his voice flat. "That is to say, I drove off the invader. They were, and I use the past tense here precisely, a nasty collective. They were, once upon a time, a super-organism comprised of billions of individuals joined through an interlinking thread of intelligence and awareness that abhorred anything and everything other than themselves. They believed they knew their god's mind and in their interpretation of that mind rationalized all they did."

He hesitated. "…And, oh, and did I forget? Did I forget to mention that I killed them all? That their planet continues to orbit about its sun, but is now sterile of all life down to its core? I will answer to my God for that." He smiled without humor, sarcastically adding, "But, of course, there is always hope, is there not? The chemistry that once evolved there may evolve yet again. Given enough time, one never knows, does one?"

Gatc'hh'en could only stare.

"Are you ready to come home now, Gatc'hh'en?" Arra'll'en asked, the tumult within him now clearly visible. "Have I answered all your questions? Is that not your intent? To return home?"

"It is."

"Then shall we, together, end your Rite by opening the energies of the ancient past?"

Gatc'hh'en shook his head. He was still reeling, a thread of despair beginning to snake through him.

"Do you know why I killed them all?" Arra'll'en asked, not yet finished, L'Batard's voice flat and even, his eyes hard and brittle. "It was not the fact they had already blown away half a continent, five hundred million of my people dead, but more to fact that they killed someone I loved. Just one; that's all it took. I'm sure if they'd known... Here, I will show you what she looked like. I carry her image with me."

An image of a tall and nearly transparent being with gossamer wings coalesced over the Loire. She floated above the old bridge, exceedingly beautiful. Gatc'hh'en in awe over her image, her beauty, and her grace, could only think of Catherine. He was thinking of the priests who had burned her and how he had felt at the time — and how she had stopped his hand, not physically, but with the example of how she had lived her life. He did not kill those responsible for her death, or exceed his wrath by bombarding the planet to sterility, because of her. Catherine had taught him well. She had made him who he had become.

He shook himself free as the image of the beautiful winged creature — his brother's lover — dissipated. "I had excellent instruction," he said.

Arra'll'en stared back, fighting for self-control. "This Rite — I don't know about this Rite. It is a cruel Rite," he said barely able to check his anguish. "Forgive me for the lie, brother, and for keeping you here. I am not right inside because of it as you can see. That is what our mother says, too. Still, she sent me. I am only able to stand here because of her."

Gatc'hh'en grasped his arm and they embraced: Gatc'hh'en and L'Batard, brother and brother. They transitioned into their natural forms and merged together, and ascended above the stone bridge, the Loire, the village of Blois, and the old Chateaux built by the French Kings hundreds of years after L'Batard died. They shone like two suns in the daytime sky casting the ancient city below in warm light and dark shadow. They hovered for a moment then accelerated upward, rising like a pair of shooting stars ascending instead of falling, the old town jolted by two sonic booms moments later, the old stones chattering before settling once again.

35

Apotheosis

Emily stepped out from beneath the canopy of oak and maple, elm and chestnut, into the open and looked upward. He was coming. She knew he would be. He said he would. She first saw him as a tiny pinpoint of brilliant light above the One World Trade Center. He appeared out of nowhere against a blue sky, dropping, then sweeping past the blank face of the glass towers, growing brighter as he approached. He appeared as a point of light without dimension. She could barely look at him without shading her eyes.

She experienced a sudden déjà vu, and almost immediately recalled the source: the hospital right after the very first time she had met him — fields of poppy and light.

Slowly climbing to his feet and turning to her he had asked her, "Who do you want me to be?" A silhouette in broken shards of sunlight.

"I don't know…," she had answered.

He had reached down and helped her to her feet, his hand, his human hand, appearing from nowhere. It was built of light. She could see through it but his touch was human. It was a real hand.

Once on her feet, he had lifted her up into his arms. She could see through the glare that he was smiling, the light fading to reveal a face in profile. He was handsome, beautiful as an angel, she had thought at the time, but now knew better. He was not an angel. He had not been sent by God. He had not been sent by anyone. He had been placed. Lovingly placed.

He had turned her so that they each faced the sun. It was blinding, golden, and pure, and they drifted upward, the poppy fields dwindling below. They ascended into crystal-clear air shot through with blades of sunlight, the two of them growing brighter, pure light. She looked downward; her parents — better times when she had been young and they had been in love — were on their knees looking up in wonder and horror as if believing that God, uninvited, had come to take their daughter to Heaven. God should not do such a thing. God should leave the living with the living. It is what a real God would do.

His wings opened — she thought they were wings; she did not see them but what else could they be but wings? And they flew across the landscape, the river drawing under them and then quickly falling away: fields and villages, mountains, rivers, the sea. They rose higher, the sky turning dark blue and then black. He held her tightly; he was not about to let go. Warm light radiated from the two of them brighter than the sun. She was wrapped in a blanket of light.

They achieved the altitude he sought. She did not think she would be able to breathe, but she could. It was not cold. The air was sweet but tasted like heated metal. They rotated slowly in profound silence. She had not realized how deep silence could be until then. She could see his wings now — they were not actually wings; he possessed a tail that reached halfway across the sky spreading out in a direction opposite from where she knew the sun lay.

The sun drifted into view. Hydrogen igniting under its own weight. A hole in space filled with light. A rare diamond blinding them. Heaven jumped, and beneath them the overwhelming blue curve of Earth drifted into view: blue, white, green, and brown, silver oceans reflecting the sun, and a thin layer of transparent silver in which hung thin clouds of vapor. All this while the crescent moon hung in the black emptiness with stars like tiny diamond chips scattered everywhere.

"That's not my home but it is something like it," he had said, indicating the blazing sun. "I am made of the stuff of nebulae between the stars as you are." He pointed showing her what she would later learn was the Trifid Nebula, NGC 6514. "But I always return to the heart of our sun where it is warm," he added, referring to any one of the many stars in the core of the nebula that he called home.

He let her go, their hands trailing off, and she drifted, slowly turning about to behold him once again. He was no longer shaped like a man but like a small star. "That is your home," he had said, indicating Earth, his voice the same voice, ringing beautiful and clear. She was falling faster into the blue and gold and yellow with strings of silver. "Spread your arms and fly, Emily," he said, again a man, opening his arms like the sun rising to show her how.

· ·· ··· ·····

Emily stood in the heart of Central Park, the light coming directly toward her. It stopped fifty feet up and slowly descended, opening. She saw him then. His face, his shoulders, his chest, and arms, until he floated above her. Beautiful. Powerful. All glory. She fell on her knees and wept. She had never felt such beauty, such power, such grace — such peace.

A pair of hands reached out of the light to gently hold her own and lift her to her feet. Blinded by tears, she could not see.

How she had longed to his voice again. "Did you ask your brother?" she asked wanting to know.

"I did."

"And?"

"I will join him shortly. But first, I wanted to see you — I needed to see you."

She stood perfectly straight. Her tears streamed down. She could not stop them, or slow them.

"I'm glad you did."

"In case it does not go well," he added solemnly.

"It will go well. I do know this. Have you not made me so that I can?"

He studied her carefully, hesitant. "What I do see is that the devices I planted in you have gone further than I intended," he said cautiously.

She remained perfectly straight, facing him not at all surprised by what he said.

"I am Catherine — is that not what you intended?"

"It is."

"Then here I am."

He bowed.

"It has gone wrong, though, hasn't it? I can feel it," she said having known almost from the beginning.

"Yes, it has."

She stood very straight, facing him. Her tears had stopped flowing; she could see clearly. "You did not intend that I should become what I have become, is that not right?"

"It is."

Emily nodded. He had not told or even suggested the devices might go beyond their programming, but it was a glorious omission.

"That is why I have come. To confess," he added. "I have done you yet another great wrong. I cannot expect you to forgive me." he said. "You are no longer entirely human."

"Do you love me?" she asked ignoring his confession.

"I have through the devices given you something more too," he pushed on after a moment of indecision, ignoring what she said. "Whatever you decide to do with it is right." He turned to go.

"What else could you possibly give me?" She had known since he had descended and their hands first touched what his gift was and how she would use it.

He paused and said over his shoulder, "It is a gift I gave you once before — but this time I have given you more, far more. You may protect yourself now, if you wish."

He turned to go one last time.

"Gatc'hh'en?"

He turned half way.

"Do you love me?" she asked again.

He hesitated. "How can you ask when you are the alpha and the omega of all I have done," he said, and was suddenly gone as was the light that sourced him.

· ·· ··· ·····

Emily stood perfectly rigid for a few moments, the park slowly revolving about her; the sun, the blue sky, the clouds in it; military aircraft in the air, the birds, the trees, the manicured park, the city beyond, concrete and glass, the odd silence of the streets, the sleeping subway, nearly twenty-million people. She waited patiently for the new powers he had given her through a simple touch — a reprogramming of the devices — to take effect. Then with her new eyes she looked about. She studied her hands and saw the power in them. She covered her face with those same hands but after a moment dropped them to her side. She hesitated, then spread her arms and rose up off the grass. She ascended as high as the tops of the tallest tree in the park, slowly turning in the direction she knew she needed to go. She flew bathed in sunlight while those gathered in the park looked up and pointed, taking picture after picture with their cellphones, sending them out around the world.

Catherine Healer

What better way to promote the health and welfare of the people than to give Catherine through the devices he had planted within her the ability to heal? What could be more right? What is right for otherwise if not to promote the health and welfare of the people? And yet, he often wished he had not. He should have instead swept her up and taken her to the far side of the Earth, and there on an island in the midst of the vast Pacific lived with her forever keeping her young and beautiful. They could have had children together.

Isn't that right, Catherine? Isn't that right?

• •• ••• •••••

No dawn, only a suffusion of light that slowly lifted a night of complete darkness. Fog clung to the streets while cold morning dew ran in rivulets along the stone. Catherine dropped beside the ebbing fire. A soldier tossed a piece of wood on the coals showering her in a rain of red sparks quickly extinguished in the cold night air. Catherine leaned in close to the fire, closing her eyes. The world spun around her as she nearly surrendered to the sensation of falling inwards towards the rising heat.

A gentle hand placed on her shoulder jolted her awake. A village woman knelt next to her, her eyes wide and dark in the firelight. "Thank you Lady!" she whispered. "God shines on you, Lady!" Catherine frowned, unable to recall her. "You tended my child last night," the woman reminded her. "She is well now, resting."

Catherine reached for the woman's hand, drawing it to her, her exhaustion so deeply felt she could barely speak. "You need your rest too," she managed. She released the woman's hand and leaned back against the broken battlement and smiled. "God be with you."

Another villager replaced the old woman: an old man, his arm bandaged. He kneeled before her like the old woman had and bowed his head. "Thank you, Lady."

"Go," she said, drawing her fingers along his ragged cheek. "Go in peace."

She suddenly sat upright: a crowd of villagers, shadowed and dark in the near dawn, pressed inwards, mumbling, whispering amongst themselves. L'Batard's guard noticing them for the first time climbed to his feet. He slowly sat. The next villager in line approached. "Thank you Lady! God, bless you Lady! You have God's hand Lady! You have saved us all Lady!" They knelt one by one before her asking for her touch. Among them were several of L'Batard's soldiers. She accepted them all, fully awake now, giving each her blessing.

She had asked for her gift — the ability to remove the treasonous sins of the body as she had once described the multiplicity of disease and the corruption of the body that plagued humanity. She possessed the same power as he did, and like him, the only corruption she could not conquer was death itself. But it had been wrong to give her such power. He knew that now, but she had been obsessed, so he had. He had given it to her at a time of the Black Death, during which entire villages might be wiped out in a single day. Where was God, Catherine had asked, falling to her knees in near despair amongst the hundreds of dead lying in the street, their faces blistered and blackened? The horror. The macabre. But statistically, nothing to the host of other diseases that shortened the lives of the people, most notably tuberculosis, dysentery, influenza, and typhoid, but also the aging process, perhaps the most painful to witness. It affects not just the people for the mechanism of life that had evolved on the third planet had built within it a degeneracy that limited the days of all living creatures. In the days that Catherine knew, the lives of the people were, as defined by fate, luck and chance, short, brutish and short, and always about God or the lack of God's presence, and perhaps rightly so.

· ·· ··· ·····

In the open courtyard, the flames flickered over the last of the coals, white and black within the circle of blackened stone. She reached for his hand and kissed his open palm drawing him down to her. "I am sorry I was so angry," she said looking up. She waited until he settled. "You could have helped me, but you did not," she said waiting for him to turn to her. "Why is that?"

She did not wait for his response but instead continued, her voice soft, full of the love she felt for him. "I do not believe it was the boy's inevitable fate, or that the mind of God had already been decided. It was in L'Batard's hands to show mercy, and he did not. Some things one cannot blame God for. But you did not help and I do not understand that."

L'Batard had the day before decided to hang a young boy who had assisted the murderers who had ravaged and plundered the village. Relieving the village from the mercenaries was the reason he had diverted the column, delaying them a day and a night. Catherine had pleaded for the boy's life but L'Batard was adamant and the boy was strung up. The only concession he allowed her was that he made it quick. The boy was thrown off the battlement so that his neck snapped when he came up short on the rope.

He answered Catherine as L'Batard had answered her previously. "He commits the sins of man; he must face the justice of man."

She had replied with a gentle touch, turning him and his self-righteousness back to her. "Those are L'Batard's words," she had said. "Have you no original ones of your own?" Then asking when he didn't reply, "Do you, my love?"

He could not answer for it was true, he had no words of his own. Not then. Not now, perhaps too.

• •• ••• •••••

Dawn slipped into morning, the sun unseen, nor felt. Blois was still three days away. L'Batard would be there in two. His brother's life depended on it. The garrisoned company lined the road leading to the gate and the outside world in perfect order. L'Batard nodded to his Master at Arms commanding the newly established garrison. "In a fortnight Sergeant!" The man saluted, "In Blois, my Lord!" L'Batard spurred his mount forward, and like a living thing, a beast tamed by head and heart, the column surged forward, the guards at each echelon returning the salute of the troops remaining behind.

The column turned out of the courtyard and into the passage leading to the gate. L'Batard raised a hand to stop; horses and men jostled but kept their order. A gathering of villagers blocked the way; they stared up at the column as a body, their faces pale but unexpectedly uplifted. L'Batard spurred his mount forward to address them but the crowd inexplicably parted, lining both sides of the road, every man and woman dropping to their knees to let them pass. L'Batard hesitated, but then spurred the column slowly forward. It stepped out slowly, wordlessly, and entered the passage. The faces of the old and young, the wounded and the maimed, the few that remained untouched, were not directed toward L'Batard, nor the flying banners, but toward Catherine. They chanted, "Lady! Lady! Lady!" Some climbed to their feet to wave her on, others wept where they knelt, their faces turned upward to follow her progress, their hands lifted in prayer.

A child broke free of her mother's grasp and ran recklessly into the column. Before she could be trampled he scooped her up and spun her about and placed her on his lap then turned her to face Catherine. The child smiled and handed her a bouquet of flowers – buttercups, he remembered. Catherine graciously accepted them. She leaned across and kissed her, her fingers lingering brushing the child's hair back off her face.

"Thank you, child."

"You are our Hope, Lady!"

Catherine nodded once, tears of love filling her eyes. She then looked away, weeping. He set the child down and she ran back to her mother as the column surged forward.

"L'Batard does not know what true power is," Catherine said as they passed through the open gate, the guard saluting.

She turned to catch his expression, wiping at her eyes. "But do you, my love? Do you?"

Emily Healer

erhaps I should have swept you away to the far side of Earth and lived with you forever, keeping you young and beautiful. We could have children together.

Isn't that right, Emily? Isn't that right?

• •• ••• •••••

The camera jostled, pitched up to the ceiling, but then swung back. A reporter from Eyewitness News swung into view. He had to shout to be heard. "I'm here at the New York Presbyterian Hospital in New York..." He was nearly overwhelmed by a powerful expression of pure amazement originating at the end of a long corridor. He immediately twisted about to determine the source. The hallway was jammed with doctors in white lab coats, nurses in their blue and green scrubs, patients in hospital issued garments tied at the neck. He turned back to the camera. "...The same as happened at CHONY Children's Hospital a couple of hours ago is happening here right now! I don't know what you want to call it, but the word around here is impossible!"

He raised his microphone above the heads and shoulders of those pressing in close. Only the odd phrase was distinguishable, each indicating excitement and wonder. The camera shifted, opening the field of view. Staff and patients stood about in stunned wonder. The image blurred and then bounced into position. "You see me?" The camera steadied, then found the reporter. "Good, good…" The camera bloomed then focused. "…Okay. …Okay."

An explosion of pure amazement at the far end of the corridor cut him off. He twisted about, stretching to see. The camera pitched then steadied. He was quickly back, his eyes wide, excited.

"I see her! I see her!"

He wheeled back for another look, the camera attempting to follow but focusing instead on the back of the heads of those who had pushed themselves between the cameraman and the reporter.

"I see a woman, quite short, blonde hair, young, early twenties. She's glowing!"

The crowd parted, forced apart by the cameraman pushing forward using his camera as a wedge. The camera caught the reporter wrenching about to check again, but then immediately returning to report on what he was witnessing, utterly amazed.

"She is beautiful! Beautiful! Quite a sight!"

He glanced over his shoulder as if torn to turn back but then reported, "I can't believe what I saw." He shook his head with amazement. "It can't be happening." He turned again to look, straining to find her through the crowd but then immediately returned full of excitement. "She's coming this way…" He turned about forgetting about the camera.

The young woman he had described floated into view. Her eyes were closed, her hands open, her palms turned upward bathed in a halo of sunlight as she walked suspended above the floor. She was beyond beauty, not possibly human. Sublime. Glorious. Those within range, including the reporter and the cameraman, reached out to touch her. Their hands played over her arms, her face, and her hair, then reluctantly trailed away as she moved along, opening the crowd before her, their arms reaching out to her too.

The camera pitched up but then quickly recovered as it focused on the back of her. There were no gimmicks; nothing to raise her above the floor; no special lighting, no wires. The camera followed her until the closing crowd once again wrapped itself about her.

The reporter drew the camera physically back to him. He was still obviously affected. "You've got me? Yeah? …Yeah?" He attempted to compose himself. It took a moment. "Okay…. Okay…" He fought to remain calm. "Who was that?" he pointedly asked the general audience watching all this unfold from the homes, at work, or out on the street, in the bars, stores, and subway. He was calmer, looking right into the camera lens. "Better yet, what?"

He again glanced over his shoulder drawn to yet another eruption of wonder. "She doesn't look human, not to me," he said turning back, regaining some composure. He speculated. "I've heard some ask if she might be the alien, or at least one his emissaries; if so, then to me it's clear that the alien is not here to kill us, or burn us up, but to heal us! That's gotta be the message! All that stuff about the BMO blowing up and taking us must be just wrong!" He was fighting for control; the excitement and emotion of the moment was sweeping him along. "She's healing the sick, everyone who is here, dying, or just ill, in the wards…" His voice broke. He fought for control and regained it. "The alien wouldn't be healing us to just to blow us up. It is not the End of Days. it can't be! It can't be!"

The camera shifted but then immediately returned. The reporter had fully recovered. "Whoever she is, she is no doubt the same woman who was sighted earlier in the park, and the same reported at CHONY. Eyewitnesses there reported her to be an angel; well, I don't know about that — we didn't have cameras at CHONY — but we do now at New York-Presbyterian. It's all being recorded, so you can decide. I think you will agree, though, that this is history, people. This is history… But why it is happening, no one knows."

Another cry filled the ward and he was propelled forward by the crowd out of the field of view. The camera caught up and focused on him. "But if not real, then it is one hell of a good trick!" Yet another loud cheer drowned him out. The camera jumped toward the source. "On me! On me!". The camera immediately flipped back but instead centered on a woman, a nurse, just over his shoulder. She was straining to see what was happening.

The reporter shoved his microphone in close. "What do you think is happening here?" he shouted.

She glanced at the reporter then seeing the camera turned to face him. She self-consciously brushed a loose strand of her hair off her face before she spoke. "She is stunning! I don't understand it! I don't get it, I really don't!"

"Is she human?"

Her eyes opened wide with surprise. "Of course! What do you mean?"

"Some are saying she doesn't look human."

The nurse laughed. Her name-tag indicated she was Carolyn Burns, RN, Pediatrics. "They're nuts!" she shouted. She glanced back to see what was happening at the end of the corridor.

"What is she doing?" the reported prompted.

She turned back. She gripped the microphone, almost swallowing it, looking directly into the camera lens. "She's doing what we often can't! She's healing the sick!" She straightened and laughed, then shrugged, stepping back and staring into the camera as if it was all too incredible. She shrugged. "Don't ask me what's going on, don't!" She laughed again. "It's like a dream! We'll all wake up tomorrow, I'm sure!"

"What is she?" the reporter asked again, pressing the microphone in closer yet.

She grabbed hold and shouted. "I'd say an angel! She's gotta be an angel!" She laughed. It was clear she didn't believe what she said and equally clear she had no idea who, or what, the mysterious woman might be. The camera shifted back to the reporter who smiled and shrugged, his shoulders raised, his expression saying, "See? What can I say?"

He extended his microphone to a man immediately adjacent to him who identified himself as Dr. Neil Bobroff, Head of Radiation and Oncology.

"I have never seen anything like it," he shouted into the microphone. He was more comfortable with the camera, only glancing at it. "It must be some kind of mass hysteria — I can't really tell from where I stand."

A commotion further along the hallway, momentarily distracted him. He quickly returned. "I do know this: Patients who moments ago could barely sit up, are now gathered about in this hallway apparently healthy and claiming they are cured. If that is true, it is, indeed, what many are calling it — a miracle. I have no other word that comes close to describing what's happening here. It is quite beyond me; I am having some difficulty absorbing it in fact." The doctor's attention jumped to something of interest near the Nurse's Station just a few feet away.

"Did you manage to talk with her?" the reporter asked drawing him back.

The doctor quickly returned. "No, but I saw her up close. She brushed right past. I felt an electric shock. She's wired into something. She's burning hot too — temperature wise."

"Did she say anything?"

"Not that I know or heard."

They were nearly swept away by another commotion that drew them apart.

"What did she seem like to you?" the reporter asked forcing the doctor back yet again.

"Beautiful. Very peaceful. Serene."

"Like an angel?"

"There's no such thing — that's crazy stuff."

"The Alien?"

"Give me a break, no! Couldn't possibly be! She's human! At least of a sort — I don't know how a normal person could do all this. She looks... She looks human. Beautiful."

The doctor grasped the microphone to ensure he would be heard above the bedlam. He stared into the camera. "I cannot comprehend what's going on but we will, we'll figure this out — there is a reason for everything."

Another roar interrupted him and the camera jumped.

Theories

E leanor used her credentials to fly directly from Kahului, Maui, to Los Angeles, California in a United Airlines Boeing 787 held in reserve for just such a requirement. They were escorted by six Lockheed Martin Lightening II F-35 fighters. She was one of only six passengers, the Boeing 787 the only aircraft in the air on the western seaboard of North America and the only aircraft to land at LAX that day.

She was met by the FBI and was taken in a long snaking convoy of armored black Suburban's from the airport to the Pasadena Convention Center. The convention center had evolved into a state of bedlam. The science teams and supporting staff remained cloistered, pulling in gigabytes of raw science data from the few remaining assets in orbit, as well as a much greater number of ground-based observatories, including previously top-secret military sensors, and even high-end amateur images from parts of the planet not well covered. Thousands were gathered, the support staff setting up networks, food services, and cleaning services while the science members gathered in the big hall with the image of the Bright Maneuverable Object front and center. It was now dazzling white and more than twice as bright as only a few days ago, but still unusually and unexpectedly small; there was still no discernible diameter; it remained a pinpoint of energy.

The image and associated data, optical flux from x-ray to infrared, temperature, radiation levels, orientation, were updated once a minute from data provided by JPL's Europa probe now in orbit close to the BMO. The object may no longer be spinning; it was difficult to tell, at least in visible light, but in ultraviolet the surface was shown to be torn apart from the inside out. Whatever was inside was boiling mad and ready to break out. In both wavelengths, streams of blue and white filaments erupted from the surface, twisting as they reached upward into open spirals. The stream followed tightly bound lines of an invisible magnetic field only to disappear in a tight arc into the black emptiness of space. Radiation levels were off the charts. If it were not for the fact the JPL probe had been designed to operate about Jupiter, it would have long ago been consigned to space junk.

• •• ••• •••••

Eleanor entered a small room off to the side of the larger auditorium. Ramanujan was studiously studying the back of his hands but was otherwise patiently waiting. He looked up as she entered. "Welcome back, Ellie." He stood and accepted her hand. "Wonderful to see you."

She acknowledged him with a curt nod. "There has always only been one object," she began as she sat, nearly calm, opening her laptop. "That is all we ever detected; at no time until L2 does the data show more than one object — and that notwithstanding the mysterious merging of two separate objects during the flyby. We still don't know what that was. It looks like the alien got a boost from whatever it might have been. There is speculation there may be two of them, but we just don't know; let's hope not. That's all we would need."

She flipped through her notes until he found what he was looking for and then tracing the entry with his finger read directly from them. "Dr. Monserrat and Dr. King helped me get this data. The very first observation by Pan-STARRS came thirty-two days, six hours, forty-two minutes before the Jupiter flyby. It was magnitude eighteen, still quite bright. We assume that was a course correction to place the BMO into position for Jupiter. It subsequently went dark less than twenty-four hours later so that when Dr. Matheson attempted to reacquire he failed."

She continued without the need for notes, looking up. "We have verified that the switching from bright to dark and back is, as we suspected but couldn't prove until now, representative of the energy required to make the course corrections. When bright it is expending energy but when dark it is presumably quiescent; in cruise-mode so to speak."

She continued without pausing. "Extrapolating back, we've determined two other possible observations of the object both very faint, less than magnitude twenty because of the distance. Extrapolating back any further may be somewhat speculative, and even though we do not have any confirmed tracks to verify this, from the data we do have we believe the object likely originated approximately 43 AU from the sun in the Kuiper Belt"

She closed her notebook. "We are prepared to publish if necessary. I hope their quick and don't sit on it too long — I may not get a chance to see it in print."

She stared across the table unsmiling. "Do you now know what it is, Ram? A dead comet? Black Hole of some sort?"

"It is a Black Hole, as we've all surmised but it must be a very special type of Black Hole." He contemplated her blank expression. He smiled then added, "We believe it to be a Primordial Black Hole, or PBH. We thought they are very rare — apparently not. But if it's what we think it is, then all the mountain-sized mass has been compressed by gravity to be only a few atoms in diameter." He quickly continued as Eleanor sat back astonished. "But what is not known is how many PBH's there might be and how they are distributed. Up until now, it has been assumed that the density of such objects is statistically very low making the probability of the alien — or aliens — finding one relatively close by extremely unlikely."

"You cannot argue with the reality of it," Eleanor calmly stated, entirely focused, still amazed.

"One way to test that theory is to determine if the matter and energy being released is pre-baryonic. And it looks like it very much is from the energy signatures we've been observing. It is quite astounding, really; absolutely so."

When Eleanor didn't immediately reflect his enthusiasm, he asked, "What other news other than what you've reported?"

"The spin has stabilized. It's now rotating at two point six revolutions per second with less than zero point zero one percent deviation. It is very stable. Not wobbling. Its spin axis is nearly exactly normal to Earth's equator, which seems hardly arbitrary," she added evenly.

"That's interesting."

"Do you think?"

Ramanujan smiled and wagged his finger. "Don't be sarcastic — It is not becoming. What about the mass?"

Eleanor managed a smile for the first time. She and Ramanujan went back a long way. "It appears to be remaining the same — if the mass changed, I'd quit."

Ramanujan's expression opened and he nearly laughed. He clearly liked her. "There is an adage that says that what a physicist wants more than anything in the world is to change the laws of physics," he offered and continued to smile.

Eleanor, despite the tension, smiled back. She threw her head back to toss her hair out of her eyes, and her smiled opened.

"How do you know the mass hasn't changed?" Ramanujan asked.

"JPL's Europa probe has re-purposed and is now at L2," she quickly answered. "Its onboard accelerometers indicate it's being accelerated toward the object. It indicates a gravity field of zero point two five gravities sourced within the geometric center. It is the same body — changed but with the same mass I should say. Only the rate of change of unlocking the singularity — or near singularity I should say — has increased dramatically."

She looked up and added, "You must have heard that Phoenix is about ready to be launched."

Ramanujan spread his hands on the table, and after a moment said, "Yes, of course. One of my best students — other than yourself, that is — Has been assigned as crew specialist: Rosie... Rosalind... Rosalind Stewart. Do you remember her? She's a Scot — speaks with an accent. Lovely voice. Brilliant mind. Again, not unlike you — except for the accent of course."

"I hate heights," Eleanor mused and grinned. She did know Rosie. They had been good friends for a while. Of course, she knew that Rosie had been assigned. The entire world knew.

"It will be ten days before they get within range of the BMO," Eleanor said only. She'd do almost anything to be onboard the Phoenix with Rosie. "God knows what they hope to do when they get there."

"Talk, I hope."

Eleanor again nodded. "The press is here, but they're all locked in. They're going nuts. No careers made here, not from what we are observing and from what the mathematical projections state."

"And what's that?" Ramanujan asked carefully, studying the back of his hands again.

"I'm just telling you what I know, and not even that, so if it doesn't sound particularly promising, or happy, don't blame me." She took a deep breath and continued. "The truth is, the outlook from this side of things is not great. As the aliens continue to loosen the effect of gravity within the singularity, it will grow hotter and hotter and then it will likely fly apart. It would be the biggest nuclear explosion ever. It would be like a small star going nova on our doorstep. All our calculations show it would take us out for sure. Some calculations indicate it might even boil away the oceans. Either way, it will take out all life: All life," she emphasized, "Right down to the smallest microbe. They're not just killing us; they're taking out the very foundation of life on this planet." Her voice broke, but she remained steady, staring at her colleague and friend waiting for his response.

"And we're still trying to talk with whomever?" he asked quietly still studying his hands.

"All frequencies, as they say," Eleanor replied just as quietly in turn, just managing to control herself. "Nuclear flashes from our converted ICBMs, to let them know how desperate we are to talk; everything we got: lasers to flags, to people gathering in massive crowds waving their arms and shouting upward. You've seen that, haven't you? It's absolutely incredible. Every country, everywhere. The largest gathering of humanity at anytime and anywhere and it's happening all over the globe: India takes the cake at over ten million gathered."

"Yes, I've seen that in the news coverage. It is all quite incredible — And yet they're not answering and we don't know why. I'm still puzzled by that."

"I could guess why."

"Yes, well, there is all that…"

Eleanor finally said, again sighing but in control, "All the projections indicate that BMO— Black Hole, PBH, whatever it is — is going to blow up and take us all with it."

Ramanujan shook his head.

"You don't believe it?"

"If there is mind and a will behind this, the direction could change any moment." Seeing Eleanor frown, Ramanujan smiled. "Any good news to report, Ellie?"

Eleanor looked down nervously then back up. She shrugged.

"I can see that there is."

"Maybe."

He politely motioned her to continue.

"It's a small thing — ridiculous, really. When I landed at LAX, I was met by Dr. Kalinowski. He's a graduate of MIT: math and physics. Clever chap, apparently: or so he says. He showed me his badge and for what it is worth, he is with the FBI — an Analyst, he says. He told me he had been trying to get a hold of either you or Trevino but with no luck, and then he told me a number of amazing things no doubt hoping I would pass them on. He no doubt figured I was working for you; probably knew all along."

Ramanujan frowned. Kalinowski had been pounding on his door for days and he'd refused to see him. He had done as much to ask for a confirmation of his authority via the FBI liaison but it had not yet come through. They were stalling for some reason. Still, he didn't have time for everyone with an opinion or a theory.

"He claims it is not aliens but an alien — only one — responsible for all these goings on," Eleanor explained slowly. "He handed me a report from the Applied Physics Laboratory in Laurel, Maryland that describes his physical characteristics. I have not read it yet but, in short, the alien is most likely not a biological entity but a machine built upon fantastic technology that seems almost like magic to those who wrote the report. Kalinowski has no idea what the alien is up to at L2 — it seems frightening, he agrees — but he claims to know absolutely and unequivocally that the alien is not about to destroy us, and for one simple but incredible reason."

"And what would that be?" Ramanujan asked evenly, sitting back, becoming more and more convinced he perhaps should have talked with him.

"His girlfriend lives here."

Ramanujan sat back even further, completely stunned. "Well… That is news."

Eleanor squirmed nervously. She forced herself to add, "I managed to drag him through the gauntlet with me. For some reason, they took away his access card. Why they would do that to an FBI agent who claims to know what he knows is beyond me. He says they want to lock him up to shut him up. He's just outside if you want to hear what he has to say. If they want to shut him up for whatever he might know, it is probably worth hearing him out."

Ramanujan glanced at the door again astonished. "You brought him with you?" he asked. "Through all that security?"

She nodded. "I don't know what possessed me. His story sounded like a good one at the time. Pretty incredible, really. I thought it might be something you might want to hear. I'm sorry if it is not."

Ramanujan leaned forward, still astonished. "You surprise me, Eleanor."

She smiled back but nervously. He never called her Eleanor. "How is that?"

"I trust you in all things — how could you doubt that I don't?" He waved her on. "Show him in. I will give him five minutes."

Surprised but pleased too, Eleanor pushed away from the table and made her to the door. She boldly opened it swinging it wide, revealing the doubled-up Marine Guard who immediately turned and saluted. Kalinowski sat on a bench across the hall, his head in his hands. Hearing the door open, he glanced up and seeing Eleanor, immediately jumped to his feet.

"Dr. Kalinowski?"

He nodded, running a hand through his hair then self-consciously straightening his wrinkled clothing.

She waved him forward.

"I said I would, didn't I?" she whispered as he passed.

"I love you," he said whispered back out of the side of his mouth looking straight ahead. "You're wonderful."

"You got lucky," she stated flatly, closing the door behind them, but smiling. "You got five minutes — Don't blow it."

Angel

"D r. Robert Norris, I presume?"

Dr. Norris, wiping his tears one eye at a time, his other hand balancing the syringe, jumped. The fluorescent lights shone brightly; the hot water baseboard heaters ticked as the thermostat closed to adjust the room's temperature to what he had set on the dial. There had been a voice in his head. He had little time. He held the tip of the needle to the vein at his elbow.

"Please stop."

He had heard a woman's voice that had seemed to originate from the corner where there was no door, and no possible way in; it was a solid wall. Worse, she had spoken in French; worse still, he had understood her.

He refused to look. To do so would be a huge mistake. He quickly rubbed the flesh to raise the vein, concentrating, positioning the needle. He heard the rustling of a long gown as she stepped through the wall.

"My love has sent me to prevent you from carrying through with your plan to end yourself," she softly said from behind.

He recognized her voice and knew who she was. He had seen her on the television as had millions of others. It was on constant repeat on every channel side by side with the coverage of the Bright Maneuverable Object. He dared not look at her.

"You are ill. I will help," she added gently.

He abruptly drew back in anticipation of her reaching for him. The syringe flew from his hand. He scrambled for it and snapped it up just before it rolled beneath the bed. He fumbled with it positioning it again. He stood with his back to her.

"You will not accept my help?" she quietly asked. He furiously rubbed his arm trying to raise a vein.

Lights suddenly snapped off followed immediately by the Emergency lighting. She reached across and gently removed the syringe from his hand. "It is a sin to take your own life."

His throat was constricted into a knot. He could barely speak. "It is the end of the world," he managed to say, and I had no small role to play in it." She stood behind him. He still refused to look at her.

"Your role was circumstantial, that is all," she said softly and reasonably.

"I am responsible."

"You are? How is that?"

He had to strain to hear her. "I could have stopped him," he said just as quietly in turn. The room ticked.

"How is that?"

"I could have told Kalinowski all I knew right from the beginning. I knew how powerful the alien was. I knew he could move through solid walls. I knew how he could turn a body into mush and then reassemble it like humpty dumpty.

"Do you know who I am?" she suddenly asked whispering almost in his ear.

She radiated heat as if from the summer sun. He could feel it on the back of his neck. She stood that close. He turned, drawn immediately to her face. He required a moment to recover.

"I saw you on TV — everyone has."

"Look more carefully."

He studied her again and shook his head. "An angel?"

"I am Emily."

"What?" He finally recognized her. "You! Emily! Miss Dupuis!" He was dumbfounded.

Emily floated backward so he could take her all in. "Yes, it is me." She smiled. "What else do you see?" She wore a simple one-piece gown, white, trimmed in waves of blue with hints of gold. But all the elegance and saintliness was in her beautiful face, and in her eyes, her hair, in the stance of her body, standing straight, and her hands, long delicate fingers, clasped in front.

Norris' heart soared. He began to weep. He nearly fell to his knees. His legs were giving out. "I see an angel!"

"Don't cry. Stay on your feet."

"But the world is about to end!" he groaned, his hand raised in prayer begging for her understanding.

"No, it is not."

He insisted. "The power is out. It is the end. The beginning of it."

"You did not hear?" she said reasonably, and calmly. "The President and all other world leaders turned the power off on purpose. They have grounded all aircraft, stopped all traffic; there is no television, no land phones, no cell phones, and no internet. Nothing that is electronic will survive when the wormhole opens, and they know that. They are protecting themselves; it is not the end at all."

Norris nodded. He dried his eyes using his sleeve and nodded again. "I did hear that," he agreed.

"And I am not an angel," Emily responded quietly. "Je ne suis ce que vous ne pouvez l'imaginer. Do not place upon me the burden of being an angel."

He began to weep again. He fell to his knees before her. "Please forgive me," he cried, burying his face in his hands.

She gently scolded. "Oh, stop that! Stop that! There is nothing to forgive." She offered her hand. "Come, come with me." When he didn't move, she drew him to his feet.

Norris cried out. His body, his heart, his mind, had shifted with her touch. He shook. He felt as if he was floating. He was utterly amazed. He breathed in, tried to speak, then did speak. "...What happened?"

"It is odd, is it not?" Emily responded, answering him indirectly. "That although we are people, and we have souls, we are as much of the body as the soul. But our body often betrays us; it can be such a treasonous thing."

· ·· ··· ·····

The room suddenly shifted. The wall disappeared and the open vista of New York's Central Park blossomed. No lights, no traffic, but people everywhere staring upward. It was nearly dawn. Heavy dew draped the trees and lay on the grass. The pond was perfectly still, like a mirror. The sky, turning from gray, promised to be profoundly blue.

"I feel better. I don't feel the same," Norris said, in shock and unable to take it all in. Emily smiled. It was as if the sun had burst through a cloud or had suddenly risen, he thought. He had to shield his eyes.

"My love cannot teleport himself like this, but I can. We are very similar he and I but we are not the same. He does not know of this so — she brought a finger up to her lips - "*Shhhh...* But know that I love him, even so. I glorify in the differences between us. Together we are greater."

Norris climbed to his feet and grasped her free hand — how strong she was — and they stepped through the open doorway and onto the lawn of the park, feeling the forgiving earth upon which they now stood, as much as the opening of the day.

Valentina sat on the grass, her dark hair falling to her shoulders. She sat alone. She had not seen them yet. She was staring at her hands as if they did not belong to her. She lifted them to explore her face, her fingers following the curve of her neck, then over her breasts. "Look what he has done," she whispered in wonder, still not aware of their presence. "I prayed for this but I didn't expect it, not after what I have done. I am not deserving. I am a great sinner."

She climbed to her feet, spread her arms, and pirouetted about and finally saw them. She stepped back her eyes opening wide. She looked from one to the other. "You! ...You!" She approached. One step forward, and she fell to her knees. She grasped the hem of Emily's dress and kissed it, then looked up. "Am I dead?"

"No," Emily responded, reaching down and helping her up. "And my love did not return your youth. It was within my power to do so, so I did. I am certain he would have, if he had the opportunity, but he is quite preoccupied at that moment."

Valentina could only nod her understanding.

"It is a matter of conscience on my part, and the man I love. We could not let you remain as if you were not a person," Emily further explained. "You would die believing you were soulless, and we could not have that for it is not true."

Valentina cried out, throwing her head back her dark hair flying, and nearly falling to her knees again.

"You may not be the original Valentina," Emily went on to explain. "She was gone when she burned — but you are you, complete, body and soul, reborn with your new body recovered from the old body. We, my love and I, and you, and you," she turned to Norris, "are living beings."

Emily placed her arm about Valentina and beckoned Norris, wrapping her free arm around him and drawing him close. "This is what my love would have wanted you both to see...," she said, her voice like music. A Mendelssohn Choir.

The sun was rising. It was golden, promising. It would be a glorious day. The horizon flashed and there was another light: a brighter, hotter, purer light. It glowed on the horizon behind the city to the west. As they watched, it grew in strength. It soared in intensity until it was brighter than the sun. It seemed to be an explosion. The shock waves ran along the western horizon, silhouetting the far trees and the nearby buildings. It rippled, danced, remaining the purest white.

Abruptly, as if it had a will of its own, it began to rise. It was not an explosion at all; it was infinitely bright, and from the distance, a pinpoint of light flooding the entire sky. It moved against the darker western horizon, temporarily following it but then slowly climbing, then accelerating, and rising. It was a falling star against the gold of the sun, only ascending, faster and faster, outshining the sun, filling the morning with its pure white light, following an arc upward.

"Look! Look what my love can do!"

Her love ascended, illuminating the day, arcing upward towards heaven, the city safe and whole beneath him.

Phoenix

"Phoenix this is Houston."

"Phoenix here."

"Listen, John; this is Ferris again at CAPCOM."

"Hi, Ferris."

"How you doing, buddy? All good?"

"All good."

"We calculate approximately four hours of battery power remaining. We recommend you shut down all non-essential equipment at this time."

"Already done – and it's already getting colder. We're all in the Crew Module, EMU's on, helmets off, gloves off."

"Roger that. Ground radars indicate your orbit about the BMO is deteriorating; it is continually being affected by the point mass which has completely thrown off the gravitational balance at L2 — as we expected; but now that you have no way to compensate, your halo orbit is falling apart. You're going down in. It is just as the five of you figured out for yourselves, buddy.

"Understood. Thanks for the confirmation Houston."

"In two hours thirty-two minutes you're going to eject first the weapon followed by the SM, then the ATV. The ATV and SM are the

292 · JOHN TALISKER

same as for re-entry protocol; we'll talk you through the weapon ejection. We're uploading the protocol for that now."

"Roger that — we see it."

"Listen, John… We have a few minutes. We have Dr. Ramanujan on standby here again if you or any of your crew wish to talk with him."

"Standby…" The Phoenix commander, US Navy Commander John D. Jennings, returned in a moment. "We're good for that. Rosie has been using everything we've got left to study the thing, eyeballs mostly. She's taken lots of photos. She just indicated she's downloaded the first of them just now. You should see them coming up."

"We see them. They're coming in slow. Wish we still had that high gain."

"A working life support system would be better. I'm turning the COM over to her. She's ready when Dr. Ramanujan is."

"Okay then… Caltech, this is CAPCOM, Houston — Derrick Ferris, here. Dr. Ramanujan are you there?"

"I'm here."

"You're on."

"Dr. Stewart — Rosalind?"

Ramanujan was speaking to Dr. Rosalind (Rosie) Stewart, Ph.D., Astrophysics, a graduate of University of Glasgow, Scotland, and mission specialist. She was born and raised in Scotland, Perthshire. Like all the four crew members, she was handpicked for a mission that was from the beginning assumed to be risky, and likely one-way.

"Professor."

"I didn't think it would end up like this."

"No sir."

"You were my best grad student."

"Yes sir." She laughed, but was quite clearly, even as heard over the static-prone link, carefully controlling herself. "One more test, is that it professor?" she asked.

"Tell me what you see, Rosie."

"The external cameras are deader than dead, the NAV radar is out, as is the spectroscope, so it's only eyeballs. We have a telescope and, of course, a sextant and my camera."

"That's fine. Just tell me exactly what you see. Without the Europa probe, we're blind down here."

The Europa probe had been taken out as had much of Phoenix by the massive EMP that had preceded the final moments of the BMO's transformation.

"The BMO is, for all intents and purposes, gone," Rosie reported. "There remains only a very tiny but very bright light where the center of mass once was. However, our accelerometer data continues to show that something is still out there and in the exact same position and the exact same mass. We measure a constant acceleration of almost a quarter g directly toward the center point. It is a singularity, just as you predicted, sir. It is now radiating much more intensely, however."

"Okay, thank you, Rosie. It is radiating because the mass is so small – small black holes will do that - as you no doubt recall; I know you know more than you say. We have some flying observatories out of Hilo — sadly, that's all we've got now to see above the ionosphere. They indicate most of the radiation from the singularity is in the visual, stretching into the ultraviolet. The good thing is there is no appreciable x-ray or gamma-ray emission as we feared there would be."

"That's a relief."

"Does it appear to be getting brighter at all?"

"Yes, it seems to be. But that's only because we're getting closer, I think."

"Can you see anything else near it? It should be less than a second of an arc to the left. It will be very, very small at the range you are now. It will be difficult to see."

"Just a moment. I'll look ..." On cue, the Phoenix commander increased the spacecraft pitch so that the onboard telescope would have a direct line of sight. There was a short moment as Rosie checked. "I don't see anything near it, not yet anyway."

"Our best calculations show it should be only about ten meters in diameter – very small, and no doubt difficult to resolve at the distance you are currently. But you should be able to detect it from the light reflecting off it – a glint. Again, it should be very close to the remains of the BMO."

"I do see something. Wait... I have to offset the scope so the glare from the singularity doesn't wash out the background. Hang on... ...There."

"What?"

"It is a sphere — a perfect sphere made of some transparent material. From the range, I'm at, it looks like a little glass ball with a light shining on it — the BMO mostly, but I can see sun glint, too; even Earth-shine."

"Okay..."

"Is that good, doc?"

"It's perfect. It is precisely what it is supposed to be."

"I pass?"

"You pass."

"I'm handing COM back to Command — Goodbye, sir."

"Goodbye, Rosie."

She quickly cut the link. There was dead air for a moment but only a moment.

"Phoenix this is CAPCOM, Houston. Do you copy?"

"Loud and clear, Houston."

The Phoenix pitched back to its nominal flight attitude and thirty minutes later rolled onto its side and pitched up normal to its orbit. The weapon was released. First a set of four pyros followed by mag clamps allowing it to slowly drift off. Phoenix backed off nearly a kilometer and the weapon was pitched up. Four minutes ten seconds later, the weapon main engine was ignited. The nuclear weapon accelerated quickly and soundlessly, directly normal to the ecliptic and into deep space. It would follow an arc that would eventually take it into the sun.

• •• ••• •••••

Three hours after that event, the four astronauts in full EVU using internal oxygen, the spacecraft pitched up again. The command module separated from the ATV. It was a procedure that they had practiced hundreds of times. Pyros, mag clamps, and the Phoenix capsule pulled away with a gentle nudge of the ACS thrusters. Phoenix, consisting of only the command module now, rolled and turned about on its z-axis placing the heat shield directly in line with the newly formed and now clearly discernible sphere just to the left of the remains of the BMO. It appeared exactly as Rosie had said. It was a glass ball bathed in the brilliant glare of the sun with the BMO just adjacent, except it was not made of glass at all but exotic matter with a negative mass. No one knew exactly what it was made of, but they did know something very unusual would be needed to keep the tunnel open — ordinary matter would not do it.

It was an open mic. There was no time for protocol and only one thing remaining: they were going in.

"Houston, this is Phoenix. We're closing fast. I'm throttling back. We're dead center. Telemetry download continues. Fuel at three percent. Attitude nominal.

"Houston, do you copy?"

"Copy that — God-speed, Phoenix."

"...Rosie, I'm pitching down, take a close look."

"...I see it. A good shot. Sending photos. Another, another.... Oh, my God! We're getting really close. Still sending... Hope to God you're receiving these Houston! Oh, my God! I can see into it! I see stars! Thousands of stars! I see a city! A city! It has its own sun! Oh, my god, I hope you get these, I hope you get these photos!"

"I'm pitching up. We're going in!"

Low rate telemetry was held for another three minutes twenty-four seconds; voice contact was lost when they entered as was the photo stream. The telemetry indicated attitude was nominal. They had one more hour of oxygen remaining, the cabin temperature was passing the freezing mark, the batteries were down ninety percent, and there was one percent of fuel remaining. The heart rates of the individual astronauts were through the roof but strong. No ACS thrusters were firing. Phoenix was flying straight and true. Only four hi-resolution photographs were successfully downloaded. What was shown was enough to turn the entire world upside down yet again.

Emily

Emily turned toward him as he entered. She wore no jewelry, and no makeup; only a single piece gown the color of wheat raised to her neck exactly fitting her form. She was standing in sunlight. It wrapped about her turning her golden. He took her hands and kissed her, her mouth, each cheek, her forehead, and then again her mouth.

"I am very proud of you," she said as he stepped back.

"And I, you," he said. He smiled uncertainly, taking her in: all the changes he had imposed upon her. She was like the sun.

"You look exhausted," she said, smiling, accepting his compliment.

"I am, very much so."

"Did your brother help you?"

"He did."

"That is a good thing — that is what brother's do."

"You have changed considerably since we last met," he said as the sun slipped behind a cloud but the room remained full of light, the same color as sunshine in spring.

"The world wants to know," she asked. "What happened to Phoenix? Did they get through? Are they alive?"

"They are — a rough passage but they are fine, so I am told."

She smiled knowing from the way he was looking at her that he understood her beauty. "I am more like you now," she said evenly and in a low voice. "And more perhaps, too?" she suggested, eyeing him and smiling.

"That is understandable — I am a machine while you are a living being."

"So that is what you imagine the lesson of your Rite to be?" she asked quietly. "To rub that so-called truth in your face?"

"You seem to know — are you wise now too?"

She smiled again as he did but without his uncertainty. "I am."

His smile turned to the distance. "Enlighten me — I have lived a long time waiting for the answer."

She stepped in closer, aligning herself to him. "There is no mystery here — anyone who loves you will know this." She nodded slowly and then told him. "To share this life, of course. To know you are not alone despite the vast emptiness all about you." She reached up and whispered in his ear. "To confirm the truth that you are alive too and not just a soulless machine," she said, kissing his cheek. "It is how you remember who you are — not what you might be."

He nodded, visibly shaken.

She held him by his arms aligning him to her. "Look what you have become," she said smiling up at him.

He appeared startled but remained silent. He gently broke her grasp then stepped toward the window. She followed, placing a gentle hand on his back.

"If I took you with me, you would lose your biology entirely," he said not turning to her. "My sin would be too great. I could not live with it."

She calmly waited for him to say more.

"I will go alone," he solemnly added and stepped away. "You cannot come with me — I will not allow it."

She called him back. "You will leave me here?"

He stopped in mid-stride.

"How dare you."

"To be great one must dare greatly," he offered standing straight.

"Do not quote L'Batard — he would never agree with you."

He remained frozen, his back to her. "Who are you?" he asked quietly: "You are not Catherine."

She floated across the short distance to him, her body shifting. He turned and watched her change. Her hands glowed; her entire body radiated. The energy might come from the devices still in her, but her beauty was all her own.

She held the devices in her open palm, then before he could react scattered them in the air. "Take them." They fell like invisible confetti to floor.

"Come live with me and be my love," she said, "and we will all the pleasures prove, for I know you love me."

He stared, then smiled, then turned to face her fully. He held out his hand.

"Did you not say I was the alpha and the omega? Was that a lie? Am I not Catherine and Emily too? Is there no room in your heart for us?" she asked as she reached for him.

He accepted her hand, and they accelerated upward above the city — through the window as if it didn't exist, the cloud cover, and into the silence of space: Sweeping around the moon, then transiting the newly formed star-tunnel Phoenix had just sailed through, and onward in a mad cascade of color.

Catherine

Catherine smiled up at him, brushing her hair back off her face. She asked, falling back on her pillow, "What is it then? What is all this philosophizing about? Is it not enough for you to simply see the beauty, and then accept it — and then kiss me?"

He smiled then kissed her. "Anything you say — but if you do not question the world," he had said, "its philosophy, why it is, why it is not — then what are we? If we accept the world the way it is and do not question it, where does that place us? We would be no more than animals."

She smiled, nearly laughed, and wagged her finger. "Oh, I have you on this one!"

"How is that?"

She shrugged. "Are we not animals? Have we not just proven it together? You in my arms, me in yours? Coupling?"

"Now that is blasphemy," he laughed. "Man is made in God's image — women as well, of course. It sounds confusing, I know, but there you are."

She drew her knees up then tightened her wrap about herself so that only her head showed. She pitched her head back, throwing her hair out of her eyes, then smiled finding him. "I can do and say whatever I wish," she said flippantly, throwing her head back again to get the last strands out of her eyes.

"Now I have you!" he had said in triumph.

"Now?" she asked, smiling.

"You lecture me on all the meandering twists and false turns of blasphemy all the time. What gives you the privilege now to speak whenever you wish on whatever you want?"

"Because I am a woman and I can do and say whatever I wish!" She laughed, knowing she finally had him. "Have I not told you that before? You are slow, sir!"

He laughed with her. "You are impossible — and you do not mean a thing you say."

She would not be diverted. "Do you intend to burn me for my blasphemy? You have asked me that same question when the shoe was on the other foot — remember?"

"I remember."

"Then will you hand me over to the Inquisition for my minor slip?"

"We know the answer to that, do we not?"

She stared at him without smiling, suddenly serious. "I am not an animal, and nor are you. We are God-chosen. We have souls," she said evenly, staring into his eyes, daring him to challenge her this time.

He stared back but couldn't help but smile, he loved her so. "Then I say this," he said. "If we accept the world and the philosophies within, including the teachings of your God, and do not question them, then we are doomed to continually repeat the errors of the past, and we will die because we cannot grow; we cannot step beyond ourselves."

"Why step beyond ourselves?"

"To be something better."

"What could be better?"

"Truth: our truth; to know who we are, really."

"You do not know? You are saying I do not know who I am, or who you are?"

"That is right. How could we? Have we done all? Have we reached so far, learned so much, that we know everything, including all there is to understand about ourselves?"

She leaned forward. He hesitated, wound up as he was but then finally surrendered and completed the extra distance between them to kiss her again.

"You are weak," she said softly.

"I know I am."

She smiled again as he sat back and gathered his thoughts. Sunlight painted her face. Golden strands of her hair floated in the busy summer air. "I think you think too much," she said gently. "But I love you for that. You would not be you otherwise."

"Does that mean I win?" he'd asked, smiling carefully, knowing he hadn't.

She shook her head, sending her hair flying, then quietly laughing, her love for him evident.

"Of course not!"

Acknowledgements

I would like to thank Ben Ballard, Tim McGee, Oda Lindner, Jim Wood, and Arnold Davenport for their help in formulating this novel, both the content and the approach. And especially all those in the Niagara on the Lake Writer's Circle: Hermine Steinberg, Selina Appleby, and Terry Belleville with their unwavering advice to follow my heart. Special thanks to Terry for his creative work on the cover as well as for his unflagging encouragement. And finally, my family: Alison, Sarah, Will, Mitch, Ellie, and most important of all, Patti for her loving patience.

About the Author

John Talisker lives an eclectic lifestyle immersed in isolation, beautiful views, dark skies, and a deep passion for writing the best novels he can. He likes physics, mathematics, music, art, literature, astronomy, paleontology, anthropology, entomology, geology, even religion — but finds the human mind and heart the most interesting and often the most perplexing of all. He has a degree in physics, and owns a kayak. He has a cabin by a river and wonderful friends and family, without whom he wouldn't bother to write. What would be the point? Besides writing in the morning and late at night, kayaking beneath gentle rain, he likes to hike in the mountains of British Columbia or canoe in the back country of Algonquin Park. He has holed himself up on Wolfe Island where the Great Lakes merge into the St Lawrence River, and takes close-up pictures of wildflowers when he's not writing or trying to keep up with those around him who take up his time but only because they care. He is a Canadian and a proud American. He has English roots, some Scottish peat in his blood, and even a tingle of the Irish. He has a lot of good stories in him.

He can be reached at jdreid1p0.com

About the Cover

The cover was designed by the renowned artist Terry Belleville seen at TerryBelleville.com and with much thanks. It is built upon a photograph of the Starfish Prime high-altitude nuclear test explosion, part of Operation Dominic on July 9, 1962 with an explosive yield of 1450 kilotons.

Image courtesy of US Govt. Defense Threat Reduction Agency. Author U.S. Air Force 1352nd Photographic Group, Lookout Mountain Station.

About the Editing

All effort has been made to ensure this work is as grammatically correct as possible within the constraints of the author's style. It is not perfect. Please forward any concerns or corrections you might think of to the author.

Proof

Made in the USA
Charleston, SC
08 February 2017